WITHDRAWN
Damaged, Obsolete or Surplus
Jackson County Library Services

DATE DUE			
APR 1 9 '01	Aug 30		
MAY 3 0 '01	8/19/06		
JUL 1 3 '01	3.21.14		
JUL 2 6 '01			
AUG 1 5 '01			
JAN 2 2 2002			
OCT 21 02			
MAR 28 '03			
MAY 2			
SEP 1 4 '06			

3/01

JACKSON COUNTY
Library Services

HEADQUARTERS
413 West Main Street
Medford, Oregon 97501

Dc

3-02

Labette County's Ultimate Deception

G·K
Hall
&Co.

This Large Print Book carries the
Seal of Approval of N.A.V.H.

Florence B. Smith

Labette County's Ultimate Deception

G.K. Hall & Co. • **Thorndike, Maine**

Published in 2001 by arrangement with Florence B. Smith.

This is a work of fiction. All characters and events portrayed in this book are fictional, and any resemblance to real people or incidents is purely coincidental.

G.K. Hall Large Print Romance Series.

The text of this edition is unabridged.
Other aspects of the book may vary from the original edition.

Set in 16 pt. Plantin by Al Chase.

Printed in the United States on permanent paper.

Library of Congress Cataloging-in-Publication Data

Smith, Florence B.
   Labette County's ultimate deception / Florence B. Smith.
      p.   cm.
   ISBN 0-7838-9375-2 (lg. print : hc : alk. paper)
   1. Private investigators — Kansas — Fiction.   2. Labette County
(Kan.) — History.   3. Missing persons — Fiction.   4. Married
women — Fiction.   5. Bender family — Fiction.   6. Large type
books.   I. Title: Ultimate deception.   II. Title.
PS3569.M35165 L33 2001
813´.6—dc21   00-065342

DEDICATION

Dedicated to Angie Graff who helped me on fact-finding trips so I could write this story. I also want to thank Sophia and Virginia for their encouragement. Last, but by no means least, I want my husband to know that without him, I'd have given up writing years ago. I love you, darling Er, and thanks for everything.

FOREWORD

The characters of THE ULTIMATE DECEP-
TION are tried by fire, so to speak, and have survived to reflect the spirit and intestinal fortitude of
the early settlers in our great country. This is a
story of evil verses good, and the way the battle
goes is intriguing.

CHAPTER ONE

1873

Private Investigator Shadrach Koby glanced at the beautiful, enticing Sarah Anne Daniels sitting on the straight-backed wooden train seats of the passenger coach. He could see that she didn't appear alarmed, so he said nothing. The passenger car they rode in rocked from side to side much more than he thought it should. He glanced quickly toward the vestibule hoping to see the conductor, but he wasn't there. Shadrach settled his gaze back on Sarah. She sat directly across from him and her whole being shone with the renewed hope he'd given her a few minutes ago.

He wished he hadn't taken this assignment, he didn't need the money. His uncle had left him a fortune, but he wasn't a philanderer, so he'd become an investigator, which was a respectable name for *bounty hunter*. Looking at the porcelain beauty across from him, he almost wished he hadn't given her the latest bit of information about her missing husband. Shadrach was falling in love with Sarah, but she had love in her heart for only her husband.

Shadrach hadn't wanted to leave Chicago again, but Sarah had wanted him to. This time they were going to Kansas — Labette County Kansas — to a town called Cherryvale. He shuddered at the thought and again glanced out the window. He raked his fingers through his thick black hair. Trees and rock bluffs flashed passed in a blur. He wondered briefly why the engineer was in such a hurry. Again he took a quick peek at Sarah, then cast a concerned look back toward the window — *the engineer is driving this train far too fast!* he told himself.

A limb from a tree too near the railroad easement smacked the window causing him to jump. "Damn!" he muttered embarrassed by his reaction. Why was the train moving so rapidly? Where was the conductor? More to the point, why was he feeling so apprehensive about going to a town named Cherryvale? Perhaps it was the nature of the letter he'd received from a man named Troy Adams. He was seeking the award money Sarah was offering for any information leading to the whereabouts of her husband. The letter had said Adams was staying at a hotel in Parsons, Kansas and had seen the name Leo Daniels on the registry. He asked for a picture of Leo Daniels, so he could see if anyone in town remembered seeing him. If anyone did, Troy Adams said he had some startling information that might explain what had happened to Leo Daniels. He'd ended his letter, saying:

Several men have turned up missing in this area of southeast Kansas, and someone should come and check this out. I think there's a vicious killer on the loose out here. I will be staying at the

Parsons Hotel until April first. The clerk here said this man, Leo Daniels, was heading for Cherryvale, before going on to wherever he was to buy some horses.

Sincerely, Troy Adams.

Shadrach stretched out his legs, being careful not to touch Sarah. He could hear and feel the wheels clattering under him. Visualizing the sparks flying behind the wheels once more made him uneasy about the speed they were traveling. Glancing at Sarah, he saw she didn't seem perturbed. She smiled, but her smile didn't hide the tiredness he saw in her eyes. Sarah's husband had disappeared, or rather, she'd not heard from him in eleven months. Leo Daniels had left Chicago a year ago this March 15, 1872, with a large amount of money, prepared to purchase Quarter Horses for the riding stable he and Sarah were planning to build. Rodeos were the current obsession, and they wanted to accommodate the many young people in Chicago who wanted to learn to ride in these sporting events.

Shadrach squared his broad shoulders, flexed the muscles of his back and stared out the window again. This was just another of Sarah's dreams that had faded and died because of Leo Daniels. The man had promised her the world, and might have given her a part of it except for the war. The Civil War had ended seven years ago, and hundreds of thousands of survivors made their way back to ravished homes and broken families to make a fresh start. Leo Daniels was one of these soldiers who wanted to pick up his life where he'd left it. War changed many lives, and the way Sarah took the changes in Leo Daniels was something remarkable to behold.

Shadrach shifted in his seat and studied the woman across from him. Her loose yellow blouse failed to hide her full bosom which wasn't all that common on one so thin and petite. He moved forward and started to speak just as her lips spread into a smile. It was a sweet smile that carried promise with it. Shadrach hurt inside because the promise wasn't for him. His gaze was focused on her round, warm green eyes fringed with dark lashes, but he had to glance away or be lost in the depths of those green pools.

Covertly, he examined her high, delicate cheekbones, and her straight, slightly up-tilted nose rising above full, rose-petal soft lips. None of these features could compare with her seductive, expressive eyes. Sarah had a face and personality few men would be able to forget. So where was Leo Daniels? Shadrach left his seat.

"Are you going to the vestibule?" Sarah asked.

"Thinking about it," he answered.

"May I come with you?"

He reached out his hand to her. "Of course you may." He led her down the aisle of the passenger coach helping her keep her balance because of the swaying car. They reached the door that opened between the cars. They were standing on a platform in the vestibule that allowed them to see from each side of the train, but not behind it.

The wind roared around them because of the speed they were traveling. "Doesn't it seem we are going awfully fast?" Sarah called so she could be heard. She leaned over the guard rail to look down the tracks.

Shadrach took her arm and pulled her back. "Don't lean out like that! You scare the life out of me! Yes, I think we are going too fast. I hoped to see the conductor in the next car." He opened the other door and nearly fell before he was able to close it again. "He's not in this car either. Someone ought to ask him where the hell he thinks he's going."

"Leo always knew what to do in difficult situations. I'll be so happy when he comes home," Sarah cried. She was uneasy because Shad seemed so worried. She didn't like to see frown lines on his handsome, clean-shaven face. Shadrach always reminded her of a picture she'd seen in school. It was a sculptor of David, by Michelangelo. To Sarah, Shadrach's face wasn't as beautiful as David's, but in it you could see his innate pride and determined, intense eyes. He had a nervous yet agile body expressing the force, decision, and nobility in a man of strength.

Shadrach was still holding her arm as they stood in the vestibule watching the blur of passing objects. He wasn't certain if he'd been

11

insulted by Sarah wishing her husband was here, and he had no intention of letting her remark slide. "Meaning no disrespect, Sarah, but is it possible your husband may have changed his mind about returning home to Chicago. Men have been known to do such things — even men capable of handling *difficult situations.*"

Sarah jerked her arm from his grasp and faced Shadrach. "I didn't have any reference to you, Shad. You are also a man for every occasion, but I resent you implying that Leo has left me. I've been told the same thing by more people than you can imagine. I never expected to hear it from you. Lord, Shad, I thought we were well enough acquainted, and that you'd heard enough about Leo to know his nature is nothing but good, all the way to his soul."

Shad tucked his finger into the collar of his shirt and tugged, hoping to relieve the tightening in his throat. He didn't want to reveal his personal feelings about Leo Daniels. Part of Shadrach's initial investigation was to find the architect and the builders who were supposed to have been building the stable, but he found no one who knew anything about such a project.

Sarah had not been upset by this since she said that Leo had many Army friends out of state whom he could've contacted.

"If that is the case why haven't you heard from them?" he remembered plainly asking.

Her answer was that Leo had probably not signed a contract yet, or had decided to wait until he had purchased the horses he wanted. After that, Shadrach knew she'd never believe Leo had left her, so he didn't bother to tell her that his so-called bank account was nonexistent. He'd been to every bank in Chicago. He was certain if he did tell Sarah, she would say that he had used a bank in another city or state.

"Shad didn't you hear me? Haven't you learned enough about Leo Daniels to know he would never leave me. He loves me so much, I get angry when you intimate he's not coming back."

"What I meant to say is that it's possible he's been providentially hindered in some way," Shadrach offered weakly.

"Thank you, Shad. I needed to hear you say that. I've been angry, depressed, and over-wrought by unthinking friends who have no idea how strong Leo's love is for me. I know you have had some doubts after so many disappointing searches. I will not allow these doubts to upset me. My husband loved me more than his own life — the only way he'd not come home to me is if he were murdered — God forbid!"

Shadrach steadied Sarah as the train swayed furiously. This wasn't the first time he'd heard the lovely Sarah expound about how much Leo Daniels loved her. She'd told him so many times, he'd begun to wonder who she was trying to convince. Her faith in Leo was mind-boggling, and Shadrach wanted to find him just to justify the confidence she had in him.

The train had picked up more speed and was whistling down the tracks faster than before. The coach lurched to the side and Shadrach reached out for Sarah who had lost her footing. He held her a moment longer than he should have. When he turned her loose, she smoothed her shirt and turned to look out the opening between the cars.

Since Shad had gone to work for Sarah nearly nine months ago, he'd found it more and more difficult to maintain an air of professionalism, and holding her tight in his arms, even for a few seconds, didn't help. He was certain that he had never met anyone as wonderful as Sarah Daniels, had never looked into eyes the color of pale-green agates, had never seen skin so fair and flawless, had never seen hair the color of copper threaded with gold. Lord, but she was beautiful — put together by God Himself! She had him in knots — and at her beck and call.

As the train sped on, Shadrach leaned over the guard rail and saw the engine as it bent around a long curve. What was the engineer doing? He heard Sarah scream and reached for her. "It'll be all right," he yelled, refraining from taking her back into his arms.

Before Shadrach's father had died, he'd told him never to get personally involved with his clients, saying that familiarity bred contempt. What he felt for Sarah was a long way from contempt.

"Sarah, I'm going to search for Leo one more

time, but I don't want you to go with me any farther than Kansas City."

"But why?" she cried.

There was no way that he could tell her why he didn't want her along. She wouldn't understand how her smile affected him, how her voice made his pulse sound like an Indian tom-tom, or how her accidental touch would send gooseflesh over his entire body. These long train rides with her crammed in the seat next to him or directly across from him where he could do no more than stare at her beauty, were the worst — often tortuous. He couldn't name the times he'd nearly lost his composure and taken her into his arms; especially when she'd fall asleep on trains or stagecoaches and her head would tilt softly onto his shoulder. He couldn't take anymore; he'd made up his mind not to continue subjecting himself to her charm and beauty.

"Sarah, try to understand," he called, as he peered over her shoulder at the passing blur of bushes and trees, "we've been searching for Leo nearly nine months, following leads all over Texas and Oklahoma, interviewing people about dozens of possible sightings, and all of them to no avail. Besides, the traveling is hard on you. You've lost weight — look at you! You weigh a hundred pounds, more or less, and your usually cheery countenance has turned to a seriousness that doesn't become you."

Sarah touched her face, then reached out to take his arm for balance. "I can't help how I

15

look. What if you had a wife and she disappeared, wouldn't you go through countless disappointments, inclement weather, being uncomfortable, or even miss a meal or two?" she yelled above the whistling wind. She was now feeling concern over the rough ride they were experiencing.

She clung to Shadrach and fear filled her eyes. Shad spoke close to her ear so he wouldn't have to yell. "I certainly would do anything in my power — until it became fairly clear to me that I wasn't going to find her. Sarah, I didn't say you looked awful; you're as beautiful today as the day I first met you. Traveling is hard on you. I see it in your eyes — those expressive eyes, emerald green as the foliage of the wild columbine." Shad glanced at the exposed skin of her arms, ran his finger slowly from her elbow to her hand, then said, "I've never seen such fair complexion, and it weathers nicely, reminds me of a Georgia peach." He was trying to relieve her obvious concern. "I spoke about this haunted expression of yours that I'd give all I have to see disappear."

Sarah wanted to ask him how she could hide her fear that Leo had met with foul play. How could she erase from her brow the concern always with her? She lived with fear that she might be a widow. Leo would have written her a letter if he could — wouldn't he? She shook her head to rid herself of her morbid thoughts, and tried to figure how to convince Shad that she would be all right if he'd take her with him. She

16

was paying him to work for her and she could flat out tell him she was going, but she didn't want to be overbearing. "Shad, if I try harder to lift my spirits, will you allow me to accompany you one more time?" she shouted, smiling in a beguiling way that caused Shad's pulse to skip beats. "I don't want to stay alone in Kansas City. Please."

Why was he like oil in her presence? He cleared his throat and said, "All right, Sarah — one more time. But if we find nothing this trip, I'll not go anymore. I don't like taking your money when I'm not accomplishing anything."

"How can you say that? Because of your investigations, we now know that Leo reached Parsons, Kansas and was on his way to Independence when he disappeared, somewhere around Cherryvale. Please don't quit on me now! We're closer to finding Leo than we've ever been, and thank you for your compliments about myself. You've always been a perfect gentleman and I so very much appreciate you. Thank you for allowing me to go with you; I couldn't have stayed in Kansas City — not when we're so close to finding Leo. I have a good feeling about this lead, we're going to find him," she shouted.

She stepped very close to him and placed her hands on his shoulders, mainly for balance and to be heard. "And, Shad, I'm aware how hard this is on you. I know you have more to do in life than helping me. I'll pay you double for this trip."

Shadrach placed his large hands around her tiny waist and lifted her away from him. "I don't want your money!"

"What do you want?" she yelled, showing shock at his statement.

He wanted to say, I want you, but he restrained himself, and said, "I want this job to be over. I want to see you happy with your husband so I can get on with a life of my own, but it's only ·fair that I tell you, Leo may well be dead."

"You've told me that many times, but as always, I won't believe it until I see his body or stand beside his grave."

"For your sake, I hope we can settle this in Kansas." The train lurched and the coach rocked with disturbing intensity. Sarah screamed and Shadrach pulled her into his arms. He heard those inside the two passenger coaches screaming and frantically shouting for the conductor.

Shadrach made a quick decision. "Go inside and wait for me." He opened the door into the coach, and Sarah stepped halfway inside. "Go on in and sit down," he shouted, pushing her down the aisle. When he looked for a seat, he saw their former seats were occupied. "Come on, we'll try the next car," he said.

As they started back to the vestibule, the conductor arrived with obvious concern written on his face. He was repeatedly pulling the emergency stop cord. The train made a sudden vicious lurch throwing the conductor into the bulkhead of the vestibule. He was stunned and bleeding profusely from a head injury. He staggered momentarily then fell to the aisle in a daze. Sarah stepped quickly to his side and kneeled down to help him.

The conductor cried out desperately, "There's a slow order out on the bridge ahead and the engineer isn't responding!"

Shadrach grabbed the stop cord and jerked several times without any response.

"Something's terribly wrong!" the conductor cried trying to get to his feet, but failing.

Shadrach headed for the door. Sarah followed him as he exited the door. "Where are you going?" she cried when Shadrach began climbing the ladder to the roof.

"I'm going to see what the engineer is doing. Get inside and into a seat. I'll come back as soon as possible."

He climbed to the roof of the fast-rolling train and found it impossible to stand, much less walk or run. The catwalk was narrow, but on his hands and knees, Shadrach crawled rapidly toward the engine which was four cars ahead of him. A sudden whip-like sway of the train caused him to nearly fall over the edge. He was able to cling to the catwalk while trying to gain a foothold. He was struggling to hang on, and when he'd hoisted himself back onto the narrow catwalk atop the train, he resumed crawling.

Shortly, after another dozen scares, Shadrach reached the coal tender. He leaped into the midst of the shifting, dancing coal and dug his way to the other end. Coal dust soiled his clothing, choked him, and blurred his vision. For one quick instant, he thought he saw movement at the side to the tender, but the shifting coal was a more crushing matter to deal with. With one hand he was able to grab the top of the coal car and hefted himself high enough to get both hands on the edge. From there it was easy to swing himself over the top of the car and into the cab of the engine.

Shadrach saw the engineer on the deck. After a quick feel of his neck, Shadrach knew he was unconscious, probably a heart attack. He heard a sound like someone laughing and looked around. He saw no one. Where was the fireman? Then, glancing back at the engineer, he saw the blood beneath him. Had there been a fight? Shadrach didn't have time to speculate. The train was speeding down the tracks, swaying furiously from side to side. His mind was questioning how good his decision had been. He didn't know anything about trains.

He reached for the brake handle but discovered it was the throttle. He couldn't decide what was what, and bent to the floor to try and revive the engineer, but as he bent, a solid blow to his back sent him falling across the engineer. Shadrach rolled over and saw a wild-eyed man ready to sling the coal shovel into his head.

Again Shadrach rolled, but not fast enough.

The blow knocked him senseless; he seemed paralyzed. He stared at the laughing man pushing on the throttle. The fireman had gone berserk.

CHAPTER TWO

Shadrach lay very still where he'd been knocked on top of the badly wounded, possibly dead engineer. As feeling slowly began to return to his body, the urgent state of the imminent emergency hadn't escaped him. All he could think about was stopping the train. He drew up his legs and with all his strength, kicked the fireman away from the throttle. He stumbled sideways, reaching out to grab for something to stop his flight out the open cab, but there was nothing.

Shadrach managed to get to his feet. As he looked ahead he saw the town of Kansas City. "Damn!" he cried as the train bore down on a metal bridge. He could feel the wheels clattering faster and faster. Shadrach knew he had to do something. He didn't know what a *slow order* was, but remembering the frantic conductor, Shadrach knew it must be bad. He pulled the throttle back and grabbed what he supposed was the brake handle, desperately trying to stop the engine.

He heard the horrible sound of metal striking metal, leaned out and saw sparks spewing from the wheels, then knew he'd found the brake. The engine screeched to a faltering stop just as it crossed the narrow bridge. Shadrach stared back with thanksgiving which instantly changed to horror as the cars piled into each other. The baggage car uncoupled from the tender in the impact, it and the engine remained stationary. The baggage car jumped track and toppled from the bridge. One by one, two more cars followed in a crushing plunge. The remainder of the train stayed on the tracks. Passengers screamed in terror as the coaches hit the water.

Shadrach leaped out of the engine, and amid the crunch of metal and screams, made his way down the bank of the bridge. All he could think about was Sarah. Was she in the water? Dead? Some people, lucky enough to get out of the half submerged passenger cars were swimming for the bank. They were crying or in shock, some begging for help, and as Shadrach pulled men and women onto the rocks, he couldn't think of anything but Sarah. He kept searching for her, praying and hoping the car she was on hadn't left the tracks. It was impossible to determine which car she was in. He hardly had time to count, but he was fairly certain the fourth car had stayed on the tracks.

Those passengers from the remaining cars were jumping into the water to help pull struggling passengers from the train. Shadrach heard a man shriek, "I've got to get my wife out!" The man was bleeding badly, but dove back into the water. Shadrach pitched his hat aside, yanked off his boots and followed him, swimming to the coach with the man.

The man took a deep breath and dove under water. Shadrach did the same. The riled slough was muddy and it was difficult to see. The man swam through a hole in the side of the car. His wife was not breathing, her body wedged among the twisted metal.

Shadrach could see well enough to know that freeing her was impossible, but the woman's husband was determined. He pushed and shoved against the metal holding her, then sensing the fruitlessness of his effort, swam out of the car. When he and Shadrach reached the surface, the man began to sob. "I can't bear to live without her." He jack-knifed and went under, swimming back for his wife.

Shadrach started to follow, but he saw a young boy trying to swim with one arm. The other had nearly been ripped off. Shadrach grabbed the boy, and swam to the rocks where others were waiting, ready to pull them out. Immediately, Shadrach took off his belt and tied a tourniquet on the boy's arm. Then he pulled on his boots and picked up the boy. People from nearby homes and businesses were arriving with wagons. Shadrach carried the boy to one of the wagons already full of wounded and signaled the driver to head for the hospital.

He turned around and started across the bridge to find Sarah when he heard her call his name. She was on the bank below the bridge helping pull people from the water. Shadrach ran across the bridge and down the other bank to where Sarah stood.

She cried, "I thought I'd die after the wreck

until I saw the engine. You did it! You got the train stopped. The conductor is grateful. He's been talking to some railroad men who rushed here within an hour of the wreck — unbelievable how fast bad news travels! The train stopped in time to save most us." She rushed into his arms. "I'm so thankful you're safe."

"I'm sorry, Sarah, but the wreck was my fault. The fireman had evidently gone mad and killed the engineer. I had to fight him and ended up kicking him off the engine. I stopped the train too quickly. When I saw the bridge, I panicked."

Sarah looked around her. "Shh, don't say that. I saw you helping people, that little boy might have bled to death but for your quick action. Other than a couple dozen injured, I heard no one died."

"I know one woman who is dead — maybe her husband with her." Shad shuddered as he recalled the desperation of the man trying to save his wife.

"But it could have been much worse. You have to realize that," Sarah said as she stepped out of his arms. "Look, here comes more wagons and people from Kansas City are coming to help. We can't do much more here so why don't we leave? Let's catch a ride in one of the wagons going into town."

"I need to tell the railroad authorities what happened. There may be a dead fireman down track, or if he's not dead, he needs some help. The man is crazy — I've never seen eyes so obsessed with destroying something as his were. It was one of the most frightening experiences of my life."

Sarah was silent, seemingly able to understand how distraught he was. She reached out and touched his arm. "You were wonderful, a hero."

She had a way of making him feel ten feet tall. He cleared his throat and said, "I thought I spotted some officials about thirty minutes ago. I've got to find them — they need to know what happened."

"What did you say?" a booming voice called.

Shadrach saw a well-dressed man coming from the engine. He was making his way down the bank toward him and Sarah.

"Who wants to know?" Shadrach called back.

"I'm the train master in charge of this district," the man said, sticking his hand out when he was near enough. "Carl Owens," he said. "I'd like to hear what you know about this wreck. Do you know who killed the engineer? Where is the fireman?"

Shadrach briefly told Carl Owens what he knew, and what he'd tried to do. "I'm afraid this is all my fault," he said as he finished, looking at the crumpled wreck in the water.

"On the contrary, you were obviously unaware that a slow order was in effect due to high water on the Missouri River. A quarter of a mile farther up track is the Missouri River Railroad Bridge. Had you not stopped this train when you did, the train would never have made it across. In my book, you are the champion of the day. This whole train could easily be on the bottom of the Missouri. Thank God, you got it stopped."

"See, you really did save the train and passengers," Sarah cried.

Shadrach said nothing as he glanced once more at the three mangled cars in the creek. His eyes glimpsed the man whose wife had been trapped. "Excuse me a minute," Shadrach said to the train master.

"That's fine, you go on, I see my section foreman coming over there. We've a lot of work to do here. Don't leave the area before I get your name and where you can be reached."

Shadrach hardly heard the man, as he made his way to the depressed looking fellow. "Sir," Shadrach said when he reached his side, "I'm glad to see you're alive. I'm sorry about your wife. Death is never easy."

"I'd have killed the engineer for taking my wife, but someone beat me to him. He cheated me out of my very life — my beloved wife."

Shadrach glanced at the forty-fives strapped at the man's hips and decided to leave well-enough alone. He had no desire to have a grief-stricken avenger stalking him, so he didn't disclose the part he'd played in the death of the man's wife.

The man stuck out his hand to Shadrach. "I want to thank you for your effort trying to save my sweetheart."

Shadrach shook his hand and said, "I'm just sorry I couldn't have been more help."

Sarah called from above, "Shad, I've found us a ride into Kansas City. Come on, or we'll be left."

Shadrach nodded to the man, and looked around for his hat. He'd slung it aside when he'd dived into the creek. There it was, right where he'd left it. He ran to recover it, and then climbed the bank to where Sarah waited. As he took a seat on the rear of the wagon, he said, "Oh, I forgot; I'm supposed to give the train master my name and address." He jumped off, Sarah followed.

"Forget doing that," Sarah said, "we don't know where we'll be from day to day."

"This won't take but a minute. I see the train master there on the bridge."

"All right, I'll wait right here and try to get us another ride."

"Thanks," Shadrach said, wondering how she could look so good even wet and muddy.

"You're welcome." She smiled and took his hand, squeezing it gently. "I'm so proud of you."

When Shadrach Koby and Sarah Daniels arrived in Kansas City, they exchanged their city apparel for clothing more suited to the west. They had mutually decided to ride to Labette County after their sad experience on the railroad. "Anyway," Shadrach said, "we'll appear more like traveling natives riding horses and leading pack animals."

Shadrach had a theory — if mercenaries had

robbed and killed Leo Daniels, perhaps Sarah and he would tempt them again. Sarah was enticing enough by herself, that's why he'd asked her to dress temporarily in men's clothing. She'd stuffed her bright vermilion hair under her black Stetson, and bound her full breasts so he could hardly believe the way she looked — flat-chested.

She wore an oversized shirt, boots, and hat. As he looked at her, he hoped binding herself so flat wouldn't hurt her. He wanted to ask, but knew better. She might take his inquiry as forwardness and be insulted. Shadrach didn't want anything to happen to her form, or to the way she was reacting to him of late. She was perfectly put together — face and body, and he could hardly keep his hands away from her.

They left Kansas City and headed for Westport in a covered cab. Shadrach said, "If possible, and with a little luck, I hope to trail along with a wagon train as far as we can. We'll turn south when we're straight north of Labette County."

Sarah was surprised at his sudden decision to join a wagon train. "I thought the railroads had taken over carrying people west." She looked at the wagons which seemed to be everywhere in Westport and asked, "Why are there so many wagons still making the long trip?"

"Trains are for those folks with no treasures to transport, or at least nothing too large — costs too much. Wagons traveling on the trails today

29

are loaded with furniture and priceless heir-looms. Some are transporting growing fruit trees and even grape vines to plant in the perfect climate of California. Others are taking tons of special seeds, rye, red wheat, and alfalfa, and frankly, trains aren't always dependable."

Sarah smiled. "Aren't you the pillar of wisdom!"

"Are you making fun of me?"

"Never. However, I'm constantly amazed at what you know about places and people, and things."

"This is the fifth time in nine months that we've been to Kansas City. I hear a lot if I listen."

"How come I haven't heard some of what you have?"

"Men don't usually talk about such things in the presence of a lady."

"I hope it's different this time — you know — with me dressed like a man."

"Don't count on it. Anyone who gets within ten feet of you will know you're a woman. The way you're dressed only protects you from a distance."

"And how is that?" she asked, turning in the seat to better hear his answer.

"The west is short of women and full of starving men. If one of these men see us passing, they will pay no heed because from afar, you'll seem like a young man, but face to face, they'll know the difference."

"I know one thing, I'll prefer riding in trousers and boots to a dress. Hey, there's a wagon train and it appears to be ready to leave. What is Westport anyway?"

"Westport was a way station for wagons heading west or south. Since the railroads have grown so big, fewer wagons are going west anymore. Now, because of that fact, Westport is the place to make good buys on horses and gear."

Shadrach paid the cabbie, and took their satchels from the luggage rack behind the wagon. They had done things like this before, but never here in Westport. The first place Shadrach went was the livery. He purchased two pack horses, and had them fully equipped with needed gear; two tents, two stools with backs on them, pots and pans for cooking, a pickax and shovel, sleeping blankets, and several other items that made them look prosperous.

Shadrach picked a black stallion named Hominy for himself, and wondered about his other horse being boarded back in Chicago. Sarah seemed attracted to a gentle brown and white pinto named Bear, so Shadrach talked her into getting it.

"Stay here; I'll ride ahead and speak to the wagonmaster. I'll let him know that you and I would like to tag along for a while. He'll know where we should turn south for Cherryvale."

"Shad, I'm so excited. Why can't we just ride on? Why do we have to trail after a wagon train?"

"There's safety in numbers and you'd do well

to keep that in mind." He kicked his horse and rode forward.

Sarah watched him ride away and thought how well he set a horse. He rode like a man born to the saddle. Shadrach Koby was unique. Handsome could describe him, but Sarah thought of Shad as more attractive than handsome. He was certainly more attractive than Leo, but then, Shad didn't have any permanent injury to detract from his looks as had Leo.

Shad and Leo had both fought in the Civil War, and Shad had come home unscathed by sword, bullet, or emotional trauma, while Leo had suffered injury by all three. A sword had punctured one of his lungs, a bullet had so riddled his left leg that he would always walk with a decided limp. These had taken a toll on his emotional stability, but had not changed the way he loved her. While he recuperated in an army hospital, he'd whittled himself a unique walking stick. Carved on the top of the mahogany wood was a face, much like a cameo. He said the face was a replica of herself. It had been a labor of love.

Tears blurred her vision as she dabbed at them with her handkerchief. Thoughts of how Leo had suffered always upset her. She saw Shad riding back toward her and plastered a grin on her face. His answering smile was contagious, and she found herself giving him back one just as genuine. He was much larger than Leo, but why wouldn't he be? Shad was healthy and active. He had muscles on his muscles, was over six feet tall, broad shouldered and narrow hipped. Leo spent most of his time with a pen and paper, while Shad traveled all over the country helping one client or another.

Thank goodness Shad hadn't yet married or he'd be divorced — no woman could tolerate his lifestyle. He might be gone four or six weeks at a time. Sarah couldn't believe how faithful he'd been to help her. If not for her parents leaving her a substantial inheritance, she could never have afforded to hire Shadrach Koby. He'd quoted her a fee far less than the Pinkerton Agency.

Leo had never allowed her to use her parents' money. It seemed that he had much to prove to her as well as to himself. Poor Leo — the war had changed him in so many ways. Her happy-go-lucky husband had returned to her a wounded veteran; the only thing about him that hadn't changed was his love for her, and that love had been enough. She constantly had tried to support his effort to be the wage earner. He had been in the cavalry and his injury hadn't lessened his ability to ride. Horses and he got along phenomenally, so when he'd come up with the idea to buy a stable and rent horses to give lessons to those wanting to learn to ride, she'd encouraged him to proceed. She had always felt guilty about the money her father had left her because he'd made his fortune from racing horses. The worst part was the way he'd treated all his animals. He believed all horses were dumb and only learned by using the whip, which he did constantly. Sarah shuddered; she honestly believed her father enjoyed cruelty. So when Leo wanted a stable and horses, she'd jumped at the chance to rectify some of her father's unmerciful acts to his champions.

Leo owned a Quarter Horse and wanted to buy more of the breed. He had said that an army pal of his raised Quarter Horses in Fort Worth, Texas and when he had the money, he was going to contact him. Sarah had literally had to beg Leo to let her help — after all it would become as much her dream as his. Leo had finally conceded to take ten-thousand dollars of her inheritance since it was to benefit both their futures. He opened a bank account, had talked to an architect about designing the stables, then the architect was to hire the builders and begin work while Leo was in Texas buying the animals he wanted.

"What has you so serious looking?" Shad said as he rode to her side.

"Oh, nothing; what did the wagonmaster say?"

"Said he could use any man willing to work."

"What kind of work does he have in mind?"

"He needs an extra smith to help keep the wagons moving, and I happen to know a little about smithing."

"What about me?" she asked.

"He said the cook needs a helper."

"The cook? Don't the families of this train cook their own meals?"

"The chuck wagon is for the men who work on the train, those who keep it running, the scouts, blacksmiths, horse handlers, and wagon repairers. If this is something you aren't comfortable doing, I'll ask wagonmaster Burns to find you another job."

"Don't be silly, Shad. I think your arrangements are fine. When do we leave?"

"Burns is waiting for one more arrival — a Pinkerton agent escorting the wagon of a family who is searching for a brother who has disappeared — around Cherryvale."

CHAPTER THREE

Shadrach headed for the make-shift corral with his pack horse while Sarah was left with her pinto and pack animal. She was taken by the wagonmaster to be introduced to the cook. "Where is Mister Koby going to sleep?" she asked, having heard wagonmaster Burns tell him that he would be standing the third watch.

"Near the corral with the other men, I reckon."

"What about me? Do I sleep near the cook wagon or what?" she asked, feeling a bit put out that Shad would leave her without much explanation. He was usually very informative. Besides, she didn't know how to set up a tent. But, perhaps, Shad was as much in the dark as she was. She gave him the benefit of doubt. Oh, well, she thought, I've been in stranger situations than this and survived. I can learn anything if I really want to. She looked at the wagonmaster, waiting for his reply, but then, maybe he didn't know she had a tent to set up.

"I have my own tent," she said, "I could set it up anywhere."

"I expect Jelliroll will tell you where he wants you. Since your escort won't always be around, I want you under the watchful eye of someone I trust. We've lots of roving eyes around here. And a pretty girl like yourself will attract them like bees to pollen. Wouldn't want you to get stung."

"I'm twenty-two years old and have survived without being stung one time, but I appreciate your concern." She smiled at the wagonmaster so he wouldn't think her rude.

"Shadrach Koby told me of your mission, and why you're dressed as a young man — although, I don't believe your disguise will fool many." He chuckled as he looked around. "You've no need to dress as you are on this train, but, that's up to you."

A few minutes later, wagonmaster Burns assisted Sarah as she dismounted beside the cook's wagon. She liked the cook instantly, but it was obvious he wasn't too happy being stuck with her. His girth matched his height. He had white hair and hazel eyes, and they squinted as he spoke, "Concernit, Burns, I done raised my young'uns. Why you doin' this to me?"

"Do it tonight, and tomorrow, I may have a family willing to let her trail along with them."

"Maybe I can work with Mister Koby," Sarah interrupted, not wanting to be anywhere she wasn't invited to be.

"Don't pay any mind to Jelliroll. He's all bluff. You'll be fine with him tonight. We leave at first light." He looked at the cook. "You behave, you old buzzard."

The cook moaned and looked at Sarah. The man was about sixty years old, and amazingly clean-shaven, spotlessly attired, and physically smelled like a fresh bath. "I only cook for the

37

men hired to work the wagon train, and I like what I do, except I hate drivin' this dang chuck wagon. Makes me sore and out of sorts," he said.

Sarah sensed that he was sounding tough to impress her. "Wagonmaster Burns told me I was to help you cook."

"No one helps me cook," he growled.

"Then I can serve the food for you, and do the dishes. Doesn't that qualify me as a hired hand?"

"Humph, guess so. But, it would surely please my men more if'n you wore a dress. I jus don't cotton ta a gal in trousers."

"I have a dress. If you say I should wear one, I will."

"Would please me if ya did."

"Then I will. Now, where should I set up my tent?"

"Tent! I figured ya could sleep under the chuck wagon, and I'd sleep behind it."

"If you don't mind, I prefer the tent. I need a place to dress and bathe."

"Bathe! Oh, Lord, yer a city gal, ain't ya? Well, bathin' don't bother me, but ya'll haul yer own water. Or, like me, ya can bathe in cricks we'll be campin' beside."

"If needing a daily bath and my privacy makes me a city girl, then I am."

"All right, set yer tent behind the chuck wagon." Jelliroll said he'd sleep under the chuckwagon, so she unloaded her pack animal.

With everything removed from her horse, she looked around and wondered what to do with her mounts. The cook saw her dilemma and offered to take the animals to the corral. Sarah was most grateful and began untying the straps to her small tent.

She stood a long time trying to figure what to do. It surprised her that Shadrach had left her to do this by herself. She'd just assumed that he would set up her tent, but she wasn't complaining. In retrospect, she preferred the trail to riding on a train. Her last ride was enough to last a lifetime. She was still studying the tent when Jelliroll returned.

"What ya doin'? I thought ya'd have this up by now."

His disbelieving attitude and stern voice was more than she could take. Tears filled her eyes and she quickly turned away, but evidently not fast enough.

"Lord, yer a city gal and a greenhorn. Okay, ya stop blubberin' and do what I tell ya. We'll have yer tent up in five minutes," he said grabbing up the tent posts.

Sarah gained control and went to work, doing everything that Jelliroll said, and true to his word, the tent was up in a few minutes.

"Thank you," she said, smiling at the huffing and puffing round little man. "I think I can do it by myself the next time."

"Good, I'll show ya how to take it down and pack it up in the morning, but pretty gal, if ya want a bath, and aren't willing to jump into a crick, don't turn those big, green eyes on me —

remember, ya fetch yer own water. For now, if ya jes want ta wash up, the water bucket is over there." He pointed at an oak barrel tied onto the chuck wagon. "It's really fer cooking and clean-up, but ya can use a pan full ever now and then." He gave her a wide, toothless grin.

Sarah knew she'd made a new friend. She filled a pan of water and carried it into her tent, having decided to take a sponge bath. She removed her clothes and wiped down her body with the cool, clean water which removed the dust and made her feel better. Donning her blue muslin dress made her feel very much like a woman. She'd had to dampen some of the wrinkles to get them out. Her satchel was too full to allow anything to escape deep creases.

She allowed her hair to fall freely over her shoulders, dampening it slightly so it would curl around her face. She tied a matching blue ribbon in her hair to keep it off her face. Glancing into her small mirror, she smiled, wondering what Shad would say when he saw her. She knew he'd be happy to see she'd unbound herself. He'd amused her with his questions about the binding hurting her. She sighed as she left the tent to help cook.

"Miss Sarah," Jelliroll said as he fixed supper, "yer about the prettiest gal I've seen in a long time. How come yer husband strayed off?"

She frowned, not certain what to say. She knew Shad had said something that had gotten back to the cook, and that thought made her

40

angry. Angry at Shad, not at Jelliroll. He was just trying to be friendly. "Don't believe everything you hear," she said, hedging a little. "Some of your men are coming. Are you ready for me to dish this food out?" she asked, picking up a ladle, trying to change the subject.

"Mighty thoughtful of ya. See ever'one gets only one slice of cornbread before they start askin' fer seconds."

"I'll do it," she said stepping behind the serving table as men from the makeshift corral washed their faces and hands in pans of water that Jelliroll had sat on a long bench beside drying towels. When they came with their tin plates in hand, she was ready.

"Hey, Jelliroll, when did you get help?" one of the men asked.

"Today, and this one's a tenderfoot, so watch yer mouth, and mind yer manners. Miss Sarah, meet the gang, Jack, Richard, Gerry, and Tex."

"It's good to make your acquaintances," she said.

The two not introduced stepped up. "I'm Granite, this is my brother, Stonewall."

"I'll try to remember all your names, and I'm glad to meet each one of you." She smiled as she placed cornbread and beans on the first man's plate, then served nine more men. "Is this all?" she asked the cook, wondering why Shad wasn't with them.

"Two more, the blacksmith and his new helper are coming. Look behind you." Jelliroll pointed at the pair walking toward the wagon and signaled them. "Come and get it before it's gone."

Sarah hardly believed her eyes. The usually immaculately dressed Shadrach Koby was filthy, and so engrossed in conversation with the blacksmith that he hadn't even looked up to see her. He'd just washed his hands in the pan of water provided, but his clothes and face were smudged and black with soot. She cleared her throat and placed a slice of cornbread on his plate.

He looked up, and dropped his tin in the bean kettle. "What the . . . am I dreaming?"

She smiled. "I don't believe you are." She fished out his plate and wiped the bottom.

"You know this little lady?" Jelliroll asked protectively.

"We've been friends a few months," Shadrach said, seemingly unable to shift his gaze from her face.

The cook took a plate for himself, and said, "We call her Miss Sarah around here." Then he walked away and sat down with his crew, but kept his eyes on his new helper.

Shadrach said, "All right, *Miss Sarah,* let's eat over there, under that sycamore tree, so we can talk. Why did you shed your trousers? I thought we were in agreement about the way you were to dress."

"I'm still in agreement, and I'll dress like a man when we leave the wagon train and are traveling alone. The cook wanted me to wear a dress;

I'll change back when it's necessary," she smiled. "Have you met the family traveling to Cherryvale?"

"No, not yet, but I met the Pinkerton man. He told me plenty. It's really odd that his client's brother and your husband both disappeared so near the same place. Sarah, I'm beginning to agree with you; we may be on Leo's trail this time."

Shad's statement gave her renewed hope. "This conversation may take half the evening. I want to hear everything he told you," she said, glancing at the meadowlark singing in the tree over her.

"I'm willing to tell you what I can remember." Shadrach didn't want to tell her all that the Pinkerton man told him; much of it was too frightening. Samuel Bell, the Pinkerton agent, had told him a lot about Cherryvale. "The town is located on the Osage Mission-Independence Trail which is a winding, beaten path across Eastern Kansas," Bell said. "Cherryvale is nestled among gently rolling hills surrounded by meadows of rich farm land. It derives its name from the many wild cherry trees growing in profusion among the wooded areas and along the winding, peaceful paths of water flowing into one of several rivers. Beneath the land, it is said, lay pools of oil and volumes of gas. Although the state of Kansas prohibits the sale and manufacture of spirits, illegal booze, gambling, and houses of ill repute are in abundance."

Samuel Bell said the town was divided east and west by the railroad tracks, and that Shadrach had better keep his client away from the west side. "No lady is safe over there after dark," he'd remarked.

That was scary enough for Shadrach to contemplate, but what Bell told him about missing men in the area was worse. "A man named Bill McCrotty left his home near Osage Mission with over two-thousand dollars and disappeared. When his family traced his trail they found him clad only in his undergarment face down in a field. He'd been hit in the head, and had his throat cut.

"Another man, John Greary, was found dead in the same fashion, and the two-thousand dollars he carried was missing. Other reports were that a Johnny Boyle had disappeared in the same region."

Shadrach shuddered thinking about some killer, or killers, roaming the vicinity of Cherryvale. Lord, but he didn't want to subject Sarah to such a blood-thirsty country.

As Shadrach ate beans and cornbread, Sarah studied him covertly. She asked herself as she had many times, how this man had so easily won her confidence.

As they sat eating together, children were playing hide-and-seek. One young boy stumbled over a root in the excitement of the game and fell on his face. Before Sarah could react, Shadrach was on his feet, picking up the boy. He brushed

44

dirt from the boy's face, checked his front teeth to see if the hit to the ground had loosened them, then said, "Lift your feet really high when you aren't watching the ground. You'll not stumble so easily." Shadrach patted the boy's shoulder and sent him on to play.

Sarah knew that act of kindness was one reason she was drawn to Shad. He was gentle and caring. Before he sat down, he asked, "Would you like a cup of coffee?"

"Why yes, thank you." She handed him her tin cup. His fingers touched her hand. The sensation was wonderful. She drew a long slow breath as she watched him walk toward the fire. No one's touch, other than Leo's, had ever thrilled her so much. Shad was as considerate as he was exciting.

She nodded politely as he returned, carefully taking the hot cup he was handing her. "I can't tell you how lovely you look this evening," he said.

"Why can't you?" she asked, teasing him the way he often did her.

"It might go to your head," he joked back. "Too much vanity is a curse."

"I don't believe I'm vain — am I?"

"Not in the least, but you have every reason to be," he said, then smiled. "Have I ever told you how much I like the color of your hair?"

"Not really," she answered starting to feel uncomfortable under his gaze and the way the conversation was drifting.

"When the sun shines on it, I think of copper thread woven with gold and silver."

"Why thank you, Shad, that was a sweet thing to say. I think it's part of my job on this train to help the cook with clean-up." She looked around and started to get up, but Shadrach took her hand.

"I honestly don't have the words to describe you as I'd like," he said eyeing her appearance in the lovely dress she wore. He saw she was nervous. "I hope I haven't said anything that has upset you."

Embarrassed by the trend of their dialogue, she said, "Speaking of being upset, did you know that you've already made me feel bad once today."

"I have? How?" Shadrach asked, his eyes glowing with concern.

"What did you tell the cook or the wagonmaster about my husband?"

"I only said that he'd not come home in eleven months."

"Thanks a lot. What would have been so difficult about saying Leo Daniels has been missing for eleven months?"

"What I said means the same as what you said. I'm sorry if my words were offensive."

"Don't get sensitive on me," she said quickly, "I'm just trying to understand why you are suddenly bad-mouthing Leo."

"I'm not bad-mouthing Leo Daniels." He thought about the ten-thousand dollars Leo was

46

probably carrying and wondered about telling Sarah what he'd learned from Pinkerton Agent Bell, but he quickly dismissed the idea. What she was now upset about was minor to what he wanted to tell her.

"It seems to me you are," she said glancing around trying to decide how to get off this subject. "I see cook is cleaning up. I'd better go help him." Sarah stood, and walked away. She could see that she'd hurt Shad's feelings, but he'd also hurt hers.

"Hey, Miss Sarah, I wasn't certain ya'd be here for clean-up," Jelliroll sang.

"I'm here, ready to work."

"That's my gal!" Jelliroll said, as he poured hot water over a bar of lye soap.

"What can I do?" she asked.

"Ya wash and I'll dry and put away."

From that first meal, Sarah enjoyed every minute helping Jelliroll. She discovered that his name was given him at birth because even then he said he was as broad as he was wide. He said no one ever poked fun at him because of his shape.

Sarah knew why they didn't. He was agile for his weight and completed his share of chores. As she turned to speak to him, she saw Shad walking toward the corral. As always, his walking away or toward her made butterflies in her stomach.

"Hey, pretty gal, ever go to a hoedown?" Jelliroll asked.

"I don't believe so, what is it?" she asked.

"Fiddles, guitars, mouth harps, jugs, and wash boards all playin' toe-tappin' music ta dance by."

"I've never had the pleasure," she said, smiling at him. She'd been to all kinds of dances, never one called a hoedown, unless it was similar to a barn dance.

"Every night on the trail, there's usually music or story-tellin', and once or twice a week, there's a dance. Wagonmaster Burns said we'd have a short dance ta-night so ever'one could get acquainted. I'd be flattered if'n I could escort ya."

"You know that I'm in mourning over my missing husband," she said, searching for a way to say no politely.

" husband wouldn't want ya to pine away fer him. If he loved ya as much as ya seem to love him, I'd say he'd be happy to see ya enjoyin' yerself. Havin' a dance or two with me or one of my boys is just innocent fun. I'll be with ya to see no one gets out of line. Whatdaya say?"

Sarah glanced at the corral, and not seeing Shad, said she'd be delighted to go with him. She knew Shad was probably too upset with her to go anyway, and she felt bad about being so short with him. Maybe it was she who was being insensitive? She needed to apologize. *No, she would not.*

CHAPTER FOUR

As Sarah considered telling Shadrach she was sorry, she decided again that she had nothing to apologize for. Shad was definitely not dealing with Leo's disappearance the way he used to. Perhaps, she should just dismiss him, and let him get on with his life. . . .

That thought didn't set too well. Why did the possibility of not having Shadrach Koby at her side cause a lonely feeling to roll over her? She closed her eyes and turned away.

"Ya all right, Miss Sarah?" Jelliroll asked.

"I'm fine, just tired."

"Why don't ya go rest. We've an hour to wait fer the dance ta start."

"Thanks, I believe I will." She wiped her hands on her apron, and walked to her tent only a few yards from the wagon. She was enamored by the birds who didn't seem afraid of the people and horses. A warbling red bird perched on a limb near the wagon didn't even flitter a feather as she walked past. Inside the tent, she removed her dress and laid it across her satchel so it wouldn't be wrinkled for the dance. She wasn't really excited about going, but first impressions are important, she told herself as she lay down on her bedroll.

When the fiddle music started, Sarah came

49

awake with a start. She expected Jelliroll any minute, so she combed her hair and slipped into her blue dress. She rubbed some coloring on her cheeks, a rose cream that her mother had taught her to use sparingly. She had taught herself to rub a small amount on her lips to deepen the natural color and give her lips a sheen.

Sarah spread the blanket over her bedroll, then stepped outside the tent; she didn't see Jelliroll anywhere. He could have called for her and when she didn't answer, gone on deciding to let her sleep. She walked slowly toward the people gathered around the huge center fire.

The first person she recognized was Granite. With him was his brother, Stonewall, and when they saw her, she was greeted heartily. "You hear about the horse kickin' Tex?"

"No, I didn't. Is he badly hurt?" Sarah answered.

"Jelliroll took him into Kansas City to see a doctor. Broken ribs probably. They'll be back directly. The dancin' is startin'," Granite said nervously, "could I have a dance with you, Miss Sarah?" he asked and bowed, his hat crumpled in his hand, and a hopeful expression on his face.

She started to decline, but just as she was about to speak, she saw Shad escorting a pretty woman onto the smooth, grassy area where the dancing was taking place. Seeing him with the light-haired woman's arm looped over his seemed suddenly infuriating to Sarah. She took Granite's arm and said, "I'd be happy to dance with you."

As they danced around the area, Sarah tried to laugh and be happy like the others around her. Every time her eyes met Shad's she looked quickly away and wondered why she was behaving like a jealous woman. She had absolutely no claim on Shadrach Koby. Before the dance ended, she was dancing with Stonewall, then the next ones with Jack and Richard. Every few minutes, one of the men she was dancing with would stop and introduce her to someone. She'd met the Murphys, the Smiths, Blacks, and Winchills — all heading for California.

Several dances later, she asked Gerry to get her a drink of water. When he left, she glanced around and saw Shad carrying two cups of refreshments toward the yellow-haired woman. She smiled at him and he said something that made her lift her chin and laugh. Shad seemed completely captivated by her.

When Gerry returned, Sarah drank the water, then excused herself and as unobtrusively as she could, made her way toward her tent.

She removed her shoes and dress, then turned back the blanket over her bedroll and crawled into bed. The light from the fire flickered through the flap she'd opened to get a breeze. She crawled out of her bed and pulled the flap shut, afraid that Shad might come to see why she'd left. Why had she? She didn't know and that made the situation worse.

Again, under the blanket, she curled up and buried her face in the pillow, but could not stem the tears that came. She'd never looked forward to evenings, or quiet times without Leo, and tonight things were no different. Alone, she could release her agony. However, her concern for Leo's welfare took second place to the humiliation she felt concerning her adolescent behavior. One moment, Shad dominated her thoughts, then her thoughts would quickly change to her missing husband.

"Why did you have to leave me?" she cried, tears wetting her pillow. In the blackness of the soft nest where she'd escaped, she rejoiced about one thing. She still remembered the things about Leo that she missed the most — his smile, his touch and his even disposition. Her grieving heart cried for the time when her world was full of hope and love. Had she really expected that she and Leo would live happily forever? Her life with him had ended too quickly.

Leo Daniels had been her mainstay for so long it was hard to think of going on without him. Leo Daniels! Shadrach Koby! Their names wrenched deep groans of agony as she drew herself into a tighter ball. The memory of one had given her life meaning and the deepest sorrow she'd ever known. Shad — he'd invaded her thoughts, and she didn't want him in them.

She questioned the faults inside her, trying to decide how much, if any, of the episodes with Shad were because of her shortcomings. In some respects, she counted herself innocent, but in others, she had to accept blame where she had doubts.

She fought the indignation that made her feel like a fool because of jealousy. She dug her fists into the blanket, blind to everything but the truth that she was acting like a fool, and that she'd been somewhat unfaithful to Leo by even giving Shad a second thought.

Despite herself, she found herself trying to find a similarity between Leo and Shad, but nothing came to her mind. She sighed dejectedly; she knew Leo, and had never doubted him. She thought she knew Shad, but decided she didn't; he would show his faults before long, of that, she felt certain.

"Ohh," Sarah wailed, "the whole world seems wrong! Is it any wonder that I want to cry?" Listen to yourself, she scolded, you've lived long enough to recognize self-pity when you hear it. At that moment, she knew the answer to her question. "I want to bawl because I've been fooling myself," she cried. "I'm just self-centered, and I lack the sense of trust! I'm such a mess! I feel like a child. *Oh, God, why am I so weak?*" she sobbed, remembering her sainted mother who admonished her to pray in trouble as well as in happiness. She tried to think of the words her mother had often prayed when her father was being so obnoxious to her. . . . *Oh, Lord, the only one who knows all, why am I often tempted to question why? I do not dare because I know my mind is too feeble to understand Your mysterious and mighty knowledge. My faith is so small it is almost invisible to my eye. If it were but the size of a speck of dust, would I even then understand? I doubt it; oh, my God, help me! I plead this day, even this hour that my faith increase, not so much that I may know the why's of Your doings, but only that I can accept Your decisions without questioning, that I might have complete and absolute faith in You. It is I who am weak and You, my Lord, who is strong. Let me have the gentle peace only the Comforter can give, for it is my heart which is broken, Mend my heart, I pray. I can bear the scars but not the pain of an open wound. Stitch it gently for You know how tender and easily hurt I am. You made me this way, so don't allow me to suffer more than I can bear. Provide for my endurance. Give me courage to face tomorrow. Remember to watch over me, for I am faint. Let my life count for something more than defeat. Lead this crippled and cowardly saint to victory. Amen.* Sarah wiped tears from her eyes realizing that her mother's prayer was hers also.

She'd no sooner spoken that tearful prayer, than all the things she'd been sobbing about began to dissipate. Then she saw the clear image of Shad, arrogant, brash, and handsome as it flitted across her tortured mind. She could still feel his hands on her waist as they'd stood in the vestibule of the train. He'd moved her away from himself. She even remembered his smile, rare as it was, and realized that she had probably not been behaving properly and needed to make some changes in herself.

After a while she pulled herself from under her blanket. For a moment, the evidence of her feelings dazed her. Her bed was a twisted wreck, her face hot and sweaty, and her eyes stung from salty tears. She had to make a trip to the bushes, and the thought of that chore set her to crying again. What was she doing here, anyway? "Searching for your husband," she spluttered. "So what if you've never roughed it any way but like a city girl. You've never spent a night in a tent, you've always slept in hotels, eaten food you've prepared and served from your own kitchen . . . why didn't you stay in Kansas City?"

Distraught, she rolled over against the edge of the canvas tent and wondered numbly if she should just leave on her own in the morning. A few minutes later, in the shadows, she stumbled toward the trees and tried to think of nothing. She returned feeling some better. With a new clearness of mind, she began to analyze her feelings and organize some plans. By the time she fell asleep, she'd decided on her next course of action.

She would stay with the wagon train and prove to herself that she had grit. She'd become a cowboy and prove to Shadrach Koby that she was not helpless. She'd do whatever was required to find out what had happened to Leo, and as bad as it hurt to admit it, she knew something terrible had happened or he would be by her side. Maybe all these decisions would help her develop a tougher frame of mind. If it were possible, she wanted to show herself as well as Jelliroll that she was a capable person. If Shad continued to behave like a gentleman, she would conduct herself like the lady she was, and keep her emotions reined tight.

Sarah was now entertaining an idea she wasn't certain about, but had decided to see if it were possible to put into action. She wanted to drive the chuck wagon for Jelliroll. He hated driving it, said it was a tough job and hard work, but that was what Sarah wanted. It would help time pass, and keep her from thinking. She couldn't spend the day just riding — that would drive her into despair she didn't want. In the past, she'd attacked unpleasant chores with a vengeance and found her mood soon changed.

Sarah wanted to ride her pinto sometimes, and was certain that wouldn't be a problem. She'd been riding since she was six. Tomorrow, she would ask Jelliroll if he would let her drive the chuck wagon. She'd driven buggies, surely a chuck wagon wasn't so much different.

Her last vision before going to sleep strangely comforted her. Shad gave her a wide, warm smile.

The following morning, Sarah awakened early. She smelled sweet clover, and heard birds singing. She rolled over and stretched. A look to her left revealed an empty bedroll — a slept-in bedroll. Had Jelliroll slept there? She didn't have to wonder long because she heard a crunch and looked up to see Shad ducking to enter the tent. He was fully dressed, running a comb through his dripping wet hair, and the sight of him made her heart race. She muttered to herself, "Don't let your defenses down."

Sarah swallowed a couple of times and tried to slow her fast-beating pulse. "Why did you sleep in my tent? What will people think?"

"Jelliroll had to stay in Kansas City and I didn't want you alone this far from the others."

"Jelliroll was going to sleep under the chuck wagon!" she cried.

"So was I until it started raining. Did you want me to get my bedroll soaked?"

"Of course not, but what about the appearance?" she asked.

"No one saw me enter, and no one is up yet, so don't worry. I'm leaving."

She felt as if she were over-reacting so she said, "Brrr, you look cold." She tried to sound a bit friendlier now that she understood he was only protecting her. The chuck wagon was some distance from the corral and the other wagons, but Lord, how people would gossip if they saw him leaving her tent. "Don't tell me you've been swimming in some stream?"

"I bathe every chance I have. It's refreshing, but chilly." He leaned over and deliberately shook his head over her.

"Oh — oh!" she gasped, springing straight up.

"A little cold water won't hurt you, but I guess a hot house flower like you is only used to heated water and herbal scented bubbles."

He spoke softly so as not to disturb anyone within earshot. But, he disturbed her! So, he thought she was so sheltered and pampered that she wasn't functional in his world, did he? "I was just getting ready to take a dip, but I had to wait for you to finish," she fibbed. Oh! her mind chastised, why did you tell him that? She thought of Leo, how she'd once blamed him for a small white lie he'd told her, and now, she had the nerve to accuse this man of making her lie! See, God, how weak I really am!

You're a fool, Sarah Daniels, if you believe anyone but yourself is responsible for your actions. At least, she was facing this problem with truth — and she did it immediately. Perhaps, she'd improve herself yet. Shad set the small bag he carried onto his bedroll. After digging around a few seconds he handed her a towel and a bar of soap. "If you don't mind sharing my soap, you'll find it a perfect time to bathe; no one's stirring about yet. Now's the time to go."

She shivered at the thought of cold water — icy cold water. "I don't need a bath every day like men do," she said without thinking about the way her words sounded.

Shad stopped walking, turned around and bowed low, making a grand sweep with his hand, indicating she could do what she wanted. Sarah couldn't believe the arrogant way he was behaving. "You misread me," she said.

"Did I?" he replied tersely.

"Yes, you did, and I'm sorry I keep saying things to you that I don't mean." She needed to bathe as often as any man, but she could see he didn't intend to dispute her words. What a temperamental man, she thought. Maybe she had found the flaw in Shadrach Koby.

She struggled from her sleeping roll and slipped her feet into her dew-laden shoes. Ohh, she thought, as her socks grew moist. She was embarrassed at the way she must look — wrinkled underclothes, smudged cheeks and tangled hair. It didn't help a bit to have two amused black eyes watching her every move as she tried to get into her robe while holding a blanket up in front of her. When she was finally decent, she threw the blanket down and grabbed up her satchel, then headed for the tent flap.

Shadrach gave her a wide berth as she walked determinedly passed. "I wanted to tell you that I met the family searching for a missing brother. Roberta and her husband James are nice folks. They have a three-year-old boy who is having some trouble adjusting to traveling. When we leave the train, we'll be traveling with them to Cherryvale. After talking to Roberta, I feel the two of you will get along famously."

Sarah turned and faced Shad, placing her hands on her hips. "Is she the one you were dancing with all evening?"

Shadrach reared back on his heels and

grinned. "I danced with her every dance that she wasn't with her husband. I noticed that you seemed to be having a good time."

She didn't answer because his grin infuriated her, but mainly because she felt like such an idiot. She ducked out of the tent and headed for the stream. Why did she behave like such a fool? She walked on, looking back twice before reaching the stream. Why was she suddenly having so much trouble dealing with Shad? When she was certain she was alone, she opened her satchel. It struck her suddenly, that she had few changes of clothing. That meant she must wash her dirty clothes often, and in this murky water. She slipped out of her robe, and no matter how much she wanted to remove her under-clothes, she couldn't convince herself to take them off.

Finally, she gritted her teeth and did what she had to do. The bath went fine even wearing her underclothing until she couldn't figure out how to get out of the stream without getting mud on her feet. She heard a "baloup, baloup," sound coming from the waters edge. She covered her mouth to smother the scream that threatened. All she needed was for Shad or some of the others to come to her rescue.

She saw the frog leap from the bank and for all she knew it was after her. How she got out of the stream, she didn't remember, but she did notice after she dressed that her feet weren't too very muddy.

Dawn came brightly. The sky grew like a slow blooming pink and blue flower that stretched out as far as her eyes could see. Sarah stood watching the marvelous reflection in the water. She washed her soiled clothes so she could carry them back to the wagon. After breakfast, she could hang them inside the chuck wagon to dry as they traveled.

She smiled, looking at the red streaks from the sky reflecting in the water. She'd walked into the icy stream, bathed, and returned to the grassy bank in three minutes, thanks to the green long-legged frog. Dressing in clean undergarments and another dress, yellow and a bit wrinkled, took another three minutes. Her wet, tangled hair was a mess. Despite feeling chilled, she brushed her hair, then braided the dangling curls into one thick rope.

It felt good to be clean. Her reflection looked satisfactory. She closed her satchel. "You look just fine for the job ahead of you," she remarked to herself. "Take heart and pray that Jelliroll lets you drive the chuck wagon."

She picked up her satchel and carried it and her wet clothes toward her tent. The shimmering water drew her attention back to the sky. She had never been in the position to pay much attention to a sunrise. It was by far more spectacular than the sunset.

Voices came floating softly on the morning breezes. The wagon train was coming to life.

When she arrived at the chuck wagon, the first thing she saw was that her tent was down and gone. Next, she saw that Jelliroll had returned and was busy preparing breakfast.

Sarah could tell that he was exhausted. He'd obviously not been to bed and she didn't know whether to approach him now about driving or wait until after breakfast.

CHAPTER FIVE

"How is Tex?" she asked, deciding to wait a while before asking Jelliroll about her driving the wagon. She really didn't know what he would say; he'd been so possessive about his duties, cooking and such.

"I'm afraid not too good. He won't be makin' this trip with us, got somethin' broke inside."

"Will he be all right?"

"Doc said he needs lots of time and prayers."

"I thought you were going to show me how to take down my tent," she said looking at the place where it had stood.

"The blacksmith's helper had it down and loaded before I got here. Who is he anyway?"

"His name is Shadrach Koby," she said.

"I forgot, lay that stuff in back of the wagon and come here. I'll teach you the art of pancake making."

She didn't have the heart to tell him that she knew how to make pancakes, so she did as he asked. As she cooked, he gave her an appraising glance. "I see yer an early riser. That's good." He gave her a light tap on the arm, telling her to move over so he could see, then he checked the bacon sizzling in the skillet next to her griddle. "Ya look different — more comfortable, I think," he remarked.

"I feel better." He was being nice and friendly,

and was pleased with her ability; now was a good time to approach him with her desire to drive the chuck wagon. "Today I'd like to know if there is any reason why I can't drive this wagon? I will harness and unharness the horses, feed, water, and rub them down like you did yesterday."

"Ya talkin' crazy, gal. That rack of torture will kill ya in one day."

"I'm not exactly a novice," she half lied, "please let me try."

"I'll let ya, as long as ya do yer share of the work here, but ya have no idea how rough ridin' this ol' buggy is on the trail ahead of us."

"If I can handle the horses and the wagon, can't I be excused from the kitchen detail?"

"It's fine with me, pretty gal. I'd rather do kitchen chores anytime."

"Really?" she said, hardly believing him.

Jelliroll gave her an astonished look. "After ya've followed in the footsteps of a man for a week or two, ya can tell me which ya prefer."

Sarah could tell she'd said the wrong thing to the wrong person, but it was a little late to retract it. She listened intently as Jelliroll continued, "Both man's and woman's work is hard and requires skill and efficiency. But a woman's work won't rupture yer guts, herniate a testicle, or fill ya with the miseries so's ya can't even smile. My thoughts are these: being independent is fine until ya drive it too deep, then it's a pain in the — behind!"

Sarah's cheeks radiated heat because of his words. She knew he was exhausted, but he'd let her know she was asking for trouble. "I'm sorry if I've sounded a bit haughty. I only wanted to give you a break from driving," she said weakly.

"Ah, it's okay. If ya think tradin' the animal care for the kitchen detail is a fair exchange, have at it. Go on to the corral. Someone will show ya which horses are mine. The harness is in the wagon." Jelliroll waved her on and went to the skillet to pour more pancake batter.

Despite her chagrin, Sarah tried to act composed. She smelled the coffee and decided to take a tin cup full to Shad. Gingerly, she poured two cups and walked slowly and carefully to the corral.

Shadrach saw her coming and came to meet her. His gaze swept over her. "I see you survived your bath." He took the coffee. "I trust you're invigorated after your plunge. I thought about following, but gave the idea a second thought."

She ignored his double-meaning remark. She knew he probably said that because other women expected men to be aggressive that way. Anyway, his eyes said he was only teasing.

Shad listened with interest to her plan to care for the chuck wagon team. Then someone called for him. "I'll check on your progress," he told her, preparing to leave. "I predict you'll be ready to give up before the first water stop." Again, his eyes said he was joking.

"I won't either!" she retorted.

"We'll see, won't we?"

Sarah couldn't recall how she managed to get through the first part of the day, unless it was Shad's challenge. What he didn't take seriously about her was her stubbornness! If it killed her, she would show the grandiose investigator what she was made of. The wooden seat had no padding, no back rest, and no arm rest. Every muscle in her body was constantly tight, alert to a harder than usual jar. Each wheel turn was a jolt, but any clump of buffalo grass, a small or large rock, or a watershed rut was like a blow to her body. The muscle spasms between her shoulder blades were almost unbearable.

There was a two hour respite from the hard jostling of the wagon when they stopped at the Shawnee Indian Mission just a few miles into Kansas. Shadrach offered to drive the next few miles, but Sarah refused him. He studied her a moment, then shook his head as he walked away.

As the train continued, Sarah didn't know whether she would make it to the Mahaffie House and Farmstead, northeast of Olathe, where the train planned to spend the first night, not that it mattered to her at this point. Jelliroll rode his horse beside the chuck wagon and told her that the place they were going to stop for the night was built in 1865 by J. B. Mahaffie. "It was the first overnight stop on the trail to Santa Fe. Stagecoaches stop twice a day on their way to

Lawrence and Fort Scott," he said before riding ahead to see why the wagonmaster was halting the train.

Sarah learned they were making a slight detour because of a flooded creek running too fast for the wagons to cross safely. In only a mile they found a safer fording place and every wagon rolled across without trouble.

Shortly, the wagons began a slow crawl west. A couple of hours later, Shad was back offering to drive. Again, Sarah politely refused to relinquish her job. By mid-afternoon she was calling herself stupid. She ached like Job must have with his thousand boils. She paraphrased a statement from Job, and grinned — *Though it kills me, yet will I show him.*

She let her mind run back a few yesterdays, and allowed the memories to block out the pain she was experiencing at the moment. She'd survived a train crash, and she'd survive driving this rack of pain. She hadn't really started to hurt, at least pain like she was feeling now, until they'd stopped for that short time at the Shawnee Indian Mission. Now, every jostle made her want to cry.

From the mission which was a school for Indian children and adults, they'd followed the Santa Fe Trail to some land which had a good well. The men who owned the land and water well allowed the wagon trains and live stock free access to rest and water. The watering hole was the first real rest stop after leaving Westport, especially for the animals. To Sarah it was like an oasis in the desert, not that she'd ever been in a desert, but she had a vivid imagination. Sitting on the ground with her back resting against a tree was a relief she couldn't describe.

Olathe, Kansas, would be the next stop on the Santa Fe Trail. As they traveled along, Sarah noticed Shad riding beside a covered wagon some distance ahead. Then, the same woman she'd seen him with at the dance, suddenly stepped onto the edge of the wagon seat and onto the horse with him.

Sarah clutched the reins of the two-horse team she was driving and bent forward, once again assailed by a feeling that must be jealousy — but why? She loved her husband; what did it matter who Shadrach Koby was interested in? He only worked for her. "Get ahold of yourself!" she whispered. Then, as she continued watching, it seemed that Shad and the woman were looking for something. He'd turned all the way around — was he trying to see if she was watching? Don't be paranoid! she warned herself. Then, abruptly he stopped the horse, the woman leaped to the ground and ran to a small child nearly hidden in the tall prairie grass. She took the child into her arms and it was very obvious that she was extremely happy even though she was crying.

As Sarah watched, she felt ashamed, knowing Shad was only being a good Samaritan as was usual for him. She chastised herself for getting so upset — she hadn't even known Shad's mission, yet was willing to judge him.

At last, the wagons made it to Olathe. They stopped for the night near a creek west of the Mahaffie house. Sarah was aware of the true meaning of being bone-tired, and she dreaded the routine that was to follow. Without being too obvious, she looked around for Shad, hoping for a little manly help, but he was nowhere to be found.

Wagonmaster Burns was informing everyone that he hoped to reach Gardner, Kansas by nightfall the next day. Sarah knew this was near where she and Shad would leave the train.

As Sarah stood beside the wagon wondering what to do first, she heard wagonmaster Burns telling the two people who were looking for a missing brother that this site had always been a rest stop on the Santa Fe Trail. Sarah listened and her interest was aroused. She wanted to ask several questions about traveling the trail, like how many miles they made in a day, how long it took to reach California, and were they ever in danger from Indian attacks? As she waited a short distance away, she decided not to be so stand-offish and walked toward the wagon.

Burns was still talking, "Gardner is where the junction of the Santa Fe and Oregon Trail begin." His voice faded, and when he saw Sarah, he called her over to meet the folks he was talking to. "Sarah Daniels, this is Roberta and James Jenkins, and their son Johnny. I understand they are on a mission similar to the one you're on."

"I'm glad to meet you," Roberta Jenkins said, stepping forward to shake Sarah's hand.

The young boy ran forward and pushed Sarah away. His mother grabbed him, and apologized, saying, "Forgive him, he isn't happy making this trip. I've met Shadrach Koby, and he's told me how delightful you are, and of your efforts to find your missing husband. Perhaps we can get together and compare what we know concerning our loved ones."

"I really want to do that. Don't you have a Pinkerton man with you?" Sarah asked.

"He only escorted us to Westport. That's all we could afford. Shadrach has asked if you and he can follow us to Cherryvale and I want you to know how happy I'd be to have you along. I worry about Johnny and will feel a lot safer if James has another man to help in case of trouble. Naturally, I'm delighted to have another woman to keep me company, to share our grief and our hope of finding our loved ones alive and well."

"Oh, Mrs. Jenkins," she muttered, "please know that I'm also glad to be traveling with you and your husband." Sarah reached out and tousled the boy's head of yellow curls. "I'm really thrilled to be traveling with you, Johnny. How old are you?"

The small boy held up three fingers.

"Three years old, that's a wonderful age."

"Is not!" the boy yelled, then ducked his head

and buried it into his mother's skirt. Roberta Jenkins picked him up. "I'll call you Sarah if you'll call me Roberta, and my husband is James. I'm sorry Johnny is acting so naughty."

"Don't worry about him and me, we'll get acquainted eventually. I'll be happy to call you Roberta," Sarah said.

"If you'll excuse me, I need to get Johnny ready for bed."

"I'm ready to go there myself," Sarah said, waving at the little boy who peeked at her.

Sarah slowly turned away, deciding she must talk to Roberta as soon as possible. She drew a deep breath and went to her duties. No one was around to help her.

To stop short of a job completed was not her nature. Sarah unhitched the team, checked the harness for weak places, and marked the pieces she wasn't certain about to show to the blacksmith or Shad. She checked the animals for rubbed spots, and fed and watered them before she returned to the chuck wagon. To her surprise, she saw her tent was already up and knew Shad had been busy. After helping serve the supper, and eating a few bites, she announced to Jelliroll her intention to go to bed. Never in her life had she felt fragile as an egg shell — like she would crack if she moved too fast.

Her announcement obviously disappointed the men listening to her and Jelliroll as they talked. There was to be another hoedown after the evening chores to celebrate their first successful day on the trail, and they wanted Sarah to attend. For a moment, Sarah considered making the effort — but she couldn't.

"Thanks for wanting me, fellows. When I'm not so tired, I'll be there."

"Sounds great," Granite said, lifting his tin coffee cup in her direction.

"You go on to bed," Jelliroll said, taking the dish pan and soap out of her hands. "I know how tiring it is to drive this pain rack." He kicked the iron wheel of the chuck wagon.

Sarah suddenly stood on tipped-toes and kissed his cheek. "Thank you, Jelliroll. Don't worry, I'll be fine."

Somehow, Sarah managed to get her clothes, soap and a drying cloth, and made her way to a place of privacy. She quickly took a creek-water bath, and then limped to her tent. To her surprise, she found her bedroll already laid out and waiting. How very thoughtful, she mused, assuming Shad had prepared her bed when he'd seen her leave for the creek; she knew it wasn't ready when she'd gathered her clothes. She eased herself painfully to the ground.

In a few minutes, she heard the musical instruments warming up, then wagonmaster Burns making a speech. She listened with growing interest to some of the history about the trail. He recited some true experiences about some happenings at this exact locale. He said he'd gleaned these tales from journals and eye-witnesses.

Sarah heard Burns introduce Shadrach Koby.

72

She didn't look, but she did listen. He was an eloquent speaker, and his knowledge, a constant source of surprise to her. He said, "Over this and several other trails in the area have come and are still coming, explorers, traders, missionaries, soldiers, miners, mountain men, and immigrants, all pioneers. . . ." Sarah dozed off.

Later, she jerked painfully awake with a muscle spasm to hear Shad still speaking, "There are two thousand tortuous miles of the Oregon Trail that branches off the Santa Fe at this point. You who are taking that trail will see with fearful monotony the graves along the way. . . ." Sarah slept again.

When the music began, she once more awakened with a painful jerk, hurting so badly that sound sleep eluded her. The gaiety of the people made her almost feel worse. How anyone had strength to move amazed her. She dozed off and woke with a loud moan. Another spasm drew her leg double. The musicians played on.

Someone spoke from close by, but she couldn't identify the voice over the music and laughter, nor did she know exactly where it came from.

She suddenly realized whoever had spoken was speaking to her. She opened her eyes and couldn't see who it was at first, then she saw Shad, an indistinct hulking shape in the darkness, someone she sensed more than saw.

He knelt beside her with a cup of water and some powders. "This will help the pain. Where are you hurting the worst?" he asked.

"All over," she said, wondering about his concern, "my arms and shoulders mostly."

He pushed back the blanket of her bedroll, and spoke softly, "Now, what I'm going to do is rub your muscles — nothing more. I'm going to use a liniment that doesn't smell very good, but it'll help ease some muscle cramps. You won't sleep a wink if we don't get these kinks out. You little mulehead! Why wouldn't you listen to me? I knew you were overdoing it." He unbuttoned her gown and gently eased it off her shoulders. "Now, turn over on your stomach."

Sarah was astounded at herself, but she didn't think she could move — she couldn't even lift her arms to stop him from unbuttoning her gown. "I can't," she moaned.

Shad tenderly turned her on her side, and she finished the action by falling onto her stomach. He slipped her gown down further and rubbed the liniment over her back. His hands moved over her shoulders, his fingers massaging gently down her arms.

Leo flashed painfully into her mind — she'd often done this very thing for Leo when he'd overdone. That memory hurt about as much as her muscles. What would he think if he could see her at this moment? She'd have nightmares over this. However, even though she couldn't explain the reason for it, she felt no guilt at the hands of Shadrach Koby, the man in whom she had placed a lot of trust.

74

She tried to relax as his massage continued. His explanation of what he was trying to do sounded good enough that she felt it worth taking a chance on his integrity. Several times she almost stopped him, but the rhythmic vibration of his fingers felt heavenly, and the possibility of a pain-free body was too much to resist. He couldn't see her anyway — but he could feel her. The deep shadow caused by the tent saved Sarah from total embarrassment. A saying that she'd once read in her Bible popped into her head, and she wished she hadn't recalled it: *Men love darkness rather than light because their deeds are evil.* Its implication made her gasp. Her pulse hammered furiously with a sudden spurt of adrenaline.

"Relax," Shadrach's voice soothed, "I can't get the kinks out with you tight as a stuck axle!"

Sarah couldn't explain why, but her muscles slowly began to loosen. His fingers worked like medicine. He manipulated her shoulders and arms, his manner as cool and impersonal as a mother. Wonderful fingers moved constantly, stopping when a groan indicated he'd touched an especially sore spot. Then, in a few seconds, he would begin again.

"Over you go," he said, helping her roll onto her back. She managed to grab her gown and covered her breasts before she had completed the turn onto her back. He began his magic finger-march over her upper shoulders.

Sarah thought her heart would stop when he

did that, but as it turned out, she needn't have worried. Shad stayed away from touching any part of her that would have brought an objection. The deep, acute edges of pain floated away under his moving hands.

CHAPTER SIX

Sarah lay quietly enjoying Shadrach's hands as they eased away her aches and pains. She asked sleepily, "Who taught you to do this?"

"My grandmother."

"Is she living?" Sarah asked, having been soothed into a pleasant lassitude.

"My grandparents, as well as my parents are long gone," he said. "All right, let's roll you over once more."

Sarah felt more secure on her stomach. Shad's hands moved skillfully up and down her spine.

"I lost them all at the same time. A terrible prairie fire caught them and they couldn't get away fast enough." Shad hesitated, then began again, "I was scouting ahead of our family's wagon and didn't know there was a fire until it was too late." Shadrach sighed, and so did Sarah.

She tried to breathe deeply, but the effort hurt her ribs. She turned onto her back trying to breathe without pain. "I feel like my ribs are broken."

"You've probably pulled your rib cage away from your breast bone, right here." He trailed his finger between her breasts and pushed on the sternum.

"Ouch!" she cried and grabbed his hand.

77

She'd forgotten about her nightgown being around her waist.

"Don't be afraid of me, Sarah. I'm trying to help you. That tender spot proves what I think happened. Those powders I gave you will help."

"When will it take effect?" she asked, covering herself.

"I'll give you some more if you're not feeling better in an hour or so."

"Shad, I'm sorry about you losing your entire family so tragically, and I'm so grateful for your concern and help. I'm also sorry that I was so stubborn today. I'll never act that way again."

"Can I depend on that?"

"You sure can."

Shadrach laughed. "That's a promise I hope you'll keep. It's one thing to be independent, and another to be stubborn. No one, most especially me, would have thought any less of you if you'd conceded and allowed me to drive part of the time."

"Tell me more about your family," she said, and turned onto her stomach again.

"Father was a genius. As a child I worshipped him. He taught me more than I ever learned in school. He was a lawman and I learned many a trick about capturing lawbreakers.

"My grandmother kept all the old ways of living from Germany, and she could cook like no other woman on earth. She taught me to rub away aches and pains. By the time I reached the ripe old age of fifteen, I was going to college. My grandparents lived with us, a custom brought from Germany, and I loved every minute of our life. When I left school, my father talked us into moving to Colorado. He'd received word that a job as sheriff was his if he'd go to Denver. I was twenty-one and ready for any adventure. My father's tales of capturing lawbreakers, whether by a gun or by a trick is what started me into tracking wanted men and searching for people who have disappeared. After the fire, I traveled alone for a while, fought the war, then went to Chicago to visit an army buddy, and stayed.

"Each client I have has a different story and each one is like nostalgia to me. Every trip is filled with ghosts from a bygone era. Sometimes it's hard to return to Chicago, but a man can only spend so much time away from his chosen livelihood."

His voice was rich and soft in the darkness, gentle as his fingers on her back. She sensed the languid tone of his voice was part of the ministrations meant to comfort and soothe her. "Do you think your father wanted you to be a lawman?"

"I'm here to tell you, he did. Father wanted me to know everything he'd learned and tried to cram his forty years into my twenty. He wanted me to be a Pinkerton man, and in Chicago, I was a Pinkerton Agent for five years, then decided to work for myself."

Sarah cleared her throat, and said, "I'm

feeling better. Why don't you go on to the cele-bration?"

"I thought you might want to hear about the brother of Roberta Jenkins," he said ignoring her suggestion.

"I would, if you don't mind."

"Roberta and Robert are twins. This no doubt is behind the determination of Roberta to find her brother. The two of them and Roberta's hus-band were share-cropping in eastern Missouri. But they'd been saving and planned to buy a farm together near Guthrie, Oklahoma. Circum-stances arose that prevented them from leaving together. James Jenkins was afraid the man in Oklahoma would sell the farm before he could get there, so he sent Robert with all the cash the three of them had saved to pay the man and get the deed. Robert could get things ready for James and his family.

"Robert never arrived in Oklahoma, and after several exhaustive investigations, they found out that Robert was seen in Cherryvale. He'd told the hotel clerk that he'd forgotten something at the inn where he'd stayed the night before. No one has seen him since."

"What inn did he stay at?" Sarah asked.

"That's the big question. When they get to Cherryvale, James Jenkins is going to search for any inn within a day's ride of Cherryvale. I may go with him. It's possible that whatever hap-pened to Robert also happened to Leo."

"It makes sense to me that someone may have

waylaid them," Sarah said. "How long has Robert been missing?"

"Eleven months and three weeks."

"Dear God, that's the same for Leo!"

"I know. This may be a blessing meeting the Jenkins," Shadrach said.

"I can't wait to have a talk with Roberta," she said.

"You know her?"

"I met her earlier when we stopped. The similarities of Robert's and Leo's disappearance is a good beginning this time," Sarah said.

"It's becoming more clear to me all the time. James Jenkins and I are already making plans."

"I've never heard him say a word," she said. "He only nodded when we were introduced."

"He's quiet, has more on his mind than the average man, but he's smart as a whip. It'll be a pleasure working with him."

"What is Robert's last name?" she asked.

"Smith, I believe Roberta said."

"You never tire of doing this line of work, do you?"

"Actually, I look forward to each new client with more relish than I did the last one."

"You're a strange man," Sarah muttered, "you don't fit into any mold. Society has one for city folks and one for adventurers — in some ways you don't seem to belong to either."

Shadrach chuckled. "You mean I should fit one or the other?"

"Yes. Most men do."

"I've never noticed anyone criticizing either of the lives I lead. I do both well. That's all I can do. It's been enough for me."

"But what it you were ostracized by people because of one or the other? What then?"

"I'd continue to live as I am. I'm happy. What people think has never bothered me. I'll never change, because if I do, I might become as shallow as they are." He paused and shook his hands.

"Your hands are numb! Why don't you stop now," Sarah said.

"When I'm finished."

She closed her eyes, amazed at herself. She couldn't remember ever being so engrossed with another person's personal life. Shadrach Koby was certainly a very fascinating person. There was something special about him that she couldn't name. He made her feel at ease whether they were dining at a fancy restaurant in the sophisticated backdrop of Chicago society, or eating off a blanket under a sycamore tree on the Kansas prairie.

Sarah sighed and surrendered herself to the wonder in his hands and fingers — conscious of his nearness and baffled by it. At last her eyes grew heavy and she drifted into the sweet painlessness of sleep.

She awoke to the tantalizing aroma of coffee and struggled to sit up, then lay back, unable at the moment to rise. She had slept well and if she didn't try to leave her bedroll, she was free of pain. She heard a wood thrush tittering in the sycamore tree near her tent and wondered if it was singing to its mate. "Mmmmm," she purred, "that coffee surely smells good." Memory came rushing back and she remembered that she should be up tending the animals. She stirred, tossed aside her blanket, then staggered determinedly onto her sore legs. Every muscle felt like a bruise, yet she could stand. That was more than she'd expected last night.

Shad's soothing hands were like a dream remembered, pleasant to think about, but without reality. She tried walking and found she could move just fine. The world slowly regained its old stability. She'd survived. She peeked out the tent flap at the tree trying to see the happy bird who was still singing. The insects and night beetles hadn't yet stopped their noisy night tunes. At first the sounds had annoyed her; now, they were rather comforting. She picked up her satchel, left the tent, and moved silently away from the wagon for some privacy. The woods were shadowy and eerie this early in the day, but she wasn't afraid, just cautious. She could see well enough to follow the path toward the stream. She wondered, as she went, who had made such a distinct trail in this wilderness. Something stopped her! She could not have named the warning that was as strong as any shout. Her lifestyle these past few days had made her quick to sense small omens of danger. It might have been a singing bird who suddenly stopped its song. She only knew something had alerted her that didn't fit an expected pattern.

As she strained her ears and eyes on the path ahead, she saw what it was. At least twenty deer were drinking at the stream. She was on an animal trail. A feeling of being one with nature gave her a new set of sensations. She stood spellbound and waited.

Sarah walked softly to the water's edge after the deer had left, wanting to apologize to a family of raccoons and a lone opossum who had fled when she'd appeared. There were little footprints everywhere.

She washed her hands and face, combed her hair, brushed her teeth and almost blindly dressed in the semi-light of dawn. Voices and busy sounds from the circled wagons told her that the others were awake and eager for the day to begin. Others were coming to the stream. She waved at a couple of ladies she'd met yesterday.

As Sarah approached the chuck wagon, she paused, seeing James Jenkins loading hers and Shadrach's pack animals with their tents and bedrolls. She surmised that Shad and he had made traveling plans. It surprised her more when she saw Shadrach frying pork chops, making skillet bread and scrambling eggs. "Where is Jelliroll?" she asked, realizing how unusual this was since Jelliroll was so covetous of his cooking.

Shad greeted her with a nod. "He's not feeling

so good, so I offered to cook for him. He said he always did the cooking, but I convinced him to let me just this once, especially since we'd be leaving the train today. How do you feel?" he asked, his black eyes smiling into hers.

Her blood gave a sudden surge, and she dropped her gaze from his probing eyes. Without looking back at him, she said, "Thanks to you helping me, I have lived to see another day."

"Did you know Jelliroll once lived near Harmony Grove which isn't far from Cherryvale?" Shadrach asked.

"I didn't; when did he tell you?" she asked.

"This morning when I found him tossing the contents of his stomach. He was moaning, wishing he had a home to feel ill in. I asked him where his home was, and he started talking about Harmony Grove." Shadrach poured her a cup of coffee.

"Did he say what the town is like?" she asked, sipping coffee gingerly.

"Harmony Grove or Cherryvale?"

"Both."

"As near as I could figure, Harmony Grove was hardly more than a church where all community activity took place. I think Jelliroll is just tired of traveling. He wants to settle down and be a farmer."

"Isn't he a little too old to start farming?" Sarah asked.

"I think so, but Jelliroll has other ideas."

85

"What did he say about Cherryvale?"

Shadrach didn't want to tell her about the rumors he'd heard about men in the area disappearing. "Jelliroll said that Cherryvale is fairly centrally located to four large cities, Tulsa, Kansas City, Wichita, and Joplin. Independence, Kansas is ten miles from Cherryvale as is Coffeyville. He says the Chautauqua Hills south of Independence are beautiful. The best thing is that Cherryvale is well equipped with a public well and plenty of watering troughs to welcome weary travelers, and for the people who are immigrating to Indian Territory in Oklahoma and Texas. But, the cemeteries hide the joys and heartaches of many. It's a rough town like Dodge City or Abilene. The railroad divides the town. Jelliroll says I shouldn't ever allow you on the west side of town."

"He doesn't know that I can take care of myself," Sarah said lifting her chin in a defiant gesture.

Shad grinned. "Watch it! You promised not to be so stubborn."

"All right, I'm sorry — I guess."

"Listen Sarah, prohibition in Kansas has caused bootlegging and corruption. Gambling and prostitution usually follow, so you can see that it will be best if you stick close to me when we arrive in Cherryvale."

Sarah bristled at Shad's lack of confidence in her ability to defend herself, but she had promised. As she gazed at him, she couldn't stay mad.

He had sounded quite sincere and he was only trying to protect her. As she was deliberating about the subject, he turned and smiled at her. His smile washed everything in her mind away — all she could think about was the way he looked at her, the sheer magnetism of his masculinity, the effect his deep voice had on her senses. It was like the touch of his fingers brushing against her bare skin.

Shadrach looked at Sarah who seemed quite serious as she studied him. He smiled again and said, "Jelliroll is over by the corral sitting under a tree. He really isn't feeling too perky this morning, but if you want to go talk to him, he'll tell you the same thing about Cherryvale."

She shook her head and stood to her feet, prepared to go to work. "I'll talk to him later, but I believe you, Shad. You've never lied to me."

"Here, you're not going anywhere. You sit down and drink some more coffee. Breakfast is almost ready. While I'm thinking about it, slip these into your pocket." He handed her a small package containing some more powders like he'd given her last night.

Sarah didn't know what was wrong with her — the way he looked at her made her tongue-tied, short of breath, and weak. She obeyed him like a child might do as she took the packet and shoved it into her pocket. "Is — ah — is Jelliroll very sick? Can I do anything?" she asked, as she sat down.

"He told me all he needed was some rest. I

think he drank a little too much last night and it's upset his digestive system. He should be fine about noon. Are you feeling up to driving the wagon a few hours? We'll leave the train and turn south about noon, and Jelliroll should be able to take over then. If you don't think you can, I'll have one of his men take the reins when we pull out. I just didn't want you to think I didn't have faith in you."

"I'm fine. Don't take anyone away from his assigned duties. I am perfectly capable of driving, and thank you for recognizing that I am. I did all right yesterday and I'll do better this morning." She hated herself when she sounded so defiant.

Shad only smiled at her. "Looking at you now, I'm not so sure you are able, but don't worry, if you have any trouble, I'll be close by and can take over."

"I know you mean well, but I'm all right. I'm going to the corral and start with the horses," Sarah said, starting to stand from her chair.

"Oh, no you won't. I've already taken care of that chore. Granite is going to bring the horses and hitch the team after breakfast. You sit still and enjoy my cooking. If you can drive, that's enough."

Sarah watched him, actually grateful she didn't have to hitch the horses. Shadrach was a showman at everything. A French chef couldn't have been more flamboyant with his gestures. He was not a person who adhered to clearly defined roles regarding his duties or those of

88

others. She'd noticed the respect everyone showed him. Even wagonmaster Burns sometimes appeared to be listening to something Shadrach was suggesting. Most anyone would admit that Shad had a confident air of authority about him.

He lifted the coffee pot from the flames and refilled her cup. Sarah was nervous and without thinking took a large swallow of the steaming brew — then groaned. She dropped the cup, choking on the hot mouthful, spewing what she hadn't ingested from her mouth. Bending over in pain as the liquid reached her stomach, she hardly knew when Shadrach grabbed her. It took a moment for her to regain her breath. A cooked tongue and stomach weren't the type of injuries that you liked to be rescued from.

Shad let go of her arms which he'd lifted above her head, but he didn't move away. Her heartbeat quickened when his arms encircled her. He paused only to flip his Stetson off his black hair before claiming her lips. His strong arms seemed tighter than iron bands binding her body to his.

When he lifted his lips from hers, she grabbed for her mouth.

"I'm sorry," he cried, realizing that she'd burnt her mouth on the coffee. "You're so inviting that I forgot that you'd just scalded your mouth."

"Ah — my mouth doesn't hurt anymore," she whispered, or if it did, she wasn't noticing. How could she be aware of anything with what had just happened?

His embrace softened around her, yet he drew her back even closer. She felt intoxicated by the scent of his shaving soap. Before she knew what was transpiring, she was tasting his lips, the soft warmth of his tongue. He wasn't hurting her, but she was shocked, and not at him, but at herself. Her blood raced through her like liquid fire. Suddenly, she realized she was kissing him back, but didn't care. She didn't care what he thought, didn't care what anyone watching might think, didn't care about anything save the wonderful overpowering desire he'd ignited in her.

CHAPTER SEVEN

Shadrach released Sarah, but couldn't let go, so he pulled her back. She didn't resist when he claimed her mouth in another kiss. Their lips were like magnets.

His kiss lingered longer and more tenderly than any kiss she could remember. She didn't want to break contact. She stood on her toes and pressed her mouth harder to his, not wanting the moment to end.

Shadrach moaned softly, slid his hands down around her waist and lifted her away from him. "I shouldn't have done that," he said. "You're a terrible enticement, Mrs. Daniels." He sighed. "Do you know how very beautiful you are?" He reached out and cupped his hands on either side of her face. "And look what I've done to you."

"What have you done?" she asked breathlessly, pondering why he'd called her Mrs. Daniels.

"I think I've kissed last night's stars into these green eyes — I've got to let you go!"

"Why?" she asked, shocked that she'd let this take place, and befuddled that the glory of it still held her fast. Had he reminded her or himself that she was a married woman?

"The pork chops are burning," he replied, stepping a few inches from her, "and so am I."

His voice had not lost its softness, and her own

trembled when she answered, "Then you'd better tend them both. No one likes burnt chops, or scorched men!"

Disappointment that she'd allowed this to happen overtook her, but she fought hard not to show it. She could hear the leaves of the cotton-woods rustling in the morning breeze, hear the songbirds, see the undulating hills around them, then she looked at the wide, cloudless sky and re-membered the sunrise. She turned to Shadrach to tell him that she was sorry this had happened, but she saw that he was looking at her and smiling. She found herself wishing he'd take her back into his arms. He seemed able to erase from her memory who she was, Mrs. Leo Daniels. Glory! had she taken leave of her senses?

She could not fathom her feelings. Had it only been a year since she'd thought Leo's kisses were thrilling? Had she totally lost her morals? The memory of Leo's kisses paled into colorlessness as Shad's kiss blared as brightly as the breakfast fire. She didn't know what to do or say. Her heart thumped wildly, but something spoke to her, something from deep inside said, you ter-rible hypocrite! You have no right — you are en-couraging a relationship that is sinful. You'd better be careful, Shad is different, and won-derful, but it's still wrong!

Roberta Jenkins came around the wagon, and said, "Sarah, I wanted to offer you the comfort of our wagon when we leave the train for

Cherryvale. We can talk and read as we travel. I have many journals I've collected."

"Journals? You mean like the one wagonmaster Burns read from last evening?" Sarah asked, thankful for Roberta's sudden appearance.

"Wagonmaster Burns was reading from my journals. When I told him about them he asked to borrow one."

"I truly enjoyed hearing what was read," Sarah said.

"They tell about other people who have traveled on the Santa Fe and Oregon Trails. It helps to know some of the trouble we might encounter, even if we are leaving to blaze our own trail." She grinned at Sarah. "Please say you'll join me, we need to talk."

"I'll be happy to accept," Sarah replied. She found the yellow-haired, blue-eyed woman very interesting. "It will probably be around eleven or twelve o'clock before we separate from the main train."

"I'll be looking forward to visiting with you," Roberta said as she waved and headed back for her wagon.

"Good," Shadrach said. "I'm glad you're going to ride in their wagon; it's a lot more comfortable than a chuck wagon without any springs to lessen the jolts. It'll take a couple of days for you to stop hurting." Shadrach wiped his hands on his apron before removing it. "I'm going after the men, then we'll eat. You just sit there and drink your coffee — saucer it this time. I won't be long."

His gaze lingered a moment on Sarah, then he left, and she looked uneasily after him wondering what she was going to do now that she'd opened a door that should've stayed shut.

When wagonmaster Burns stopped and poured himself a cup of coffee, he asked what she thought of the Jenkins family.

"I don't know much about them, but they seem quite personable," she answered.

"I feel sorry for them, they've lost every cent they have, but the lady won't give up her search for her brother."

Sarah studied the wagonmaster a few moments. "Do you have any idea how it feels to lose someone you love and not have the finality of death to help heal your grieving heart?"

"I'm afraid I don't," he answered sheepishly. "I'm here to tell you goodbye as I'll be busy when you and the Jenkins leave the train. I want to wish you success in your search, and to tell you that I admired your grit yesterday."

"And I want to thank you for everything," she replied. Sarah smiled, not knowing what else to say.

"You don't have to thank me for anything, Mrs. Daniels. Even though I know the reason for your trip, I'm surprised at your willingness to face the hardships ahead. You are quite a delightful young lady. I'm sorry you and Shadrach missed the hoedown last evening. I had a marvelous time — ah — I mean everyone had fun."

Was he questioning Shad's and her where-abouts last night? If so, why? She hadn't given a thought to anyone missing her. She'd thought that only Jelliroll and Shad knew why she hadn't attended. Was wagonmaster Burns just trying to be friendly or what?

When he smiled, Sarah returned it cautiously. She didn't know the man well enough to determine if he was teasing her, making fun, or speaking sincerely.

Shad and the men returned. Sarah was glad to have the conversation change to the day's planned miles and to learn some of the obstacles she must prepare to overcome this morning on the trail.

Jelliroll felt too bad to eat any of the breakfast that Sarah took to him. "Thank ya, pretty gal, but I think sleep is the cure for what ails me."

Sarah told him that she was going to drive the first few hours, so he could sleep in the wagon. He thanked her and she helped him to the chuck wagon and made him as comfortable as she could in the narrow space he was using for his bedroll, then she returned to help Shad.

After breakfast and the clean-up were finished, Shadrach checked the team that Granite had hitched to the chuck wagon before going on to his other duties.

Sarah noticed as she climbed into the wagon seat that Shad had folded a blanket to make a pillow for her bottom. She saw Shad riding his black stallion, Hominy, and that he had tied her pinto and the two loaded pack horses to the rear of the chuck wagon. As Shad rode ahead, she saw how he gazed back at her every few minutes.

The wagonmaster lifted his hand, and shouted, "Move 'em out!" Sarah shook out the reins, and the chuck wagon began moving westward behind forty other wagons. It became an instant torture rack, a jolting bed of pain. She tried to find a more comfortable position, but there was none. With grit born of her innate determination, she set her teeth, almost convinced the wagon had square wheels. They passed by natural ponds Sarah knew would be perfect for a farmer with lots of cows. She visualized the future when farms would be everywhere. They were passing a limestone cliff with water running out of the cracks. She saw a squirrel drinking from the water and was suddenly thirsty herself. Reaching for her canteen, she drank, then hearing a crow, she looked up. It wasn't a blackbird, but a hawk. Its wing span was wide as it soared above them. Keeping her mind on what was around her kept her from dwelling on the roughness of the ride — and on Leo — and on what had happened that morning with Shad.

"Are you following the trail?" Jelliroll yelled.

"I'm trying, but it's rougher than any road I've been on before," she said.

"I'll say it is," he replied, as he crawled through the opening to sit beside her.

"Are you feeling better?" she asked.

"Some," he answered, and for a long time he sat quietly watching her. "Hey, pretty gal, I'm older and wise as a ol' hoot owl. I think ya got a problem, and if ya want to talk about it, I'm a good listener."

"There's nothing wrong with me other than I'm aching like a boil."

"Don't try fibbin' ta me. Yer fallin' for Shadrach Koby, ain't ya?"

Sarah twisted around and stared at him. Tears welled up in her green eyes. She tried to speak, but couldn't for a few moments. Here was a man so sensitive to her that he could tell she was suffering. How could she not talk to him. She had no one else to discuss her problems with. "Oh, Jelliroll, I'm afraid to think about him. I'm married to a wonderful man and shouldn't be thinking of anyone but Leo Daniels."

"I saw Shadrach kiss you this morning. Has he made any other advances toward you?" he asked as gently as a father might have questioned a daughter.

"If he would, I'd feel better," she cried, "then I could slap his face. That was the first time we ever kissed. I'm so ashamed. I don't deserve my husband's love." She drew a shaky breath as she dodged the low-hanging branch of an oak they were passing beneath.

"Stop hammerin' on yerself. When yer young and healthy, it's not hard to long for love and companionship after a year of being separated from yer man. If Mister Daniels is alive, do ya honestly believe he hasn't sought out the company of a lady all these months?"

"I sincerely don't believe he has. You didn't know him, Jelliroll, and I do. I know he's been faithful to me. The same can't be said for me. God forgive my weakness."

"I'm glad to hear ya say that, and if ya mean it, ya ought to stay away from Shadrach Koby," Jelliroll said.

"I know but I don't think I can. I might even love him!" She didn't know what it was about this short, round man that made her feel as if she'd known him forever. He was like an uncle whom she'd never had — like a father she could talk to. Not like her father whom she dared not say a word to.

Jelliroll looked at her. "Ya can't love two men!"

"What am I to do?" she cried, having never felt so disturbed. She wasn't even certain anymore what love was — whatever it was, it hurt and made her feel full of awful guilt. She glanced away from his penetrating eyes, and looked at the wild growing fir trees. She saw yellow butterflies drinking nectar from red verbena, and wanted the conversation she was having with Jelliroll to be over.

"It's useless to reason with ya, pretty gal, but let me tell ya something I told my niece when she left home for school." He reached over and took the reins from Sarah. "As ya probably already know, seein' ya've been married, there's several ways to get a man thinkin' about puttin' a ring on yer finger and a weddin' certificate in yer hand. No man goes shoppin' for eggs and bacon when he's a chicken and a pig at his beck-and-call. What I'm sayin' gal, is this, stay away from Shadrach Koby until ya find out about yer husband, otherwise, ya'll be tempting yerself as well as him. Most men are shoppers when it comes to women. I doubt Shadrach Koby is any exception. If ya don't wait until ya find out about yer man, ya'll live with guilt and regrets all yer life, regardless of which man ya end up with."

Sarah couldn't believe the man's frankness, but he was absolutely right and very sincere.

She thanked him. "I've always done exactly as my mother taught me," she said, "and I've never had any regrets until now."

"Temptation isn't the sin, pretty gal, it's yieldin', so listen, I'm only tellin' ya what any father, brother or uncle who cared about ya would say. Stay away from temptation until ya find out about yer husband."

Then, Jelliroll changed the subject and said a surprising thing. "Miss Sarah, if'n it were possible, I'd sure like to leave this train and go find me a place to settle down. Been thinkin' bout Parsons or Cherryvale ever since I heard you was headin' there. I've been doin' this fer seven years; I'm tired, startin' ta feel my arthritis, and I want somethin' easier."

"Tell me how you think you can farm when

you are starting to ache."

"Cherryvale is great farming country. It has good soil." Jelliroll leaned back and closed his eyes. "As I recall, when I lived in the area, Cherryvale had no name yet. It was nothin' but wild polkweed, clusters of sumac, persimmon trees, and buckbush."

"Never heard of buckbush. What is it?" she asked.

"I don't know what it is, but it's mean. It appears to be a shrub, and sends out long runners that Indians cut and weave into baskets. They think it's worth cultivating because of the little red berries no bigger than buckshot. Maybe that's where its name came from, but it's a pest. Grows so fast it can choke a field of corn before it tassels. Anyway, near there at Harmony Grove is where me and the Mrs. settled down."

"I hadn't realized you were married," Sarah said suddenly very interested.

"I was, years before the damnable war. We made a fair living and were happy. Then the war changed everything. I was too old to join the Union, but the Confederates were more desperate and took me in to train as a cook. I took my wife, Hanna, to Joplin, Missouri to catch a train to Tennessee. Her aging parents needed help and I felt Hanna would be safer in a town with family, but she wasn't. She and her folks became victims of war — killed by fellow Americans for reasons so questionable that I've never figured them out." He took a deep breath and began again.

"When I went back to our old homestead, I found border ruffians had nearly destroyed it. I left there a disillusioned man. I went to Kansas City and signed on to a wagon train. Since I was a cook in the army, it was easy to get a job."

"What would wagonmaster Burns do for a cook if you left him now?" Sarah asked aware of the sorrow in Jelliroll as he'd talked about his family.

"Granite and Stonewall could do it. Cookin' is all Stonewall really knows."

"Then why don't you just leave?" she asked.

" 'Cause of the way I be feelin' of late. If'n I get sick on the trail, I'd have no one to fetch me ta a doctor."

"Did you and your wife have any children?"

"Never did," he said.

"If you're serious, you could follow along with us as far as Parsons or Cherryvale. I'm certain Shadrach and the Jenkins would have no objections. Shad always says there's safety in numbers."

Jelliroll was pensive a few minutes. "I think I'll go talk to the Jenkins, then if they don't object, I'll talk to Shadrach and wagonmaster Burns." He stopped the wagon and asked if he could ride her pinto. "My horse is with the wranglers driving the extra mounts."

Sarah said yes, but as she watched him heading for the Jenkins's wagon, she saw her pinto struggling under Jelliroll's weight. She wondered briefly if a man could break a horse's back. The conversation she and Jelliroll had was still very much in her thoughts. A question loomed in her mind about what he'd said concerning her and Shadrach.

"I want to cry," she said to herself. "I'm so deceitful — I didn't even try to stop Shad from kissing me. In fact, I encouraged him. *I'm sorry, Lord, I'd promised to do better, but have failed again.*"

Sarah gasped, wondering how she could promise the Lord something that she didn't think she could do. She knew how one lie could snowball into another until she would probably end up hating herself. What am I to do? She'd never felt so distraught, and didn't feel for a moment that she could ignore Shad. "Listen to me, Sarah," she said to herself, "do nothing more! You've already done it. It doesn't matter now, what matters is how you conduct yourself in the future. The important thing is that you're aware of your shortcomings. Don't cry," she told herself, as she wiped her cheeks, "you'll be all right."

"Are you hurting bad enough to cry?" she heard a voice say beside her.

Sarah jerked around and saw Shad riding beside the chuck wagon, leading her pinto. "No, I'm all right; where's Jelliroll?"

"He picked up his own horse and went to talk to Burns. Why the tears, Sarah?"

She sniffled and crinkled her nose at Shadrach. She might as well be honest. "If I can be truthful without hurting you, I would like to tell you what's bothering me."

"Please do, but wait a minute."

Sarah watched him ride behind the wagon and knew he was tying Hominy to the wagon with Bear. In a few minutes, he climbed into the seat beside her.

"Did the blanket help soften the jolts?" he asked.

"Not really," she said, "but thank you for being so thoughtful."

"I'm not surprised, you don't have enough flesh on your bones to pad anything. All right, what is it you want to tell me?" Shad asked.

"If you'll hear me out, I'd like you to know my most sincerest feelings."

"I'm listening, tell me!"

CHAPTER EIGHT

Sarah swallowed hard, but said, "This is embarrassing for me. This morning I realized something that has probably been happening for a long time. I think a lot of you, and I believe that you have feelings for me, but both of us are wrong to have allowed our emotions to get away from us. I have a husband that I desperately want to find. Until I have good or bad news about him, I don't ever want to lose control again. The guilt is too depressing. Please don't be angry with me because I know I was as much to blame as you for what happened this morning."

Shadrach looked straight ahead for a few eternal seconds, then turned to face Sarah. "Thank you for being so straight-forward. Well, at least the pressure's off. Frankly, I was feeling a mite guilty myself, but Sarah, what happened wasn't anything I'd planned."

"I know that, Shad, but it did happen, and now we must take charge. It can't happen again."

"I don't know what you can do to stop it," he said.

"What I can do!" she cried. "I thought it might be up to us both." Sarah snapped the reins above the horses with a quick flip of her wrist, and shouted, "Catch up, you plow-horses!"

Shadrach stared at her. "I don't believe you

sometimes. While we're talking, I'd better tell you that Jelliroll is joining the Jenkins and us when we leave the train, or did you already know this?"

"We were talking and he told me how much he wanted to settle down where we are going so I told him I thought it would be all right if he trailed along with us."

"Don't you think you could have asked me what I thought?"

"Why should I? You didn't ask me what I thought about us trailing along with the Jenkins. Shad, I don't like the way you keep trying to manipulate me. I'm an adult and can make my own decisions. When I'm in doubt, I'll ask for advice. You said there's safety in numbers, and Jelliroll can shoot a gun if need be, and I'm glad he's going with us. I'm happier that he has his own horse. I thought Bear would buckle under his weight," she said trying for a little levity after her statement.

"I didn't realize that I was being so domineering with you. I'm sorry. Here comes Jelliroll now. I'd best get back to my duties."

"Please be glad he's joining us," she said.

"All right, I'm glad he's coming with us. I have to go. I'll not bother you any more until we reach our turn-off."

"That's fine with me," she said, hating herself when she sounded so miffed, but so did he.

Sarah stopped the wagon and Shad climbed back through the wagon to get his horse. He and

Jelliroll talked a few moments. She heard Jelliroll ask if Shadrach had any objections to him riding to Parsons or Cherryvale with them. Shad said he liked the idea and shook hands with Jelliroll. Sarah could tell that Shad was sincere.

He pulled his horse around the chuck wagon, then rode forward to the head of the train without once looking back. Why did this annoy her? She shook her head, determined to stick by her decision to stay away from Shadrach Koby.

Jelliroll tied his huge chestnut mare and a pack mule, obviously loaded with his belongings, to the chuck wagon. There were now five animals trailing behind on long leads. Jelliroll crawled inside and sighed.

"Are you all right?" she asked, looking over her shoulder.

"I will be when we leave this wagon from hell. I swear the wheels are warped."

Sarah didn't say anything, Jelliroll had spoken her sentiments exactly. Besides, her words to Shadrach had shocked her, but it felt good to be spontaneous and able to speak her mind. She even had a lighter heart after baring her soul as she had. Inhaling deeply, she thought how wonderfully fresh the air smelled. She found it hard to resist the urge to stop the team and pick wild flowers that stood straight and proud, beckoning her from both sides of the trail. There were white, purple and blue bachelor buttons, black-eyed Susans, purple-tassled thistle and sunflowers. The scent of sweet clover filled the air.

The undulating plains, interspersed with watershed gullies leading nowhere and everywhere grew with magnificent greenery. Huge birds glided through the air above her in the morning sun. They posed quite a contrast to the small bluebirds she saw sitting on scrub oak along the way. A cloud passed over, offering a moment of shade. Above her another contrast, a line of fleecy white clouds paralleling the Santa Fe Trail.

The wagons made a sharp turn off the road. Sarah heard Jelliroll moan. She looked over her shoulder and saw that his face was contorted in pain. She stopped her team to get him some water. She would give him some of the powders that Shad had given her.

"Here," she said, "take this medicine and put this cool cloth on your forehead."

"You're a fine person, pretty gal."

"From the looks of this trail, we're both going to hurt worse than ever in a few minutes," she said, heading around the wagon. She stopped and picked several Lilies of the Valley, drew deeply of their aroma and stuffed them into her bodice. Once she'd seated herself, she yelled and the team moved forward. She urged them to move faster as they were trailing too far behind as it was.

The wagon bounced over a deep rut and plunged down a sharp dip. "Hang on!" she yelled. "I think it's smoother up ahead!"

Her white-knuckled grip relaxed, and she stood up to see better. Sarah kept her concentration on trying to avoid deep holes or rocks. She wished she had more experience. She could see the trail ahead. It didn't look better as she had first believed.

They began to pitch over watershed ruts and rocks. Tortuous! Poor Jelliroll! The punishment for him must be bad. Sarah tried not to think of the pain in her own bones. Again, she remembered Shadrach's fingers, and enjoyed the tiny shivers that shuddered through her as her mind settled on his touch and the kiss he'd given her that morning.

By noon, the Jenkins, Jelliroll, she and Shad stood to the side of the trail and waved goodbye as the wagon train left them in the middle of a wilderness.

James suggested that they make some decisions as to who was to scout and who would drive the wagon.

Shadrach thought they should start moving south and tonight make chore assignments.

All agreed, so they sighted a straight line south and began moving.

That evening after they stopped, Sarah and Roberta cooked a supper that wasn't the best meal either had eaten. They had fried bacon which they crumpled and stirred into a pan of gravy, then ate it over biscuits that were left over from the day before.

Sarah took some food to Jelliroll who hadn't left the Jenkins's wagon. He ate it with relish, telling her that it was good. Sarah was delighted to see him feeling better.

When she went to help clean up, Roberta insisted that Sarah go on to bed, saying she would clean up. Sarah ached too badly to argue.

Shadrach and James had set up the two tents near the wagon, and Shad was sharing his tent with Jelliroll who had managed to get out of the wagon on his own. He said he was feeling one hundred percent better.

Inside her tent, Sarah lay a long time without sleep because every muscle in her burned as if someone had branded her. The only reprieve she'd had was the bath that she and Roberta had shared in a nearby stream before they'd started supper.

Shad hadn't offered to minister to her aching body although she went to bed almost hoping he might. Her thoughts about him continued to generate a wonder in her heart that opened new avenues for her to explore. But with this wonder came warnings for her to beware. After she had told Shad how she felt, he was polite but aloof. This should make her happy, but it didn't.

It had been a good day despite everything. How long had it been since she'd felt like this — bone-weary and ready to drop? Never before in her life.

The following day, the routine seemed easier. Each person took a responsibility for a certain chore or chores. Shadrach and James took turns with Sarah and Roberta driving the four horse team; that way none of them was overtired. The girls alternated cooking with Jelliroll. He did breakfast and they did lunch and supper. Sarah took charge of clean-up, and Roberta, the care of young Johnny. Jelliroll was happy to be riding ahead as scout. He was good at finding fording places for the wagon, and of evenings, he helped Shad set up the two tents. Shad and James handled the animals, the hitching and unhitching, the nightly fires, and the hunting of fresh meat. They also gathered wood for the breakfast fire which the first one up was to start.

Jelliroll surprised everyone when he produced a mouth harp. He could play many songs and seemed to enjoy the evening, playing softly as Roberta rocked Johnny, and while Shadrach and James talked about tomorrow.

The next evening they camped by a lake in Miami County. This day made Sarah unable to think of anything but a bath and a bed. The wind had been unrelenting, blowing dirt at them most of the day.

The others, as they did each evening after the wind had lain, gathered around the fire exchanging experiences, making plans for when they reached Cherryvale, and listening to

Jelliroll play. The only items of significance that she had seen during the day were several stray cows. Of course, the men rounded them up and now they were five adults, one child, one mule, nine horses, and three cows. One of the cows was fresh, so milk was a blessing, but rather hazardous to get. However, James seemed to have a way with the animals and said he'd have the cows tame in a week. Sarah loved his confidence.

Roberta said little Johnny had an ear ache, and she wasn't going to bathe. Sarah decided to go by herself. She missed a bathtub more than any single comfort, but she'd agreed with Roberta that clean water, hot or cold, in a tub or not, was always a blessing. Therefore, she reluctantly lowered herself into the lake behind a clump of trees. The area had an abundance of weeping willows. Sarah didn't recognize some species of trees, but there was no mistaking the willows, oak, sycamore, locust, and hedge apple.

She tried to relax as she eased herself deeper into the cold water. How she despised being chilled, but soon the cold water numbed her aching body, and she found herself feeling thankful for unexpected relief. Trumpet vines with their orange-colored, bell-shaped flowers grew wild, climbing through the lush trees.

Prepared, in case she encountered another frog, she left the lake carefully. She dressed in her gown and heavy robe, then haphazardly washed out the clothes she'd just removed, knowing they were as filled with dirt as her pores had been. She was making her way back to the wagon when the quiet evening suddenly exploded in angry voices.

They weren't far away. She walked below a four-foot grass covered limestone cliff that ran along the narrow creek which drained into the lake. The mens' voices came from above, and totally shocked her — Shad and James Jenkins yelling at each other! Why were they arguing? They had seemed so congenial!

Before she figured how to make her presence known without it seeming she had been eavesdropping, she found herself sitting on a rock below the cliff doing that very thing. She'd heard Shad's raised voice, and it chilled her. "I don't care what you say, for your wife's sake, you can't give up your search. Even if he's been missing a year instead of months, we both know Robert Smith and Leo Daniels are probably dead. Roberta will never give up finding her brother anymore than Sarah will give up finding her husband. They have to know whether they are dead or alive.

"Think about the future with your wife, man! If she lives with unhappiness, you'll not be happy. Your son deserves to grow up in a happy home and he won't with two miserable parents."

"You're not married, Shadrach, so how would you know what I'm going through? I've lost most every dollar I've ever earned, and spent what's left on what seems a fruitless search, and my wife hasn't the time to do anything for me, or with me. Why have I done this, you ask? To keep my wife happy, but how much longer is this going to go on?"

"I'm not married, but I'm in love, and this search for Sarah Daniel's husband is hard on me also. I'd like to settle down and raise a family, but until I find Leo Daniels, I'm obligated to stick it out with Sarah."

Sarah thought Shad's words the most cutting words she'd ever heard.

James nearly shouted in his obvious distress. "The difference between us is that you're getting paid to search, I'm not. That's why I'm appealing to you, try and talk Mrs. Daniels into abandoning this fruitless search. Since Roberta thinks a lot of her, she might listen to her if you'll help me."

"Can't do that, James. I'll mind my business, and you'll have to tend to yours," Shad said.

"Maybe you ought to try following your own advice. I wasn't the only one who noticed that you and Mrs. Daniels preferred to be alone rather than join in the wagon train's festivities. It's mighty convenient working for a rich woman you can pass the lonely hours with, isn't it?"

"I could knock your head off for saying that, but I won't because I know you're distraught, but you listen to me — Mrs. Daniels went to bed right after supper. You saw how hard she'd driven herself that day."

"Didn't I see you kissing her the morning before we left the train?" James insisted.

"That's none of your business!"

"I've discovered that people who use that expression usually have something to hide."

"You can speak clearer than that, James! Say what's on your mind and let's get this settled," Shadrach snapped.

James Jenkins's voice softened, "Shad, this is ridiculous. Why don't we just drop it and forget any of this was ever said."

"I'm sorry, James, but I'm not willing to do that. Not when you've impugned Mrs. Daniels's virtue and my veracity."

"Both of my statements were out of line," James said, "your integrity I'm beginning to know, Mrs. Daniels's virtue would be conjecture on my part. She is a quiet woman — somewhat of a mystery."

"I haven't completely figured her out myself," Shadrach said. "On the surface, she appears to be one thing, but other times . . . I can't figure her out. I just want to find her husband so she can start a new life, then I'll be free to pursue a life of my own. Regardless, I'll defend my actions and the lady's integrity."

As Sarah waited for Shad and James to walk back to the wagon she heard James speak very contritely, "I apologize for implying that you and Mrs. Daniels were together — *inappropriately together.* That was ungentlemanly of me and said in anger because I don't like seeing Roberta so certain she is going to find Robert when I know she won't."

"James, think about it!" Shad pleaded. "You're treating your wife as if you were her father. Try to understand the pull of her spirit for her twin brother. I've heard that twin siblings think alike and sometimes feel the same pain, the same joy. If she has no indication that Robert is dead, maybe he isn't. Give her the benefit of your doubts. Let her know that you love her and will go on searching until she says it's useless. If she feels you aren't fighting her, she might be more receptive to you. She needs you more than you need her even if you don't think so."

"She hasn't slept with me but twice in all these months — you know what I mean — let me make love to her. It's driving me crazy."

"Roberta may need to know that you love her no matter what, that you are one hundred percent behind her effort to find Robert, and that finding him means more to you than money. She may be suffering, thinking you're resentful of her because the money is gone. Guilt can keep Roberta from responding to your need to love her."

James was silent for a long time. "You're sure smart, Shad, and you're right, she and Robert have always been aware of what was happening to each other. Why, I remember the time he and I were plowing the field some distance from the house and he suddenly grabbed me and said that something was wrong with Roberta. He looked so desperate, I took off running for the house. When we arrived, we found her bleeding profusely. She was miscarrying our first child. She could've bled to death, but Robert knew. Thanks, Shad, for reminding me of things I shouldn't have to be reminded about. I'm sorry for what I said earlier."

"I apologize also, James."

After some seemingly endless conversation, James Jenkins said goodnight and walked away. Shadrach stood looking up at the night sky for what seemed an eternity. Sarah sat with her hands clutched to her chest. A new pain honed in on the old wounds. Only one other time had she known such agony — when she'd realized that Leo was missing. How could she have been so gullible where Shad was concerned — so trusting. Hadn't her mother often warned; *guard your affections, for out of them come the issues of life.* Sarah mentally chalked another lesson learned-too-late to the others in her life. She was a fool to have given in to Shad's advances. He loved someone else, couldn't wait for this job to be finished so he could get back to her.

Is what I'm feeling jealousy? she wondered. Did she hate some faceless woman who'd already captured Shad's heart? And here she was with a husband of her own. If he loved another, why had he kissed her? "Ohhh," she cried, throwing herself face down on the soft grass. "I'm just a fling in the wilderness to him — just a convenience. He'd said it himself, she'd heard him. That's all she was to him, a lonely woman for him to titillate — and get paid ta-boot!"

All the time she sobbed, reason kept repeating, he's not yours, you have a husband. Why do you care? Pull yourself together and get on with your life. Forget him. Let him go back to Chicago. But nothing she said lessened her anguish. She wanted to cry, but dared not — afraid that she'd never stop. Her up-and-down moods were a bitter pill to tolerate.

She went to her bedroll and wrestled with exhaustion. The gentle drone of insects, the grass whispering in the breezes, and the smell of burning wood faded away. She felt herself poised on the edge of a crevice waiting to fall, but merciful sleep rescued her.

CHAPTER NINE

The following morning, Sarah still carried a heavy heart. She went about her routine, trying to help Roberta with Johnny as much as possible. The boy had a painful ear ache and only stopped crying when Roberta held him close with his little ear pressed against her breast. She told Sarah that James wanted to take a detour to find a doctor. "Tomorrow, if he isn't better, I've agreed for him to go. James will do anything to get out of searching for Robert," Roberta said disgustedly as she tenderly held Johnny in her arms.

"Do you really believe that?" Sarah asked. "James is a good father and is concerned for his son."

"I know he is, so am I, and that was a terrible thing for me to say. He's a wonderful father and a splendid husband — especially since I'm not treating him very nice."

Sarah remembered what James had said to Shad about him and Roberta. "The question is, does he know how you feel?" she asked.

"I don't know. I've been awfully engrossed in finding Robert, but he seems to understand that."

"Does he really? You might make it easier on him if you didn't allow thoughts of Robert to domineer your life. I don't mean to be nosey, but when was the last time you allowed him to make love to you?"

Roberta turned away. "A long time," she said quietly.

"You might have a happier marriage if you spent more time building your future with James than so much time searching for Robert. You can do both, you know."

"But you're searching as hard as I am."

"The difference being that I'm searching for my husband, and if I find him, I'll work just as hard to make my marriage work. Think about it, Roberta — after Robert is found, dead or alive, your life with James goes on. If it is strained to the limit by stress and trouble between you and James, your marriage won't survive. Do you want Johnny to grow up in an unhappy home, or without a father?"

Roberta was crying. She hugged Sarah. "You're a wonderful friend. Thank you. I'm going to try and do better, but when Johnny is so sick, I can't do anything but hold him."

"Let's heat some water and keep a warm rag over his ear all night. It worked on me when I was a child. I remember." It wasn't a good memory that flooded Sarah's mind. The night she had her ear ache, she was crying in pain. Her father had knocked on her door and yelled for her to shut up. When she didn't, he'd come into her room, pulled off his belt and told her to stop yelling or he'd give her something to scream about. Her mother had come in and told him that she would take care of me. Her father had slung the belt out and hit her mother. He ordered her out of the room threatening to hit her again if she didn't go. She left and Sarah didn't utter another peep. Her father looked at her and said, "Children are just like animals, you rule them and teach them with the whip. Now don't let me hear another sound out of you."

Her father left, but thirty minutes later, her mother arrived with towels and hot water. She said her husband had left for the evening, and she started holding hot towels over Sarah's ear until the abscess burst and sweet relief flowed over her in blessed sleep.

Somehow Sarah made it through that night until the abscess in Johnny's ear burst and drained. The child went to sleep immediately, and Roberta and James thanked Sarah a dozen times.

Somehow Sarah made it through the next day with only an hour of sleep. That night, she joined the others, determined that Shad see her as an independent woman, so when the time came for her to fire him, he'd go back to Chicago and not worry about her.

After an acceptable time sitting and listening to Jelliroll play his mouth harp, she snuck away to bed. The two tents were only a few feet apart and both were close to the wagon. Later, when Jelliroll and Shad separated from the Jenkins, Sarah lay near the tent flap and could listen and see clearly because of the fire lighting the area. She saw Roberta clinging to her husband's arm.

He escorted her toward the rear of their wagon. Sarah knew they didn't know she could see them, so when they paused to kiss, she turned her eyes away, and lay very still in her bedroll.

"Roberta, honey," Sarah heard James say, "you haven't been like this in a long time. Without your love, my life has been miserable."

"I'm so sorry for neglecting you, and I offer no excuses. I just want you to hold me, kiss me and promise me that you'll never let me get so involved finding Robert that I'll do this again. I love you dearly, you know."

Several minutes of silence followed before Sarah heard James Jenkins groan. "Damn girl, you're something! If Johnny stays asleep, this is a night I'll not soon forget."

"I want to cry when you kiss me like this, please do it again!" she begged.

Another shorter length of silence, and another softly spoken endearment and all was silent. Sarah turned painfully over in her bedroll and sighed softly. All was well and good in the Jenkins's wagon this night.

Sarah thought about the talk she and Roberta had had earlier. She was a fine one to give advice to another when her own behavior still shocked her. She had finally realized that Shadrach was in love with someone other than her, and his life was none of her business, but for some unexplainable reason, knowing this did not stop the hurt she felt inside. To Sarah it was a hurt much like losing Leo. Shad hadn't made any declaration of love to her, so why did she feel abandoned and tricked? All he'd done was kiss her!

Sometimes, she found herself questioning her memory. Her feelings for Shadrach clouded her judgment. No man had stirred her as he had — not even Leo. She couldn't believe she'd allowed herself to say that about Leo. She'd never get caught in Shad's trap again. She took a deep breath, but that didn't help. She tried willing herself not to dwell on Shad's touch or his kiss, but that didn't help, either. It would do no good to deny the emotions that he had caused — they filled her very being.

No one was like him! He was already in her heart. But, her heart felt suddenly cold and lonely — oh, Lord, she agonized, what was happening to her? She curled up and tried to go to sleep, but she had to relieve her bladder. She left her tent and made her way by moonlight toward a stand of trees.

As soon as she had finished, she started back, the snap of a twig froze her to the spot where she stood. Breathlessly she waited, and when no other sound came, she released the breath she was holding; then she heard heavy breathing behind her. She whirled around in time to see a hulking figure lunge for her. She screamed as she went down to the ground, her feet and fists flying out in useless self-defense. The man was going to rape her! Her nostrils flared at the stench from the man trying to kiss her — trying to get her nightgown up over her head. She screamed for

Shadrach just before a cruel hand clamped over her mouth.

Sarah heard Shadrach's answering yell. "Where are you, Sarah?"

She couldn't answer, only twist and turn, trying to save herself. She heard James shout, "Which way is she?"

"Those trees, I think. Sarah!" Shadrach called again and she heard the frantic concern in his voice.

She sank her teeth into the finger of the hand nearly smothering her. The man grunted and turned her loose, but not before he struck her in the face. She gasped from pain and rolled away from her attacker. "Shad, over here," she screamed, scrambling to her feet to get her gown down.

"Why were you screaming? Are you all right?" he cried as he raced to her side.

"Someone tried to rape me!" She burst into tears and collapsed into Shadrach's arms.

"What's happened?" Roberta cried as she came to where they were standing. Jelliroll followed carrying Johnny and a lantern.

"Someone attacked Sarah," James said.

"My, God!" Roberta cried. "Your mouth is bleeding."

"He hit me when I bit his finger. My lip is busted."

Shadrach gave her his handkerchief. "Stop crying," he soothed, "tell me which way he went!"

"That way," she pointed into the stand of trees, and when she did, she saw the blood on her fingers. She opened her fist to see that she held a white shirt button.

Shadrach took the button and examined it. "It's not much, but it's better than nothing. I'm going after the bastard!"

"Your hand is bleeding!" Roberta cried, taking Sarah's hand in hers, examining her fingers under the lantern Jelliroll held high so they could see.

"I don't think it's my blood. I know that I scratched my attacker somewhere."

"I'll say you did," Shad said looking at her fingers. "I hope this skin beneath your nails is from his face. If it is, he'll be easy to identify. This button missing from his shirt will seal the bastard's fate. Roberta, take Sarah back to the wagon. Jelliroll, you guard them. James get your gun and horse, we're going after the cuss while the trail is fresh."

Sarah washed out her mouth with lye soap, remembering with revulsion the man's wet mouth grinding into hers. She washed her face and hands, changed her gown and donned a robe, then she brushed grass out of her hair. She sat by the fire and cried out her fear to Roberta and Jelliroll who were both most comforting. "How long have they been gone?" Sarah asked.

"Not easy trackin' at night. Why don't ya and

Miss Roberta go on ta bed?" Jelliroll said. "I'll wait up for them."

"Do you think they'll get him?" Sarah asked.

"Hard ta say. Depends on how clever the varmint is at gettin' away. Please, Miss Sarah, go ta bed."

"After awhile," she said, as Roberta took Johnny into the wagon to try and get him to stop whining. "Why don't you play your harp — maybe it'll calm Johnny?" Sarah asked.

Jelliroll obliged, and played several songs. After a while, Sarah got to her feet. "I'll bet Roberta is sleeping," she said walking toward the wagon.

"Think yer right, it's quiet in there." Jelliroll walked to the wagon with Sarah and they looked inside. "Yep, she and John-boy are both sleepin'."

"I thought we were in the middle of nowhere. Where did whoever it was come from?" Sarah asked, still shaken from her attack.

"We're close to several settlements, Parsons is only a few days away — maybe some hermit headin' fer town, or goin' home, caught sight of ya and waited to catch ya alone. Ya gotta stop bein' anxious and start dependin' on us menfolk ta guard ya. Yer always runnin' off alone, worryin' the rest of us."

"Oh, Jelliroll, I've learned a terrible lesson. If Shadrach hadn't heard me scream, I'd have been raped. The man was too strong for me. What a

125

fool I've been." Again, she began to cry.

Jelliroll placed his short arms around her and rubbed her back. "Too bad ya had to learn it this way, but praise be, yer all right. Now go ta bed. If'n ya can't sleep, ya can pray."

Sarah glanced into the wagon; saw Roberta asleep with one of the journals she so highly prized open across her chest. She had wanted Sarah to sleep with her on their feather ticking, but seeing there was little room, Sarah decided to go on to her tent.

"I'll stay right out here so's I can watch ya both," Jelliroll said, as Sarah threw back her opening flap.

She was still shaking from the ordeal, and didn't intend to sleep until Shad returned. A man like the one who attacked her might be capable of more than raping defenseless women. She took another look out of the flap and saw Jelliroll on guard a few feet away. Sitting down on her bedroll, she prayed, thanking God for saving her and asking Him to bring James and Shadrach back safely.

She suddenly felt the need to lie down and even while she prayed, she went to sleep in spite of turmoil, aches and pain.

Sometime toward morning, Sarah awoke from troubled sleep, but her eyes remained closed. She could feel someone's breath on her face, and was instantly ready to scream when lips as soft as silk touched her cheek. Her eyes flew open and she gazed into an indistinguishable face above

126

shoulders which she recognized. She knew it was Shad, that he had returned safely, that he was concerned about her, and it was like answered prayer to have him here. She didn't move as he straightened up quickly and hurried from the tent. Sarah watched him and James as they began the day's routine. Jelliroll was mounted on his horse ready to ride ahead, to scout the best route.

"You might as well wait until after breakfast," Shadrach said to Jelliroll.

"Don't think I could eat a bite, I'll be back in a couple hours, if there's a biscuit left, I'll eat it and some honey."

"We need to find a fording place on the river coming up," James called.

"I'll find one, and leave you a sign where it's safe to cross, don't fret."

Sarah dressed and made herself ready for the day. She and Roberta met beside the fire. Both were full of questions. "I don't see any prisoner," Roberta said to James.

"I'm afraid not, but not because we didn't try," he said.

"The fellow was tricky, big as a bear, but agile as a deer," Shadrach said, as he filled the coffee pot, and smiled at Sarah.

"I've never been so scared," she said. "Do you think he will surprise us again?"

"I truly don't believe he'll come near us again. He knows there are men to guard the women, so he won't try it again. Nevertheless, we'll keep watch at night until we reach Parsons — only a few more days."

"Thank you, Shad, for being there."

"Don't worry. I've got the button. Someday I'll run into a fellow with a missing button that matches the one on my pocket." He grinned and nodded, then he and James set to work hitching up the team.

The next day's routine was easier and they progressed reasonably well except for fording the numerous creeks, some wide enough to be scary as rivers. Jelliroll identified the rivers around Parsons and Cherryvale. He said the Verdigris is the principal river, entering Labette County on the Northern boundary, the Elk River enters from the west and empties into the Verdigris. The Caney River cuts across the southwest corner of the county. "Besides these rivers, there are too many streams to name. Hell, some of them have no names, but ya can count on me to get ya 'cross them in one piece," he said at the end of the day.

The following afternoon, the wagon reached a small settlement near the town of Parsons, Kansas which was the county seat of Labette County. The first sign they saw indicated that Parsons had the only horse and buggy doctor in the area. James was delighted because one of the cows had an infection on her back. James's speculated that the cow may have been stung by a bee or hornet, then in its effort to scratch the itch, had rubbed a raw spot on its back which had become infected.

That evening, they camped at a watering hole, on an arm of a creek. By day's end, Sarah had decided her lack of strength was due more to depression than exhaustion. Depression had come shortly after her terrible experience with the nameless attacker. She had heard all her life about men who would rape anyone, anywhere and for any number of reasons. She'd never considered that she would be a victim. Sarah spent hours blaming herself for the incident. Shadrach had cautioned her not to go anywhere alone without letting him know, but she was stubborn to a fault.

Roberta's husband always went with her when she wanted a time of privacy. It seemed so unnatural to ask a man, not your husband, to stand watch while you relieved yourself. So far she'd managed to slip off alone, but she was frightened every minute. Surely Parsons and a hotel wasn't too far away. Regardless, she would not go anywhere alone for a long time — not after what had happened.

Sarah had shared some of her feelings with Roberta who offered to help anyway she could. Sarah even thought about telling her about her feelings concerning Shad. If she did, Roberta might say something inadvertently to Shad, and Sarah had no wish to have him apologizing to her because she'd misinterpreted his actions. The fact that he loved another woman was never too long off her mind.

There seemed to be no solution to ease her torment. Sarah continued to feel that she'd been unfaithful to her husband, who was missing and maybe dead. To make matters worse, the man to whom she found herself attracted, was anxious to be done with his search for her husband so he could get home to the one he really loved. Because of all this, she was acting like a belligerent child.

Too tired to bathe, Sarah decided that sleep was her anesthetic. She ate and took a quick sponge bath, then went to bed. She hadn't seen much of Shadrach, and tried to make herself believe she was glad. He seemed very busy — or was she making excuses for his lack of attention? She kept telling herself to forget him, but she couldn't forget his kiss. Had it meant nothing to him?

Very late, something awakened Sarah. At first, her heart leaped into her throat, but looking out the tent flap, she saw, Roberta and James sitting around the fire talking. She didn't know what had aroused her and listened for a long time hearing nothing but snoring from Shad's tent. At times, Shad or Jelliroll, one of them sounded like a freight train. Sarah decided that was what had awakened her, so she tried to go back to sleep.

After a while, she glanced out the flap once again and saw Shadrach coming from the trees. He made his way quietly toward the tent where he and Jelliroll slept. "Is everything all right?" she asked from inside her tent as he walked past.

Shadrach drew a long-sounding breath, and ducked down to look inside. "Jelliroll snores so loud I can't sleep. I'm about ready to move my bedroll outside, but it looks like rain."

"Why don't you place your bed outside near the opening?"

"I would still hear him snoring," he said.

"Then bring your bedroll to the opening of my tent, and if it starts raining, you can move inside," she offered. "Oh, Lord, what am I doing?" she muttered.

CHAPTER TEN

Shad didn't say a word after Sarah's offer of her tent in case of rain, he just turned away and entered his own tent. Sarah didn't know if she'd crossed another line or what. Then suddenly, he was outside her tent unrolling his bed at the opening to her tent, no more than an arm's length from where she lay. Covertly, she watched him, silhouetted against the moon. He pulled off his boots, slipped his long legs under his blanket, and turned to gaze inside her tent.

She didn't know if he could see her or not; she could see him. A half hour passed in absolute silence. Thunder couldn't have sounded louder than her heart's drumming beat. Sarah wanted to talk to him, but she didn't trust herself, so she pretended she was asleep. Utterly confused about most of her feelings, she was clear-headed about one. She had to be careful. This tall, attractive man had gained entry into her heart. Such a thing couldn't happen — it shouldn't have happened!

Then, she fell asleep and didn't know when Shad crawled to her side. He leaned toward her and placed an ever so light butterfly kiss on her lips. With his mouth but a breath from hers, he whispered, "Sleep well, sweetheart, and thanks. I know how hard you're trying. Leo Daniels has nothing to complain about." And then, he crawled back outside to his bedroll. Shadrach knew he should stay fifty feet away from her, but he couldn't. No woman had ever affected him as had this slip of a beautiful girl. Every time his eyes met hers, he was lost in passionate desire for her, but his desire went far deeper than simply physical yearnings. He wanted her for his wife, his life's partner, his lover and soul mate. Shadrach knew he could never have her as long as there was hope of finding Leo. She was fighting so hard to be faithful to a memory, and that's all Leo was — a memory. Until Sarah realized that, he had no choice but to honor her desire to be true to her husband, even though Shadrach knew she had fallen in love with him. Guilt was the enemy of them both. He studied the starless sky, thinking how his circumstance matched the total darkness.

Sarah wanted to cry, because she'd awakened just as he kissed her. She heard what he said. She felt the tears running down her cheeks, and whether they were from joy or sorrow, she couldn't decide. How unbearable to be so close to him and not feel his arms around her. She turned over on her side so she could look at him. Without intent, she moved her arm toward him. She had to strain to keep from speaking, when he suddenly rolled in her direction and his hand moved over hers, grasping it ever so tenderly.

He held it until she thought she couldn't stand the shivers flooding over her. Slowly, he lifted her hand to his lips and kissed it. Sarah trembled so violently, she knew he must be able to feel it. She didn't think that all the king's horses could have held her still — not with every fiber of her being on fire, but she managed to pretend a sleepy turn onto her back to escape the numbing sensations that his nearness caused. Then suddenly, before she'd settled into her place, he'd moved to her side and claimed her lips.

Push him away! her mind cried, but she lay very still, instead. She wanted to wrap her arms around his neck and fling back her cover so he could take her into his arms. Should she pretend to wake up and do just that — or slap his face? She couldn't do either. She didn't move, allowing the kiss to continue. He was probably using her to help him forget the frustration of not being with the woman he loved. Yes, she told herself, that's the reason for his display — I've done nothing to make him believe I wanted his advances, but still, she didn't move.

His mouth suddenly lifted, and he muttered aloud as if he knew she could hear him — an apology of sorts, "Back in your bed, Koby, you're taking advantage of innocence!" His hand trailed lightly over her shoulder and down the length of her arm.

Then, he left. She heard the rain start hitting her canvas tent, saw him gather his bedroll and return to his tent. She watched for a long time before drifting into troubled sleep.

The next morning when Sarah left her tent,

Roberta told her that James and Shadrach had ridden into Parsons. "James thinks he can get a job easier in the larger town than in Cherryvale, and since we are nearly penniless, James wants to find us a place to rent. Shadrach said he had to check out a lead about Leo in some hotel."

"Good," Sarah said, "I hope the man named Adams is still in Parsons; it's been months. I'm glad James went with him."

"If James can't find work, I may have to take a job in a cafe waiting tables. I'm a good seamstress, but there's more money in tips when you serve tables. I'll do about anything to get out of this wagon."

Sarah looked around. "Where's Jelliroll?"

"He's looking the countryside over, trying to decide whether to settle here or elsewhere. Told the men he'd be back in a couple of hours. I can't imagine where he is; he's been gone that long and more."

"This is beautiful country. I'll wager it's good farm land." Sarah observed the hills, the blue sky making a spectacular backdrop for the lush greenery of the trees. "God's colors," she said, pointing ahead.

Roberta smiled. "They're my favorite colors. Sarah, do you think Jelliroll will leave us to buy a farm here? I've grown fond of him, but I don't see how he can farm alone. He is so good with Johnny, has even offered to watch him if we find a lead that takes both of us away at the same time, and it will when we go to Cherryvale.

Thank goodness it's only a few miles from Parsons. We can ride there and back in a day, and have time to do some questioning about Robert."

"Have you noticed how Jelliroll has cut down his eating?" Sarah asked. "I believe he's trying to lose weight. He'd surely feel better if he did."

"That's for certain the truth. James says that he is really a good tracker, and when he's feeling good is agile as a man half his age. I've been thinking that he might be able to help us if we get any solid leads to the whereabouts of your Leo, and my brother."

"I'm willing for any help. Let's ask James and Shadrach what they think."

"I know what James thinks. He hopes Jelliroll will stay and help him farm if we ever get a place of our own, and if not, James said he would help Jelliroll if he buys himself a farm. I figure Jelliroll will be happy if he has help; we've been sharecroppers all our lives."

"I'm really glad that Jelliroll decided to come with us. He's lonely and needs a family. Tell me about your family and Robert," Sarah said as she dipped herself some cornmeal mush into a bowl.

"My parents were older when Robert and I were born and my mother barely lived through the delivery. My father took us to our aunt in Iowa, and he went west. We've never heard from him, but then, we never knew him. Our aunt and uncle raised us until we left home. Robert is twenty-six, handsome, personable, and energetic. He's honest as Abe Lincoln, and he loves me and James. Johnny is the luckiest boy in the world to have an uncle like Robert.

"When my mother-in-law died, James's father took off like mine did, leaving him, his only son, to fend for himself. On a family trip into Des Moines, Robert met James in town and brought him home. They were only boys, twelve years old. James and Robert were close as brothers, and James lived with us until he and I fell in love and were married. Then, after we moved onto a big Iowa farm where we started share-cropping, Robert came to live with me and James.

"The three of us were share-cropping for an elderly farmer of the area. We did well, but something always came along to take our money. One week, discouraged and hurting because the crops had failed, James started drinking, and got into a poker game with our last ten dollars. God must have smiled on him. He won fifteen-hundred dollars before the game ended. James never lost a hand and was sober as an empty jug when he got home and told me and Robert what he intended to do. He spread a newspaper on the table and pointed to a *for sale* ad. The farm was in Oklahoma, and he wanted to leave the next day to investigate the property.

"I'll never forget how excited he was as he grabbed me into his arms and swung me in a circle. Misfortune seemed to follow us. One thing then another kept him from leaving. Then winter was upon us and the owner of the farm we worked for offered to let us stay the winter if we'd help him plant the spring crops. Reluctantly, James agreed, but Robert begged him to let him go on ahead and check out the farm in Oklahoma. James finally agreed, and we sent Robert and our money off to Oklahoma. We expected to hear from him by the first of the year, but we never did.

"As soon as the seed was planted, James and I left for Oklahoma, to look for Robert. I've told you the rest. Robert never arrived in Oklahoma. The man had sold the farm to another. We stopped in every town to inquire about Robert as we made our way back to Iowa to beg for our old job. We were too late because the owner had hired another family. In time, we both found work. James became good friends with this Pinkerton man, and when he told us he was heading for Oklahoma on a manhunt, we asked him to check on Robert.

"We gave him all the money we could scrape together and he promised to do his best. When we heard that Robert was seen in Cherryvale, we took every dime we could beg or borrow to get here.

"James's friend went with us to Westport, but we were nearly out of money by then, so we let the Pinkerton man go, having decided to go on our own to check out Cherryvale. Now, you know why we were so happy to meet you and Shadrach Koby. I feel like I'm sponging off you, but it's like having a Pinkerton Agent with

Shadrach working for you. Forgive me, but I'm desperate. I don't know how much more time Robert has. I only know he's not dead. I'd feel it here," she patted her chest, "if he were."

Sarah hugged Roberta, then told her about her husband's disappearance. As they waited for the men to return, Sarah realized how easy it would have been to suggest to Roberta that Robert might have lost their money, gambled it away, or been swindled, and then, being too ashamed to return to them empty-handed, had just disappeared. She refrained from saying anything, knowing that suggesting any of these things about Robert was probably as untrue as Leo having left her because he no longer wanted to be married to her.

As the day wore on, Sarah wondered if Shad and James had run into trouble, but Roberta seemed unperturbed about their being gone so long. However, they both had become concerned about Jelliroll. He should have been back by now. Two long hours had gone by.

Sarah wished she'd been able to go to Parsons. When she could again go shopping, she wanted to buy some new clothes. She was sick of wearing her two dresses. Suddenly she remembered her cowboy clothes and went to her tent, dug through her satchel and retrieved her trousers and shirt. She changed her clothes.

Roberta was surprised when she saw Sarah. "Why have you dressed like a man?"

"If the men don't return soon, I'm riding out

to find them," Sarah said.

"You can't do that," Roberta cried. "You wouldn't leave me and Johnny alone, would you?"

"Not if you'll come with me. You'd better prepare because I am going. Look at the sun. It's past noon; something is wrong. I'm not spending the night out here without the men. We don't even have a gun. Wouldn't you rather be in Parsons in a hotel?"

"Of course, I would, and I've a rifle, but what will the men do if we're gone when they come back?" Roberta asked.

Sarah looked around. "We'll wedge a note in the crotch of that tree. Now, get your rifle loaded and stay alert."

"I hate living like this," Roberta cried. "All I want is a place my boy can grow up, call home, and be safe. I don't like living out of a wagon — hitching and unhitching — hitching and un-hitching."

Her words seemed a little harsh to Sarah, but Roberta had led a hard life. She'd already told her that they'd never own a place of their own. Sarah tried to be sympathetic. She sensed that Roberta had only vented her frustration because of concern over James being so late. "We'll wait two more hours," Sarah said.

Sarah had not really talked to Shad since the night she'd been attacked. What she wouldn't give to have him making the decisions at this moment, but he wasn't here. She and Roberta had been waiting long enough. "I think we should go," Sarah said.

"Are you really that worried?" Roberta asked.

"I am."

"Surely, James and Shadrach are all right." She giggled nervously. "Unless, one of them has found a sweetheart in Parsons."

The endearment "sweetheart" slammed into Sarah's memory. Shad had called her sweetheart! The word nestled neatly in her mind, but she didn't have time to think about such things. She had a job to do and didn't know if she was up to it.

By two o'clock she and Roberta had hitched the wagon and were following as best they could the tracks of the men's horses on the trail leading toward Parsons. Sarah rode ahead, signaling Roberta when the path was clear. She worried about Johnny and Roberta. What if they ran into trouble and something happened to them? *God, I need You!* Sarah shot a quick prayer to God for guidance. She took her responsibility seriously. "I'll relieve you when you get tired," she called to Roberta.

Roberta refused her offer. The surprising thing to Sarah was that she'd come with her at all. When Sarah had insisted that she was going, Roberta had made a dozen excuses. What would they do with the animals? What would happen if Jelliroll returned and found them gone? What if they missed James and Shadrach?

"I'll stake the cows, and tie the pack horses to

a tree, then write a note *to whom it may concern* stating our intention and that if we reach Parsons without finding them, we'll spend the night in a hotel."

"All right," Roberta had conceded, "I'll go."

As Sarah and Roberta rumbled along in the wagon, Sarah observed that the hills didn't seem as high as those fifty miles back. Although the land seemed flatter, it was mostly forested. She heard a mockingbird and tried to find it, but couldn't. Johnny was squealing, and when Sarah went to see what was wrong, he'd spotted a red fox family on a bluff watching them pass. "Doggie," he cried when he saw Sarah.

"That is a mama fox, a papa fox, and two little babies," Sarah answered.

"When papa fox come home?" he asked.

Sarah was confused until Roberta spoke up, "Your papa will be along later."

Johnny squealed as he waved at the fox family. Sarah rode her pinto on ahead of the wagon, thinking how cute the boy could be when he wanted to. The grassland yielded more cattle — sleek-bodied cows and calves all roaming wild, or so it seemed. She wondered why she didn't see any homesteads or cabins. The scent of sweet clover and grass permeated the air. They passed a deserted pole barn, and Sarah knew someone had tried to raise cattle or farm in the area. Her genuine curiosity surprised her. She wondered what had happened to the one who'd built the abandoned barn. Had sickness or storms, famine or demon whiskey destroyed their dreams? She couldn't get over the lushness of this land. Weeping willows circling small run-off ponds with orange lilies growing profusely along the water's edge. This contrasted with the black, scarred trees that had been struck by lightning. Clusters of bittersweet climbed the blackened tree trunks. She wanted to pick some, but was afraid the orange bittersweet might be poison, and Johnny would demand that he have some. He was always eating berries.

She grinned as her gaze moved past a wild rose climbing along a rock cliff, then to a creek up ahead. A shuddering breath escaped her when she saw that it was a lot wider than a creek. It might be a small river. "We'll ride paralleling it until we find a place we can ford," she said to the worried Roberta.

"Sarah, I haven't wanted to mention it, but I've seen a shadow twice that might be a man. The last time I saw it, it was across this creek and a little north. What are we going to do?"

"Are you certain it was a man?" Sarah cried.

"No, I thought once it might be a bear. I wish James was here." Roberta sighed.

"So do I," Sarah agreed. "Keep your rifle handy, and I'm going to stay closer to the wagon. We'll be all right. If someone shows himself, we'll shoot, then ask questions."

"We can't do that. We might wound one of our men. We'd better first ask them to identify themselves."

"Not on your life. They need to know we're armed and ready to shoot if they try anything they shouldn't."

"I wish I had your courage," Roberta said.

Sarah laughed. "Mine is all bluff, so keep a sharp eye out for us both."

The scent of ripening wild cherry trees, along with herbs and flowers hung heavy in the humid air like a blend of perfume. The cloudless sky didn't alleviate the heavy humidity, and Roberta said, "There might be a storm brewing."

Sarah looked at the cloudless sky. "How do we handle a storm in a wagon?"

"We get wet, that's how."

Again Sarah grinned. *Brewing storm* must be a figure of speech — right along with *tempest in a teapot.* Exactly what would they do if a gully-washer came? It was a rhetorical question. She had no solutions to a hundred other things she wanted to know about — things that bothered her.

Some of her thoughts were a little frightening. Don't cross bridges before you reach them, she told her worrying mind. She glanced at the horizon, glad she didn't see any clouds forming. She tried to enjoy the changing shades of green, yellow, red, and the purples of shrubs and flowers — every color like the paints on an artist's palette.

She thought the wagon would shake apart as it crossed the rough terrain. About the time the sun began to sink in the west, they decided to stop while it was still daylight. Parsons was farther than they'd supposed. This could explain Shad's and James's delay, but not Jelliroll's.

Sarah spotted an overhanging rock ledge wide enough for the wagon, her tent, and the animals. They'd be dry in case of rain. She felt she'd found a safe place to stop with the large stream in front of them, the rock wall to their back, and the overhang above them. No one, or a wild animal could easily sneak up on them — she hoped.

CHAPTER ELEVEN

As Sarah figured out how to get the wagon under the overhang, she acted excited and confident for Roberta's sake. Sarah knew Roberta had guessed that they were lost.

Roberta stood up in the wagon and shaded her eyes against the setting sun. "Have you noticed that we are in a lovely open meadow, except for this rock bank where we are taking sanctuary? Have you seen how many tributaries crisscross this valley? What a spectacular setting! I suppose all these small waterways ran south toward some bigger, waiting river."

Roberta was wonderful, never blaming her for the decision to leave — even now when it appeared they were lost, she talked about valleys and tributaries, not wrong or right directions. Roberta lifted Johnny to the ground after the wagon was situated, and told him to help. "You're the man tonight, Johnny. You go find all the dried twigs you can carry. We'll start a fire and maybe Papa will see it and come eat supper with us."

"No!" he cried. "I don't want to!"

"All right. Do you want to look for snails over there by the wall?"

"Uh-hu," he said running off toward the wall.

Sarah sighed and turned away, not believing how easily the boy managed to get his way. A few minutes later, she and Roberta unloaded the wagon, and then, while Roberta went to gather firewood and water, Sarah unhitched the team. All the time she worked, she tried not to worry too much about the shadows Roberta thought she'd seen across the stream. She even tried not to be concerned about the men, but her efforts didn't help much, she worried plenty. Would Shad be terribly angry with her? She was so distraught she wanted to cry, but for Roberta and spoiled Johnny, she had to stay brave. Sarah had never wanted Shadrach more than she did now.

"Don't worry, he be back," Johnny said coming toward the area where she was placing rocks in a circle in order to build a safe fire. His little arms were loaded with twigs. She helped him put them down, not believing he'd decided to help. She'd never heard him say a whole sentence. She'd not heard more than one or two words at once, mostly No! and I won't! Oh, Lord! Even Young Johnny can see my concern. "I know your papa will be mighty happy to see us. We'll build a big fire for him to find, all right?"

"Big fire," he said.

Sarah opened her arms and said, "How about a hug?"

Johnny jumped into her arms and squeezed her neck.

Shortly, Sarah involved herself in the preparations for setting up her tent and cooking supper, but mentally she was sick with concern. As yet, it hadn't rained, but it seemed evident that it was raining to the north of them.

After Sarah corralled her team horses where they could feed on tall prairie grass and still get under the overhang if it rained, she watered them. Then, she started dejectedly toward the wagon. Abruptly, she heard a shrill, two-finger whistle and whirling around in the direction from which it came, saw him.

Shadrach and James were trailing their horses and cows along the edge of the stream. Shad was waving with his hat, a big smile on his face. Sarah knew they had found the note and that they didn't appear too upset that she and Roberta had left and lost the trail. Her heart raced wildly at the sight of him. Lord! It burst upon her consciousness, this was the way she'd always see Shadrach Koby. He was good-natured and genuine. He still waved his Stetson enthusiastically, looking excited about something.

Reality splintered her image of him as he leaped from his horse to the ground before her. Why couldn't she keep in mind that he had an interest in another woman? Remember, she told herself, he has made no commitment to you, and he believes you're in love with Leo Daniels! I do love Leo! her heart cried. Yet, her thoughts of Shad reached no further than the memory of his touch — his words — his caring ways. He and James led their horses under the ledge and Shadrach looked around.

"This is a perfect place to camp. You find

this?" he asked, staring at Sarah.

"Yes, and we are so happy that you found us. We were worried that we might have missed you. I thought we were lost."

"You're following a perfect path toward Parsons."

"You look happy — have you some news?" she asked trying to calm her reaction to seeing him. Why was his presence so disconcerting? Oh, Lord! Why did he impact her like this?

"James got a job and a place to live." Shad placed his Stetson on his head, then as if he'd had a second thought, shoved it off to hang against his back by leather thongs. He sniffed the air. He glanced at her. "How come you smell good even after wrestling a team out of harness?"

She just stared. Shad's gaze lingered on her face and Sarah broke eye contact so she could think. "I always gather Lilies of the Valley and rub them into my skin. Have you any news for me?"

"You're a jewel, do you know that? Did you miss me?" he asked seemingly ignoring her question.

Sarah swallowed with difficulty before she answered. She wanted to tell him that he'd not been out of her mind, that she'd worried about him, but that would have been a mild statement of her feelings. "I'd noticed you were gone. I'm glad you and James found us before nightfall. Where is Jelliroll?" she asked, evading his penetrating eyes.

"What do you mean? Isn't he with you?"

"He's been gone as long as you."

"How about that! Wonder what's happened to him? James," he called to his friend, "Jelliroll isn't back, shall we go after him?"

"Not on your life! He's a tracker — since we found them, he'll find us if he so desires."

"Will he be all right?" Sarah asked, unable to look Shad in the eye. She brushed at her dusty trousers and alternately wiped her hands, wondering why he was evading talking about finding out news about Leo.

"Jelliroll may have found himself a farm," Shad said.

"That's good and bad," she said. "There'll be some disappointed people," she looked at Roberta and Johnny standing in James's arms, "if Jelliroll leaves them."

"I understand," Shad said. "I'm hungry, have you finished supper?"

"We were getting ready to cook," she said.

"Why don't you and I sneak off and go for a ride. Those two won't miss us. Anyway, I need to talk to you privately."

His request started Sarah's pulse surging. He did have something to tell her! "Can't you talk to me now?" she asked, not certain he was serious.

"I could, but I prefer to ride with you," he said, his gaze locked with hers.

She felt breathless. He meant it! "Well," she said, fighting her trembling voice to keep her real feelings to herself, "you tempt me."

"Good, that was my plan."

His hand reached out and moved along her cheek. A finger traced the curve of her lips. "Thank you," he whispered, "I need to talk to you — I need you."

Into Sarah's mind came the vague impression of a woman she'd never seen — a woman who had felt Shad's touch and tasted his kisses. Agony sizzled like hot grease on coals and she thrust his hand away. She wouldn't be an interim romance! "Don't touch me like that," she stammered, pushing his reaching arms away. "I'll ride with you and talk if you want, but that's all, do you understand?"

"What's wrong? I've offended you — how?" His voice sounded strained.

"I — I don't want you to touch me. I mean, I do, but I don't. . . ." She shook her head, not believing she'd spoken so straight-forwardly.

"What do you want?" he asked, and the black hue of his eyes twinkled at her disarmingly.

Sarah couldn't answer his question, and fought her impulse to tell him that she knew about his being in love with someone else. She found it impossible to look him in the eyes. If she did for more than a moment, she knew she'd lose what composure she had. Don't forget, she reminded herself, you do have some self respect.

"I just want to give you a hug to say hello and I'm glad you're safe," Shad said reaching slowly out to her.

151

She couldn't imagine what she was doing, she just stood there knowing what he was intending and let him encircle her into his arms. She stiffened a second before responding to his hug.

A fantastic feeling eased into her aching heart — maybe he didn't love someone else anymore. This thought erased everything in her mind — for a moment anyway. "I'll go with you," she said when she caught her breath, "if you remember that I'm a married woman and stop doing this."

He nodded and gave her a quick squeeze. The exquisite knowledge of knowing that in this man's arms she could know untold happiness fought with another knowledge, the devastating one that brought Leo Daniels to her mind. What had Shad found out about him? Whatever it is, don't forget, she cried to her confused heart, that he belongs to another!

Although the thought filled her with despair, she refused to retain it. She cast it away. Like an insect, she brushed it from her mind so it wouldn't sting. In its place came the excitement of Shadrach Koby's tender touch that thrilled her beyond understanding.

Sarah forced a little reserve to her voice, "Let me get supper started first." She stepped toward the wagon, and began unloading the food box.

"Why can't we ride now before we eat? I'm not hungry," Shad said.

"Neither am I," James chimed in. "We ate the noon meal very late. If you want to go for a ride, go now. This is the best time of evening."

"Thanks, James," Shad said, turning to stare at Sarah. "We'll ride my horse." He bowed.

"Wait a minute, I have to change. These trousers smell like animals."

She lifted the bucket of water from behind the wheel and snuck into the wagon. She didn't want to disturb Roberta and James who were giggling like two lovers as they stood on the other side of her tent.

She took a wash pan, and half the water in the bucket to give herself a soap and water sponge bath, then took the other half of clean water to rinse the dust from her hair. As she donned her clean dress, she knew an unexpected pleasure — the dress felt good. She looked at herself, and grinned.

She tried doing something different with her hair. She'd been wearing a braid in her once carefully styled hair. Today, she brushed it up on top her head where she secured it with a ribbon which gave her a roll of tousled curls. This was fairly easy since she had naturally curly hair. She set her Stetson on her head over the knot of curls and let little wisps of springy hair fall freely around her face. Because she was so fair, her pink cheek cream made a great difference in her appearance, and caused her complexion to glow. Her yellow dress helped because it was her most flattering color, or so she'd been told.

Sarah heard Hominy whinny, then Shad's

voice. "James," he was saying, "we're going to ride a ways now, give you and Roberta some time alone."

"Surely, Shadrach. Don't worry about anything here."

"Thanks, friend," he said, then knocked on the side of the wagon.

"Sarah, are you ready?"

She lifted the canvas curtain to look out. She could scarcely believe the sky behind Shad and Hominy. In the east, it was clearing, and the late western sun shown in her eyes, making her blink. Shad smiled and his admiring glance told her that he approved of the way she looked, but her mind was flashing warnings. She returned his smile and tried to ignore the alarms making her short of breath.

"Do I ride in front or back?" Sarah asked.

"I believe," Shadrach said, lifting an eyebrow, "that your riding behind will give me better control of this stallion."

Sarah caught his double meaning and threw her leg over the rear haunches of the horse, behind the saddle, on a padded blanket Shadrach had already prepared for her. She grabbed him around the middle, realizing that either way she rode, she would be overwhelmed by his nearness. She would experience the same giddy feeling whether pressed against his muscled back or riding the other way with his arms around her waist.

Sarah couldn't help but question his sense of

honor, knowing hers was drifting dangerously low. She hoped his remained strong. She said an instant prayer to God — only one word, **HELP**. She couldn't think rationally with him so close.

The low rolling hills were covered with blackjack oak and cottonwood trees, others were smothered in a velvety blanket of summer grass, and it all made for a fascinating vista. She heard the woeful song of the mourning dove, and saw it in the tree ahead. The sun set in a myriad of colors. Several times, Sarah turned to look behind her as it disappeared. She didn't know if it appeared so beautiful because it was, or if it was beautiful because of the happiness she felt being so near Shadrach. Then she remembered the reason for the ride; he had something to tell her, but she didn't know if she really wanted to know.

They had ridden about one mile when she lost the battle with herself. She couldn't stop the shakes. A sudden little shiver ran through her — one quick uncontrollable vibration. At the feel of her tremor, Shadrach stopped Hominy.

He sat perfectly still a moment, then slung his leg over the saddle horn and dropped to the ground. There was light enough to see clearly, and Sarah's heart beat like horseshoes on hard-packed prairie when she looked into his up-turned face. The dazzling blackness of his eyes made her dizzy.

"What am I to do about you, Sarah Daniels? You came into my life and it seems the earth has suspended itself, waiting to see what will happen."

The occasional shudder that had claimed her before, now turned to outright quaking. Her legs turned to liquid.

"You're the most beautiful woman I've ever known — softness and sturdiness, fire and ice. You are in all my dreams." His arms lifted.

She closed her eyes and reached for him. What am I letting myself in for? she asked herself, as he helped her off the horse.

Shadrach's arms gentled around her. "You've set my heart on fire, do you know that?" he murmured, his rich voice deep with emotion. His hand brushed at the flyaway curls around her face, then he lifted her hat and set it on top of Hominy's saddle.

Blackbirds crowed in the cottonwoods, but to Sarah, they could have been canaries. The air was redolent with freshness. Sarah thought her heart would dance out of her body. He reached up and pulled the ribbon holding the knot of curls on top her head, then he slipped his hand into her hair and helped shake it down. It fell, full and free, around her shoulders.

"There," he said, "that's the way I want to see you."

"I'm glad I can't see myself. I'd probably cry," she said knowing she was letting herself in for trouble.

"Come here, sweetheart," he said, and pulled her into the warm circle of his arms. She figured he was about to kiss her and was prepared to move out of his arms. Instead, she didn't even flinch as his lips went right to her mouth.

Sarah's pulse leaped, leaving her breathless beneath his onslaught. Her hands moved slowly, sliding up against his chest. She heard his murmur, and tried to push away. Warning lights flashed in her mind. She didn't know how many times she'd shared a kiss in her twenty-two years, but none of them had been like this. Euphoric! His body was there and she wanted to melt into him.

Her leashed emotions wanted their guard removed. She remembered a certain joy with Leo, but dismissed Leo's image, and yearned for this rock-hard man who trembled against her — thrilling her beyond description. Hesitantly, she pulled her mouth from his, and gazed through blurred vision. Her blood, like flaming fuel, shot skyrockets from every pore.

"Where did you learn to kiss like that, Mrs. Daniels?" he asked, slowly releasing her.

He'd done it again! Damn him! "From Mister Daniels, you hypocrite! You — you did the kissing," she stammered, leaning against Hominy for support. "And you promised not to do this," she cried.

"So I did. Discretion is the better part of valor," he said, giving her a shocking stare. "And, since I seem to be lacking a little of that commodity at the moment, I think we'd better return." He turned and walked away.

"Did you find Troy Adams in Parsons?" she blurted out.

"I tried, but didn't find him."

"What were you wanting to talk about?" she asked, a mite confused.

"About us," he said, looking her straight in the eyes.

"Us! There is no us!" she cried desperately, not meaning a word she said.

"So I've gathered." He adjusted his Stetson and once more walked away.

Sarah watched him pick up a wild wheat straw and begin chewing it. She didn't move because of the weakness that had attacked her. One thing dominated her thoughts, no man had ever aroused her to such a fever pitch. The thought sent her mind reeling. Was she in love with him, or just in need of being loved? Shame burned in her cheeks as she relived his kiss. Why couldn't she remember if Leo had ever affected her like Shad? Surely she'd felt this way when she'd first met Leo. She'd heard the adage, out of sight, out of mind. Was that what was happening to her and her relationship with Leo? Had she just plain forgotten the love they'd shared? She must have, because nothing in her frame of reference came close to the thrill she knew with Shadrach. She looked up and saw Shadrach returning to her.

"It's getting late. We'd better go back," he said without even glancing at her.

His voice shook, and Sarah, wise enough to respect his effort at self-control, agreed. "We're only a mile from the wagon. Could we walk back?"

"I'd like that." He threw the reins over Hominy's head and clicked his tongue for him to follow, then took Sarah's hand. "I don't want you to turn an ankle in a gopher hole," he said when she attempted to pull away.

CHAPTER TWELVE

Sarah and Shadrach were silent for a long time as they walked back to their camp. After awhile, they began to talk about the beauty of summer nights in Kansas. Fire flies were dancing everywhere. The soft breeze was laden with the scents of green grass and wild clover.

She asked him to tell her about his plans when he returned to Chicago. She hoped that he would tell her about the woman he really loved. Sarah figured if he was fighting guilt in his heart as she was, this might clear the air between them. Something had to happen to slow the building passion between them. She felt powerless by herself.

"Well, let's see, where do I begin? I've lost nothing in Chicago. Real beauty is right here in Kansas. Here, you see radiance a dozen times more appealing to the eye than you'll see in Illinois."

"I've always found Chicago to be an interesting place to live," Sarah said. "But, I guess beauty is found in the eye of the beholder?"

"True! I realize that's a matter of opinion, but I'm prejudiced. Cattle roam and deer play out here. There, people and buggies fight for a piece of road to move on. Here, there are trees, flowers, high rolling hills, and streams that bubble out from under rocks. There, are man made fountains, cultivated gardens, and bricked roads up the hills and rock buildings, emitting coal stroke that chokes out the sunshine. Here, the water is sweet to taste, and grass is plentiful. The air smells fresh as the earth after a rain. The nights are magic and breathtaking, like this evening. You can read by starlight, and kiss by moonbeams."

Sarah decided not to comment on that remark. "You do have a way with words," she said, wondering how to ask him about the woman he loved, and what the lady might think about his description of Kansas, especially if he decided to live permanently here.

"This country is wild and rough, not manicured-looking like Chicago, and I believe I love all this open space. What a place to own a ranch."

It surprised Sarah that he would say that. Had he said the same thing to his lover? Would he bring her out here to live? Sarah stole glances at him as they walked, but kept her silence. He made no reference to the searing moment of passion they'd shared such a short time ago. Sarah began to wonder if she had been the only one who'd nearly come unglued. Again she thought of the conversation she'd overheard between Shad and James — about the woman he'd spoken about. . . . He'd probably kissed that woman the same way he'd just kissed her. Did men treat every woman the same? A moonbeam filtered through the trees they walked under, causing faint shadows to dance at her feet.

Oh, Lord! She suddenly wished she hadn't

come with him. Her chest felt as though Hominy had kicked her.

As they walked in the moonlight, clouds began to gather, lightning started in the north, and soon the moon and stars were gone. "I'd sure like to have a ranch around here," Shadrach said as if they'd never stopped talking, or that thunder had not just exploded over them. "I'd need a foreman, maybe James or Jelliroll."

Sarah gave a little hollow laugh, remembering Roberta's words about James working for Jelliroll, or vise-versa. Shadrach didn't seem to notice anything going on around him, as he proceeded to describe more about the kind of ranch he dreamed about.

"I'd raise Texas longhorns and buffalo," he said, wiping his face with his kerchief because of the humidity.

"Buffalo!" Sarah lifted her gaze from her feet and in a flash of lightning, looked at him — he was serious.

"We have killed most of the buffalo which was the main source of food for the Indians, and I believe a man could breed them back, then breed them with the longhorn. We could call the offspring buffabeef."

Sarah found that amusing and chuckled. "Or, beefabuff," she cried as she laughed.

He laughed with her, and the feeling was good. They were actually sharing a moment of lightheartedness.

"Can you really breed them?" she asked.

"Why not?"

"But what good would they be?"

"Buffaloes are meatier than beef cows, but tougher than boot leather. Beeves are more tender because they tend to be fatter than the buffalo. The offspring might be leaner and more tender, but more hearty than the beef cow."

"I've never heard of such a thing."

"That's exactly why it interests me."

"I suppose it's possible," she said.

"Of course it is," he replied as lightning flashed above. He looked down at her. "Has anyone but me ever told you how beautiful you are?"

"My husband has," she said.

He released her hand. "Sorry, I keep forgetting about him," he said.

Sarah wished she hadn't spoken so quickly. She felt her cheeks grow warm under his admiring gaze, and wondered why he kept catching her off guard this way. Her hand trembled, feeling empty and cold since he'd let it go. Impulsively, she responded, "Has any woman ever told you that you're very charming?"

"Are you telling me that?" he asked, reaching out to capture her hand again.

She gasped, feeling the blush radiating from her face to her body. She nodded her head.

"In that case," he said, "I'll answer your question, one woman has said those very words to me."

Again, she blushed, but this time it was from embarrassment because he'd confirmed, ever-so-gently, what a fool she'd been — there was indeed another woman in his life.

"We'd better hurry," she said, "it's nearly nine o'clock and it's starting to sprinkle."

"You're right. At this rate, it'll be ten o'clock before we get back." He whistled for Hominy, their helped her mount up, and to her surprise, he climbed behind her. His arms went around her waist as he took the reins.

"This is more like it," he whispered into her ear. He clicked his tongue and Hominy trotted off into the night. They both sat still, and practiced self-control in what they said to each other. Later, when they rode into their camp, they saw the Jenkins had gone to bed. Sarah helped Shadrach unsaddle Hominy and hobble him near the wagon out of the rain which was starting to come down in earnest.

Their bedrolls were inside separate tents, and she was glad about that. James had set up Shad's tent. Shadrach said he must remember to thank James. "I see Jelliroll hasn't found us yet," he said.

Sarah felt a frown creasing her forehead. "At least, you can sleep undisturbed this evening."

"I doubt that's possible," he said, and in the firelight, she saw that he was staring at her.

Lord, she thought, you'd better hope the same thing isn't true about yourself. She knew it wouldn't take much of a spark to start the passion flowing between them again.

"Maybe, I'll go over there and sleep by the fire," he said, looking at the tents sitting close together.

She'd thoroughly enjoyed the comfort of knowing Shadrach slept near her on the ground, but she knew she didn't need him any closer than ear shot if there were trouble. "That should be fine," she said trying to sound aloof.

Common sense told her that the fire was close enough. She unrolled her bedroll and blanket. Shadrach disappeared, but when she looked, his bed was only a few yards away from her tent.

As Sarah peeked out the flap, Shadrach came from the nearby trees. She ducked out of sight behind the canvas opening. How thankful she was that she wasn't in need of any privacy. She didn't have to make that dreaded trip which for her was still a degrading experience. As she thought about Shadrach, she wanted to go to him and sit and talk, but didn't.

She sneaked another look and saw him remove his boots and lay back without covering up on his bedroll. The evening was warm and lovely, or it was warm because of where they were under the overhang. Sarah marveled at the brightness of the lightning around them. The sounds of cracking lightning and roaring thunder fascinated her. All of nature seemed in a roar. She had to admit that this was indeed fascinating country.

Clearly, Shadrach was serious about what he'd been talking about. Until the last few days, she'd thought he was antsy to get back to Chicago. Now, she wondered if she thought that because she didn't know him as well as she'd figured. She was surprised about his wanting a ranch, because she'd always thought he loved the city. She guessed she didn't know him as well as she thought after all.

She and Shadrach lay silently a long time in their separate places before he got to his feet and walked to the opening of her tent. "I can't sleep for thinking about you, about us," he said softly.

She shut her eyes and clenched her fists. This is the place where I'm supposed to ask him to join me. And, as bad as she wanted to be drowning in his arms, she could not give in to her longings. Too many moral issues and too many memories kept her from answering.

Still, the thought of being held against his magnificent chest rattled her senses. She heard his rapid breathing and it excited her. She drew a long breath, trying to catch his masculine scent. The memory of his kiss sent a thrill through her, and the recollection of his gentle touch unnerved her.

Desire ran rampant. The yearning was strong, and strangely new. She burned with passion and need, and knew it, yet she didn't speak or move.

When she couldn't smother a shuddering sigh, Shadrach whispered thickly, "I want you, Sarah! Surely, you know that!"

She opened the flap and stared at him. Sarah's heart beat so fast that she thought it would explode. She asked herself if this was the way he talked to the woman he'd said he loved. Were all men like this? Did they all take advantage of any willing female? She would never know the answer to that, and at this moment she really didn't care. All she knew was that she could well be in love with him. The idea went beyond her understanding. He would never be hers, but she didn't care.

As he stepped one foot into her tent, her better judgment cried, wait! Think before you let this happen. She should refuse to let her heart and body enjoy his advances any longer. All of it, her feelings for him, the hurt, the jealous anger, injured pride, both the sweetness and bitterness were senseless, hopeless.

They both heard the approaching horse at the same time. Sarah saw Shadrach's body stiffen in the firelight. He sprang toward his bedroll to get his gun. Sarah pitched herself to the ground inside the tent to watch.

"Hey, now!" she heard Jelliroll's voice. "Don't shoot me. Sorry I'm so late. I had trouble trackin' ya'all when the sun set. Go on to bed, I'll stake my horse and join ya."

"You take the tent, I'm sleeping here by the fire. I'll watch first, then James will. He'll get you up at four o'clock."

"Great! I'll talk to ya in the mornin'. Got lots to tell ya."

Sarah wanted to hear what he had to say tonight, but knew she'd better get some rest. Tomorrow was going to be a busy day.

Sarah grinned the next morning at Johnny's excitement when he saw Jelliroll. She felt really rotten because of the frustrated state she'd been in last evening. She shouldn't have allowed it to keep her from greeting him when he'd ridden in. When she heard Roberta putting into words what she wanted to say to Jelliroll, she turned away. Too bad, Sarah rebuked herself, you can't express yourself to anyone.

Despite her personal feelings, Sarah was delighted when she heard Roberta's words to Jelliroll at breakfast. "I'm so glad that you are going to wait for a while to buy a farm. We need you, and want you to help us find Robert, then after we have tried, successful or not, James and I want to stay in Kansas and help you get started on your farm."

Roberta was nobody's fool — she was smarter than the average person. Mentally, Sarah thanked her for not hedging around the barn about telling Jelliroll what they wanted from him. Sarah didn't know what Shadrach would have done if she'd asked Jelliroll to help her find Leo. Shadrach's ego would probably have been injured — she owed Shad too much to hurt him. She could think clearly again in the light of day.

The world was fresh and clean after the drenching rain of last night, but it looked as if it could come down again. Shadrach sat on a log across from the fire where Jelliroll was busy cooking flapjacks and bacon. "Last night you said you had some things to talk about. Was it about you not finding a place you wanted to buy?"

"Naw, this is somethin' else," he glanced at Sarah, "somethin' I might not ought to speak about now."

"If you're not talking because of me, I'll leave," she said, realizing that Roberta wasn't sitting with them. She was by the wagon, trying to feed Johnny. The little rascal refused to eat by himself. Sarah found herself biting her tongue more and more to keep from saying something to Roberta about the way she was spoiling the boy. Sarah figured what Jelliroll wanted to tell them might be a man-thing.

"Ah, guess it's all right, it sorta concerns ya and Miss Roberta," he said dropping flapjacks onto Sarah's plate.

"What is it?" she asked, her attention piqued.

Roberta heard him also and came over to sit on the log with Shadrach. "I want to hear every word," she said, grinning at Jelliroll.

"Well, I was in Cherryvale by eleven o'clock yesterday. I'd decided the man ownin' the feed store might know where there could be a farm fer sell. He said I'd probably find one if I wasn't afraid of the killer or killers roaming around Cherryvale. I asked what he was talkin' about and he told me about several men and women who had either disappeared or been found dead. Seems whoever these killers were, they killed all their victims the same way — busted their heads and slit their throats.

"Well, while we was flappin' our gums, in walks this big fellow, eyes close-set, clean-shaven with a shock of neatly combed dark hair." Jelliroll glanced again at Sarah. "He had four deep scratches on his cheek. The clerk looked at him and kinda flinched like he was uneasy that the fellow was even in his store. 'Ya — ya get hold a — a wildcat?' he stuttered, sounding nervous as a bull in a cow pen. The young man giggled stupidly, and said in a heavy German accent, 'Sure did, and she tried to bite off my finger.' Again he giggled as he lifted his hand and showed us his swollen middle finger that did appear to have been bitten. I couldn't help but think this might be the fellow who'd at-tacked you, but before I up and killed him, I needed to know a little more." He looked at Sarah.

"Then this fellow asked for a sack of chicken feed. The clerk's hand shook as he filled a sack. I thought that was strange 'cause he'd seemed perfectly relaxed with me before this young man came in.

"Well, I stood there dumbfounded, not cer-tain what ta do, but well amind of what had hap-pened here the night before. When the giggler left the store, I asked the clerk who he was and he said he was John Bender, Jr. I asked where he lived, and was told he and his family lived out-side of Cherryvale at the bottom of a high hill on the Osage Mission Trail. He said they were immigrants from Germany, that John, Jr. was a mite dull-witted. His pa, John Bender Sr. could hardly speak English, was about sixty years old and mean as hell — beg yer pardon, Miss Sarah — Miss Roberta, anyway, the clerk said, the old man's wife and daughter were spiritualists, and told me I'd be wise to stay away from them, but he also said they had an inn and small grocery store for weary travelers along the Osage Mission Trail."

Jelliroll stopped to eat half his flapjack, then he poured some coffee.

"Is that all?" Sarah asked.

"No, the best part is yet to come."

Jelliroll took another bite. "Father and son have the same name, but so does the mother and daughter, Kate and Kate. In the feed store, the clerk lowered his voice and said there were rumors flying all over the area about the Benders. It seems some folks was blaming them fer puttin' curses on certain folks with their incantations, and hocus-pocus circles some said were drawn on their floor. He said the symbols spoke of demons. The clerk went on to say that town folks were suspicious of them because of the strange things happenin' — men were disappearin' or bein' found dead, stripped of clothes and money with their throats cut. Well, that was all I needed to hear. I figured this fellow might lead me to somethin' concernin' yer brother and yer husband." Jelliroll glanced at both women, then went on with his story, "I left the store and saw this John fellow headin' out of town, so I followed him. He rode along a road toward Osage Mission which I could see was a busy settlement. John Bender stopped to eat, so I did, too. I learned that Osage Mission was the center of activity there on the prairie, boasting three mail routes, a stagecoach line, trading post, and Jesuit priests who are busy doing missionary work.

"After I left there, I didn't have too many more creeks to ford and the landscape changed. It seemed barren with few trees. The fellow stopped at a wooden cabin beneath a high hill like the feed store clerk said. I stopped also, trying to keep my distance, but I hadn't fooled John Bender, Jr.

"He turned around and yelled at me sayin' I might jes as well stop fer the night. Said they had good grub and a warm bed fer weary travelers. I was of a mind to say no, but curiosity got the best of me, especially when I saw the fellow's sister. She looked like God Himself put her together. When she smiled and beckoned me with her smile and eyes, I went like a puppy dog to a dish of gravy, but I planned to keep abreast of any shenanigans they might try pullin' on me.

"She asked me what I was a doin' in Kansas, and I told her I was searchin' fer a farm to buy. She said buyin' a farm these days was expensive. I told her I'd come prepared to pay fer the right place at the right price. She gave me this peterpumpin' hip swivel — ah, ah — I'm sorry Sarah, Miss Roberta. I jes forget where I'm at sometimes."

Sarah and Roberta looked at each other in surprise. Sarah raised her shoulders and said, "We've heard about swiveling hips before."

Shadrach and James cleared their throats, and told Jelliroll to continue. He was red as a beet and for the life of her, Sarah couldn't figure out why.

CHAPTER THIRTEEN

Jelliroll said, "John Bender Jr. was obviously named after his pa, and so was this fine-lookin' gal. Kate Bender Jr. named after her ma, Kate Bender Sr. Weird folks, these four, but when Kate Jr. said she knew a man eager to sell some prime bottom land, I got to listenin' close.

"Kate said, since the man was so anxious to sell his farm, he wanted cash, now. Without thinkin', I like a fool, said that I'd come with cash. That's when Kate put her hex on me."

"Come on, Jelliroll, you don't believe that stuff, do you?" James asked.

"Never thought I did, but there was these circles and symbols drawn on the floor and when I looked at her, she mumbled some mumbo-jumbo and I couldn't turn away. I'm fifty-eight-years old, but my body reacted like I was thirty. I was spellbound by her actions, her looks, by how her body was put together, thinkin' how it would be ta touch her. She sidled up close to me and ran her tongue around her lips and I couldn't take my eyes away. It was a deliberate act to provoke me in the way she wanted it to, and it worked. I'm confessin' that I was actin' like a dang fool under her spell. Then she pleaded with me to eat a bite with her. Did I even try ta resist? Naw, I jes said sure. Hell, I wasn't even hungry. She took my hand and pulled me inside, all the time gigglin' and smilin' at me until I hardly knew which end of me was up. I figured it would be worth eatin' and bein' miserable just to keep lookin' at her."

"Damn, Jelliroll, you must be exaggerating — no woman is prettier than these two," James said, hugging Roberta possessively.

"This Kate must be an angel if she's prettier than this one," Shadrach said winking at Sarah.

Sarah laughed. "You fellows are just partial to us because you haven't seen many other women for a while. We probably get to looking better to you every day you don't have anyone to compare us with."

"Hey," Roberta cried, "don't talk them out of their opinions of us."

They all laughed and Roberta asked if anyone wanted her to make a pan of mush.

"Sounds good to me," James said.

"Well, speaking of mush," Jelliroll said, "at the Bender Inn, I was served the worst mushed-up beans I've ever eaten. The bread I ate was better. Kate told me her pa had once been a baker in Germany and had taught her how to make bread. I was complimentin' her right and left, watchin' her sashay round the room. Her ma was sittin' in a rocker jus watchin' me, makin' me feel uncomfortable. I was sittin' on one of three other chairs at a long walnut table, in front of this canvas curtain that divided the room. When the ol' man left the counter where he'd been arrangin' stuff on the shelves and went behind the curtain, I thought I saw Kate give him a signal of some kind.

"What it was that triggered concern for my welfare, I don't know, but I got quickly to my feet and moved toward the door. Sweet Kate moved with me, and tried to talk me into sitting back down. I refused, so she got angry with me and ordered me to sit back down. That beautiful face turned as mean-lookin' as her ma's. I made a dash for the door, mounted my horse, and me and Buckshot skedaddled away from there. "I rode to where we'd camped, found you folks gone and tracked you here."

Sarah listened intently to every word. When Jelliroll had finished, she looked at Shadrach. "I want to go to the Benders' place."

"Why, for God's sake?" he asked.

"To look around. If Leo was there, they robbed him — maybe there's something I'll recognize."

"Like what?"

"His hat, clothes, his walking cane, a silver button from his coat, I don't know, any number of things," she answered.

"I want to go, too," Roberta cried.

" 'Tain't a fittin' place fer either of ya," Jelliroll said. "No one's askin', but if I could give some advice, I'd say ya two gals should let Shadrach and James go check the place out — see what they think. Maybe go into Osage Mission an talk to one of the priests, go into Cherryvale and talk to the sheriff. I'll stay with ya gals, take ya into Parsons ta the place James told me about."

"I agree," James said, "Roberta, do this for me. The doctor who owns the apothecary in Parsons will show you the apartment over the store. You can tell him, I'll show up for work tomorrow morning."

Roberta wasn't happy, but agreed. Sarah knew she might as well agree. She didn't feel like fighting with Shadrach and Jelliroll. "All right, I'll wait, but not willingly. When are you leaving?"

Shadrach walked out from under the overhang and looked at the sky. "Now's a good time. The rain has stopped, but it's banking around to the west. Jelliroll, wait here until you know what this weather is up to."

"Ya don't need to worry, I'll take care of the gals and little Johnny."

"I know you will, now draw us a map, and pack us some food. I don't want to have to eat mashed beans."

He chuckled. "It'll be ready in a minute," Jelliroll said, already gathering an outfit for the two men.

Shadrach glanced across the cook fire at Sarah and he studied her a moment, then winked. "You behave yourself," he said.

She stood abruptly and went to her tent. Every time Shad did something like wink, smile at her, touch her, or hold her hand, she remembered he wasn't hers, and that was all right, she couldn't have him anyway. Anyway, whenever Shad did something that affected her, she could always depend on an image of Leo which would slam into her consciousness with a sobering jolt.

Had this Kate person charmed Leo as she had Jelliroll? Maybe Leo couldn't get away from them because of his crippled leg. I won't believe that, she thought determinedly. Her legs dug into her blanket where she'd thrown herself in frustration. She drew the cover over her head, then buried her face deep in the pillow because she couldn't stop the tears; she didn't want anyone to know she was crying. After awhile she arrived at a decision she didn't know if she could even keep.

With clenched fists, she gripped her pillow, trying to ease the ache in her heart. The ache was for Leo. She was finally believing he was dead. Jelliroll's description of the Benders and of other missing men in the area made her realize there was little hope that Leo had escaped such diabolical people, if he had come into contact with them. There was too many coincidences to believe anything but that Leo had fallen victim to these killers. Obviously, several others had also died — maybe even Robert Smith, although Roberta still didn't believe her brother was dead.

Quietly, Sarah began to reason with herself, accepting the fact that Leo Daniels was probably dead. Although she'd loved Leo with all her heart, she had to admit that she'd really been fearful that he was dead when she hadn't received a single letter from him. In her heart, she knew he would never have neglected her if he were alive. As the months had worn on, she had tried to trick herself into believing Leo was alive, and she had tried to delude herself about her attraction for Shadrach Koby.

Sarah had finally admitted that she was in love with a most improbable person, a very much alive Shadrach Koby, who was the opposite of Leo Daniels in every way. She tried to envision herself as Shad's wife, but couldn't. She had yet to really acknowledge she was a widow, but knowing this didn't change a thing. She still loved Shadrach; he had ridden into her life and taken up residence in her heart. She knew of no way to move him out. Shadrach Koby now occupied every minuscule nook not occupied by Leo. However, she had made this decision — she would have nothing more to do with Shad. He would only break her heart again. Losing Leo was bad enough, so she would not expose her heart to another loss. She could not!

Sarah stopped thinking. She lay a long time on her back just staring at the top of her tent. After awhile she had to go relieve herself. She sneaked out of her tent and walked the opposite direction from where Shadrach was saddling his stallion. She passed the overhang, walked around the most eastwardly edge, and there found a place of privacy.

Her return was cut short. A hand stopped her. She knew it was Shadrach. Frantically she thought how crazy this situation was becoming. How could this happen after she'd just settled her mind and heart? He pulled her into his arms, crushing resolve and strength from her.

"If you only knew what you're doing to me," he said against her lips.

"Then stop," she replied in a voice that masked what she wanted to say.

He drew back, and although she couldn't see his eyes, the blackness of them pierced her soul.

"Do you truly mean that?" he asked, and for all the world his voice was in a state of disbelief.

She couldn't speak. How could she lie? All she could do was shake her head under the long, hard kiss he was giving her.

He pushed her a few inches from him. "Don't ever scare me like that. It's bad enough trying to motivate through the days and nights the way I want you, and if you were not to want me — well, I can't imagine what I'd do."

Sarah gasped and stiffened. An image flashed brightly in her mind of the despicable John Bender and the way he'd wanted her. Could that be the way Shadrach wanted her? "Oh, Shadrach," she groaned, "if I told you that I was not interested in a short-lived romance, what would you say?"

He held her farther away, searching her eyes in the dim light caused by the overhang and trees. "Lord have mercy, Sarah. I'm not interested in that either. What do you think I am? The reason I'm practically insane, leaping into cold streams and biting my nails to the quick is because I'm trying to protect you from me — and you from yourself." His arms gentled around her. "You're a very warm and responsive woman. I can't let you get away from me — not until we find out what has happened to Leo. That's why you must trust me. I'll control us both if you'll let me?"

Indescribable joy filled her being. She grabbed him around the neck and sought his lips. Heavenly thoughts bounded in her mind. Shadrach knew she couldn't commit to him until she knew about Leo.

"Stop now, woman. I'm only flesh and blood. I'm going to leave now, you take it easy and trust Jelliroll — I do." He gave her a quick squeeze and left.

When Sarah heard him moving away, she raced lightheartedly for the fire where the others waited. As she and Roberta waved, she recalled everything Shadrach had said. As she replayed each sentence in her mind, she wondered if they were truly words to be so happy about. "You're a very warm and responsive woman," he'd said, "a woman I don't want to let get away — not until we find out about Leo. That's why you must trust me." A blinding moment of uncertainty crept ominously into her mind, and she felt as if a knife twisted in her heart. He'd said he didn't want to lose her until they found Leo, or something to that effect. Could he have meant he only wanted her until he was free of the job he was on? "Oh, God, what if that's what he meant?"

Shad had also said that he'd control them both if she'd let him. Sure! she thought, control me as if I'm mindless. Well, forget it, Shadrach Koby! The wonderful glow inside her faded, and though she grasped for it, the moments were evaporating into the day. Did it really matter so much? She didn't even try to stem the flow of tears. It mattered more than anything else in the world. She loved Shadrach, but given the facts, she was probably only an interim woman for him to conquer — a diversion.

Before they had cleaned up after breakfast, it was raining again. Sarah wondered if Shad and James would go on or come back and asked Jelliroll what he thought.

"Don't know," he said dubiously.

As the hours passed, the lightning grew worse and flashed constantly, some of the bolts were balls of fire bursting around them. Where the water rolled over the overhang it appeared as a solid wall of water. Booming thunder rattled the rocks above and under them. Johnny yelled, as he peeked out of the wagon, "Jelly, stop that thunder!" he ordered.

Jelliroll didn't hear him, and Sarah was glad. It was hard to hear what was being said, but she'd heard the boy's rude remark. He'd given an order, not a request.

Jelliroll looked back and saw hers and Roberta's worried faces and hurried to their side. Sarah caught her breath when she saw the concerned expression on his face.

"What is it?" she asked, as he took her out-stretched hand.

"This toad-strangler isn't letting up. I can see the water is rising, I'm tryin' ta decide what ta do."

"What can you do?" she asked, seeing the volume of falling water.

"Find us a place on higher ground."

"Are we in danger?" Sarah asked.

"We are. There are many tributaries, creeks, and streams in this valley. If this keeps up another hour, this place will be covered with water."

Roberta gasped and clutched her son to her breast. Sarah tried to conceal her true feelings and said, "Tell us what to do and we will."

"That's my gal! While I go out there and decide where we should go to be safe, you and Roberta load the wagon and hitch the team. What I hate most is leaving ya two here ta worry. Ya've proved yerselves capable of handlin' the wagon and team, but ya ain't never driven in mud and ya will have ta this time. I don't know. . . ."

"Between Roberta and I, we'll do it," Sarah said with dubious confidence.

"You could come with me and let Miss Roberta do the hitchin', then I can come back and drive the wagon."

Sarah wasn't certain if he was telling her he didn't think they could drive the wagon or not.

Johnny was screaming and throwing anything he could get his hands on. "Roberta needs to hang on to Johnny, I'll drive!" she said a mite sarcastically. She hated that she had sounded as she had, but Johnny was getting on her nerves. She found herself suddenly wishing for Shadrach.

Shad wasn't here, so she would do whatever was necessary to save them all. Anyway, Shad had enough worry trying to find Leo and Robert. Another problem facing them came flying into her mind. She tugged Jelliroll to the rear of the wagon.

"What ya doing?" he asked, gathering some loose items to throw into the wagon.

"What about these animals? We can't leave them to drown."

"I'll take my mule, and we'll tie the four horses on a long lead behind the wagon."

"What about the cows?" she asked.

"I don't know. I guess I could try leadin' them to higher ground right now, then pick up my mule when I get back."

"I'll be ready when you get back," Sarah said trying to sound confident for Roberta who had come to see what they were doing.

Roberta couldn't help notice how worried Jelliroll was; she pulled the chain holding a cross from over her head and gave it to him after he'd mounted his horse. "God go with you, Jelliroll."

"What's this?" he asked, then seeing the cross, slipped it into his pocket. "Yer a generous person, Miss Roberta. I'll not forget this kindness." He grabbed the leads to the cows and rode out into the awful storm.

Near mid-afternoon, darkness, much like a starless night, grew more frightening. Rolling black clouds moved ominously across the sky. Lightning flashed all around them. Sarah and Roberta were glad to be where they were when the wind and rain increased. Then, almost before their eyes, it too quickly changed into a deluge! She and Roberta were ready and waiting for Jelliroll. Where was he? Why didn't he come to tell them which way to go to get to higher ground? The wagon's canvas top couldn't hold back the pounding torrent being blown beneath the overhang straight at them.

Jelliroll abruptly stuck his head into the wagon. "Ya gals all right?"

"Everything's getting soaked! What are we to do?" Roberta cried, grabbing a rag to wipe Johnny's face. "Oh, poor baby." She shuddered, badly frightened and apprehensive. "Did you get the cows to higher ground?"

"I did, that's what took me so long. They don't move like horses. I've got them staked and waiting for us. Miss Sarah, do you have any rain gear?"

"Not really, but don't worry about me; how far is this place where we'll be safer?"

"Not far. Looks like yer both prepared. We're ready to move out."

"I scared!" Johnny cried.

He reached out and patted his cheek. "Ya

don't worry, son. I'll see yer safe." The lantern spluttered. Sarah adjusted the wick. It went out.

"Stay calm!" Jelliroll yelled, as he moved to the side of the wagon where some supplies were kept tied on a shelf. Shortly, he was filling the lantern with coal oil. "Miss Sarah," he said firmly, "always check the lantern for fuel each morning, then ya never get left in the dark."

Sarah had to respect his thoughtfulness of her, and his kindness to Johnny and Roberta, and she had to trust him — she had to!

"Miss Sarah," he yelled, over the fearful thunder and hammering rain, "we have a dangerous situation here! Yer gonna have ta drive harder than ya ever have before, but yer capable, so don't panic. I'll keep an eye out. If I see yer in trouble, I'll get to ya quick as possible. I'll go ahead of ya with my mule. Roberta, if ya see the horses tied ta the rear gettin' in trouble cut 'em loose. They'll swim ta safety."

Jelliroll gave Sarah a smile meant to convey confidence, but it sent fear pulsing through her. She sensed they had big troubles ahead of them. Again, she wanted the only man she really trusted to be here, but he wasn't. She must put her faith in Jelliroll.

CHAPTER FOURTEEN

Sarah yelled and snapped the reins above the team horses, and the instant the wagon wheels left the rock ledge where they'd been, the wagon nearly bogged down in the soaked grass. She maneuvered it, trying to follow the blurry figure of Jelliroll ahead of them. Mud churned to the hubs, but the horses finally pulled the wagon to more solid ground.

Jelliroll lifted his arm and signaled with the lantern for her to keep coming.

Sarah flipped the reins over her team and yelled. The horses began digging in deeply to move in the slick grass and oozing mud. They gradually plowed their way to the rockier ground behind Jelliroll.

Lightning lit the sky and the earth like noonday, revealing a frightening scene. The shallow tributaries to the big creek had swelled to river size and the water ran in torrents as though it was plunging down mountains instead of gently rolling hills.

The prairie was under water, and if not for the yellow lantern Jelliroll carried, Sarah would have no idea where she was going. Even the hooves of the horses were under water. She could hear them splashing as they trotted at her command, but the roar of rushing water plus the violent thunder made the team hard to handle. She had wrapped the reins around her gloved hands as she strained to hold the frightened animals.

Ahead of her, Jelliroll frantically waved the lantern from his horse. Sarah wanted to scream at him to come take the reins. The situation had turned critical! You can do it! she encouraged herself. She glanced back in a flash of light and saw the frantic look on Roberta's face as she held tightly to her obviously scared and screaming son. "Don't panic!" she cried. "Hold the horses back! Use the brake!" Roberta cried, offering what help she could.

Sarah repeated her instructions over and over, and felt Roberta's hand on her shoulder as she hung onto the wagon frame with one hand.

"Sit down!" Sarah cried when she looked behind her. She saw that Roberta held Johnny with one hand on her hip, while trying to encourage her to keep going. "Hang on to Johnny! We're in trouble!" The wagon tilted dangerously to one side.

The brake helped her control the frightened team. When the wagon righted itself and rolled ahead, she took another breath, but then it bogged precariously low in the rising water. Sarah screamed.

Jelliroll shouted, "Yer doin' fine, keep comin'!" He rode back to the faltering wagon and grabbed the team's lead and pulled them, encouraging them to plow harder. Soon they were doing better and he leaned over to hand the reins back to Sarah. He gripped her hand.

"Want I should drive?"

Sarah saw the look of concern on his face and told him she was fine. "I'll do it, show me where to go." Jelliroll waved and rode on ahead.

She and Roberta both screamed when the wagon again tipped far to the left and began floating. The horses were swimming hard, heading for the steep incline that led to higher ground.

The wagon tilted ominously above the raging water. The shouts of Jelliroll, frightened horses, mingled with the sounds of the wild storm were the worst things Sarah had ever experienced. She was going to die! She knew it! She had her whole life to live! *"Nooo! Oh, Lord, no! I don't want to die. Save us — save me!"* she cried lifting her eyes toward Heaven. Her heart sounded like a thrashing machine thumping against her chest; then she saw Jelliroll give her the signal to turn left in the raging torrent. The horses still didn't have their footing back, but she pulled the reins hard in the opposite direction she'd been floating.

The horses were screaming, their heads arched high to stay above water. She panicked. Jelliroll shouted encouragement to her when he saw her trying to stop the team. The water was still rising. Jelliroll yelled, "Yer about ready to cross a creek. Turn! Turn!"

Finally, when she realized what Jelliroll was saying, she gripped the reins already wrapped around her hands and lifted her face to heaven again. "God, help us!" she cried, and then yelled at the team, pulling hard on the reins to get them to turn more to the left where she could see Jelliroll waving the lantern.

Her heart stopped momentarily when the reins slackened and her team and wagon dropped deeper in the water, but the team was swimming together. Before they had traveled twenty yards ahead, she took advantage of the nightmarish time it took to cross the swollen creek, to tighten the reins and release the brake that she'd locked from instinct.

The breath she'd been holding gave out before the horses finally stumbled and found their footing, and in spite of their panic, they began pulling, and she gasped as she drew a new breath of air into her lungs. In moments, the horses moved together, and Sarah felt momentary thanksgiving when the wheels hit bottom and rolled up behind Jelliroll and his mule.

She brought the horses to a stop and sat where she was, too filled with adrenaline to move or respond to Roberta's exuberant hug.

The continuous string of lightning slicing through the ominous sky illuminated the ground. Sarah wiped away rain and shielded her eyes. An extra brilliant flash of lightning allowed her to see everything. And hear it! Before, she'd thought the sound was thunder. Half the roar was from water rushing down every wash and gully, obliterating the old creek banks and creating new ones. She knew now how flash floods formed, and the rapidity with which they developed. Had Shadrach and James escaped the deluge? She had to believe they had. One look at Roberta told Sarah that she was worried about the men also. The rushing water was still rising.

She'd seen high water in Chicago, but nothing to compare with this. Rains like this were the cause of death and destruction. Her gaze riveted itself to the white swirl of angry foam. Behind it came uprooted trees and a deer. The carcass floated swiftly by. She shivered uncontrollably with the realization that one of them could have lost their lives.

An uncomfortable feeling gripped Sarah's mind. How could she have ever entertained the idea that her life was over because of Leo's presumed death — because Shadrach may love another? She'd just fought a raging flood to save herself, and knew that instant how shallow her feelings had been. She buried her head in her hands, and above the pound of rain and continuous roll of thunder, she cried, *"Forgive my self-pity, my self-centeredness, and my selfishness! Thank You for saving us — for saving me."*

"Amen," Roberta cried.

Sarah jerked around at the sound of her voice. She'd momentarily forgotten she wasn't alone.

"I've never seen you pray before," Roberta said.

"That's not much of a reflection on me, is it?" Sarah answered.

"I don't think I know what you mean," Roberta replied.

Sarah tried to explain, "It isn't very flattering to discover you're just part of the silent believing crowd, and obviously, that's what I am. Sometimes, it takes a night like this to let you know — real quickly — where your priorities are. I'm ashamed to say, mine have been all wrong."

Too much was happening for Sarah to say anymore. Jelliroll wanted her to move the wagon higher, and Johnny was fighting mad because he wanted out of the wagon to ride with Jelliroll. The boy was kicking and scratching his mother's arms. Roberta's plea for him to "be a good boy" went unheeded.

When the wagon and animals were safely assembled above the violence of the water-covered prairie, Sarah sat humbly with Roberta, and they were both silent. Even Johnny sat quietly beside his mother. Sarah noticed Roberta seemed more distressed than she should after what they'd just been through. They'd made it! They'd won over mother nature. "What's the matter?" Sarah asked feeling nothing but exuberance over her accomplishment.

"Something you said is the same thing I've heard before!" Roberta said. "James has said to me on several different occasions that there are no unbelievers when they're facing death, and now, that I've faced death, I just became a believer."

Sarah, still shaken from her experience, grabbed Roberta and hugged her. "You're wonderful. If there was no other reason for this flood, it's been worth it. I've come to know what a genuine person you are, and to know you're trusting enough to call on God during trouble, then to have believed in Him, makes me happy."

"Thank you, Sarah. How come you know so much? You know, deep things like about God."

"I had a godly mother who never let me forget that I'm a child of the King. I have to be truthful though, until this trip, I'd been slipping away from the faith of my sainted mother."

Jelliroll rode to the back of their wagon. He whistled and stepped over the tailgate from his horse, turned and tied the drenched animal to the wagon. He gave Johnny and Roberta a bear hug as they left Sarah's side to greet him. They talked softly a few minutes, then he climbed into the seat beside Sarah.

"Yer the wonder in this night, Miss Sarah. What you did took courage! I'd be proud to shake your hand!"

Sarah numbly pulled off her glove, and when Jelliroll took her hand, she collapsed in sobs against him. He held her until she'd regained composure. "I'm sorry to act like a hysterical woman," she wailed.

"Believe me, Miss Sarah, yer tears do not minimize what ya've done. If this rain would stop, ya would see that my eyes are wet too. I had to make a fast decision. I directed the wagon across

193

the creek to safety, but I could have lost by doing it. If I'd waited another few minutes, I might've lost us all. The water is five feet deep where we were camped, and swift as the Missouri after a spring thaw. When I saw yer determined face, saw ya look up toward Heaven when I flagged ya on, it gave me courage. I'd just made the biggest decision of my life and ya and Miss Roberta trusted me. My tears are from thankfulness." He was silent a moment. "Forgive me, Sarah — I can call you jus Sarah, can't I?" he asked.

"Of course."

"Forgive me for being so hard on ya. Yer a woman to be admired. I'm proud to know ya. If I could marry two women I'd take ya and Roberta both." He gave her a squeeze and released her.

She glanced at him, blinking as the rain beat upon her face. "What a nice thing to say."

"Despite this flood, I'm still going to buy a farm out here. I'll wait until we find yer husband and Robert Smith to decide jus where."

As a horrendous streak of lightning flashed close to them, Sarah glanced around and saw they were on top of a hill surrounded by rushing waters. For a moment she felt like Noah without an Ark. "How will we ever get back on the trail to Parsons?" she asked.

"We'll do it, have no doubts," Jelliroll said as he went about securing the wagon so it wouldn't roll backwards. He then unhitched the team and staked them with the other animals.

Sarah realized how really devoted Jelliroll had

become to her and Roberta. Despite the coolness of the night, the continuing rain, he was huffing and puffing as he worked. He had lost some pounds, and Sarah had noticed how carefully he ate, taking very small portions, and no second helpings. She was proud of his determination and perseverance.

They all waited in the wagon for the storm to subside. Johnny was behaving dreadfully. Sarah had a strong impulse to whack his bottom, but tried to practice the patience she saw Jelliroll exhibiting. He was truly a wonderful man, he loved the boy regardless of the fact that Johnny was spoiled rotten by his mother. Finally, the child dozed off and the rest of them were able to catch a few hours of sleep despite the water that dripped over them as the rain continued.

The rain didn't stop until about seven o'clock the next morning. Sarah was the first one to awaken. She looked out of the wagon and saw the clouds had cleared and the sun had risen into a sky that looked so wonderfully blue that she stared upward, mesmerized.

She went to her pack animal and was delighted to find some clothing dry enough to change into. Shadrach had taught her to wrap everything in the waterproof material he'd purchased with their outfit in Westport and she was glad she had obeyed. She prepared herself for the coming day while hiding behind the animals in case one of the others awakened.

As she dressed, Shadrach's and James's

whereabouts were heavy in her mind. Had they escaped the flood? Were they out of their mind with worry about them? Perhaps they were out of the valley before the flood came. The men probably had faith that Jelliroll would see that they were safe. She prayed all was well with them. The thought of Shadrach warmed her heart as she stood looking at the muddy mess the wagon was in.

Jelliroll emerged from the tent, and seeing she had dressed in different clothes and combed her hair said, "Yer about the sweetest gal I've ever known to still be so purty."

"Jelliroll, you make me blush." She looked over his shoulder at the water that was slowly receding and asked, "When do you think it'll be safe to leave our perch?"

He grinned. "I 'spect we best stay put fer a spell. We better find some wood we can dry so I can make some coffee."

As they gathered small limbs that were already nearly dry in the rising heat of the day, Jelliroll had decided they would stay where they were for one more day and night. "The creek will return to its banks in another twelve to eighteen hours. If this heat keeps up, the ground will dry quickly. The wagon is in need of de-mudding as are we," he looked at Sarah and chuckled, "all but ya Miss Sarah. Besides this, it won't hurt ta give the team time ta rest."

Roberta yawned and stretched her back after she jumped from the wagon. "What a miserable night. The one thing we can be thankful for is the food box under the mattress stayed dry, but all the bedding and clothing need to be washed or hung to dry."

"The wagon was in water. How did the food box stay dry?" Sarah asked.

"James caulked every crack in the wagon so it would float if we had to ford a river in deep water. He also caulked the food box just in case."

"I'm sure glad you have a look-ahead type husband," Sarah said grinning at Roberta.

"So am I," she said.

Sarah looked around them and sighed. "Well, I guess we can handle this mess. We have all day."

"Get me the tin with the coffee; after I have two cups, I'll be ready for the task ahead of us," Jelliroll said.

Roberta and Sarah lifted the box from the wagon and filled the coffee pot with water from the clear water in the barrel that was tied to the wagon.

Roberta took the brass tub hooked on the side of the wagon, and found a bar of lye soap. She said, "I'll place this over here to the edge of the water where it looks cleaner than straight ahead of us. Muddy flood water doesn't clean very well. I'll wash the clothing if you'll help me with Johnny, and if Jelliroll will keep a fire roaring hot. The mud we have to wash away needs plenty of hot water, and it will need changing after each load or two."

Johnny evidently didn't like what his mother said, and began to stomp and scream.

Sarah tried to distract the boy, but nothing worked. Finally, Roberta took him by the hand and lead him to a bush where a butterfly fluttered, and Johnny just slapped at it, trying to smash it. Sarah shook her head, wishing she could have the boy alone for one hour. She thought a little discipline would straighten him out, but the boy wasn't her responsibility.

Jelliroll began stringing rope from tree to tree to hang the wet bedding to dry. He and Sarah gathered more wet wood and laid it out in the sun to dry so they could build a larger fire in a few hours. The fire they had going was strong enough to boil coffee, and water to make a pan of cornmeal mush. When they were sitting around the fire eating breakfast, Roberta suddenly threw up her hands in despair. "Oh, shoot!" she cried.

"What is it?" Jelliroll asked.

"I'd forgotten that James took the satchel containing his clothes and set it on a rock shelf under the overhang in order to get a change of trousers for his outfit. We left it when we had to get out in such a hurry!"

"Don't worry, we can go by the place and get it, if it wasn't washed away."

"Thank you, Jelliroll," Roberta said, relief evident on her face. "We don't have any money to buy more."

"But you soon will have. Did James tell you what his job was?"

"Doctor Johnson owns the apothecary but can't always be in the shop and people are complaining, so he hired James to wait on customers, keep the store clean, take messages for him, and in an emergency, James is to have me stay in the shop while he goes after the doctor."

"Why, Roberta, that sounds like a wonderful job," Sarah said.

"I thought I might advertise that I'm a seamstress, and between the two of us, we can start saving for a place of our own." Roberta glanced at Jelliroll and rushed to help him carry the tub of water to the fire.

Jelliroll's and Roberta's spirit of sharing the work astounded Sarah. Usually Roberta was busy with Johnny, but if there was a job to do, she just carried him on her hip and kept working. The pioneer spirit lived with vigor in her and Jelliroll. As Sarah helped, she felt a sense of pride to be a part of something worthwhile — a feeling she couldn't define. She wasn't a helpless female. After this trip, Sarah knew she was up to most any challenge.

At this moment her desire grew to learn more about making do with what one might have — like Roberta seemed able to do. Others, on other wagon trains, had risked everything they owned and held dear to reach some promised land, just as the three of them were doing. It was people like Jelliroll, James and Roberta who were making this nation a land of opportunity. They were the ones from whom children like Johnny would hopefully inherit a spirit of adventure and survival.

CHAPTER FIFTEEN

That afternoon when they'd hung the wash to dry, and had washed away all the mud from the wagon, Sarah decided to bake a cake. There was a black tin box, resembling a twenty-inch cube with a vent on top that Roberta called an oven. It was supposed to bake whatever was inside when set over wood coals. Sarah hoped she could use it properly; Roberta said she'd never had the courage to try baking in it. Jelliroll said he'd never cooked in anything but a skillet. At the moment, Sarah thought nothing beyond her efforts.

The only dessert Sarah had ever baked successfully in her entire life was a cake. Roberta had a well-supplied food chest, and miraculously it had stayed dry because of her husband's thoughtfulness.

Sarah made a spice cake. She used an iron pan, much like a skillet, to bake one large round layer. While it baked, she read excerpts from Roberta's collection of journals written and lost or left behind by some folks who were traveling west. She thought to ask Roberta if she wanted to read with her, but she saw that she had laid down in the wagon with Johnny and fallen to sleep. Sarah wasn't surprised. She'd never seen anyone work harder than Roberta.

The first statement that caught Sarah's interest in the journals was a remark someone had written down supposedly made by Horace Greeley in a letter he'd written to the editor of the New York Tribune in May of 1859. *"Rain, mud most profound, flooded rivers and streams, glorious soil, worthless politicians. Such is Kansas in a nutshell."* Sarah smiled as she turned the pages. Things hadn't changed much, she thought.

She read account after account of heroism and horrible atrocities committed by white men and Indians alike. One account was of an Indian attack against a wagon train. Thirty to forty people lost their lives and their scalps. One driver's wife saw this carnage and survived with her child to tell about it. An Arapaho chief called Two Face took her for his woman. The woman told a story of brutality and outrages that fiction couldn't parallel.

After fourteen months of extreme horror and suffering from the shame and abuses heaped upon her, the Indian traded her to an army post for arms and ammunition. The colonel of the post, after hearing her story, sent three hundred soldiers out, and they captured Two Face and a couple of other chiefs. They placed the Indians in irons. The colonel sent a message over the telegraph to General Connor.

The general wired back, "If you have them in chains, hang them in chains." The colonel did that deed at once. They took the three Indians from their cells, tied chains around their necks, and drove the wagon they stood on from under them. They died in horrible convulsions.

When the colonel returned to his office, a message handed him was from General Connor. "Colonel, I was a little hasty. Bring them to Julesburg and give the wretches a trial."

The colonel sent the following message, "Dear General, I obeyed your first order before I received the second."

The lady later married, and Sarah supposed and hoped she was living happily. Sarah was in awe of the lady's determination to survive.

She stuck a straw into the center of the cake layer to see if it came out clean; it did and the cake was done. The lady who had survived such trauma stayed on her mind. Sarah wondered if she herself could have been so courageous. The few Indians that had passed them never stopped or spoke to them. She found them interesting to think about, and thought they might be getting the wrong end of a rifle, the way the government was moving them around so the white man could settle their land. Sarah thought reservations were no more than prisons and didn't blame the red man for rebelling.

While the cake cooled, she made a vanilla milk pudding and poured it between the layer she'd sliced into two pieces. She made a molasses frosting to cover the top and sides. It looked delicious.

That evening after they had devoured it with relish, she went to bed feeling proud and contented. She'd contributed to the spirit that abounded, and her only regret, that Shadrach hadn't been able to share the amazing evening of comradeship.

The next morning, they left to return to their not-so-safe rock haven with the overhanging ledge to pick up the satchel containing James's clothing. Jelliroll said they had drifted so far, and crossed so many creeks, that it would take them a little longer to get back to where they'd been.

That morning, as they rolled over practically dry ground, Sarah could hardly believe how quickly the hot sun could change the landscape. The earth was actually beginning to crack where the water had dried up or drained away. Where they drove, the area turned from a relatively sparse number of trees, to thick timbered areas. Groves of cottonwood shimmered yellow in the sun. Several huge shag-bark hickory trees grew ahead of them. There were fields of Queen Anne's Lace, wild baby's breath, Indian fire-bushes, and larkspur.

"What a picture!" Roberta cried as she came through the pucker hole to sit with Sarah.

"Wouldn't you think all that water would have killed everything?" Sarah asked.

"I guess it's all part of nature," Roberta answered.

Sarah observed the gullies, watershed ditches, hedge rows of scrubby trees, and rock ledges. She saw the rocks moved by the water and deposited in piles to dot the land.

She'd seen such piles before, but usually they

were called slag piles because they were around coal mines. Sarah wondered if there were such mines in Parsons or Cherryvale. Ahead of her team, a covey of quail walked across their path. The mama bird led fifteen babies in single file behind her. Sarah held the team back to allow them a safe crossing.

They approached a narrow creek, and when Jelliroll flagged them across, she hardly believed how easy it was. Fear of fording water was not so intense after having experienced the flood. But, as the clop-clop sound of the horses' feet changed from the splash of water to the dirt, she sighed with relief and relaxed.

The creek had splashed over rocks and she could still hear its raucous music, and noticed a hawk, winging across the bright sunny sky. The morning passed pleasantly enough, but Sarah was quite ready to stop when they reached the creek beside their old campsite. She called the place, Rock Creek.

"Since it's so late, I say we best stay the rest of the day and one more night out here before we head for Parsons," Jelliroll said. "If Shadrach and James come back, we'll still be here."

"That's fine with me; how about you, Roberta?" Sarah asked.

"I think we'd feel better if we wait. Johnny needs to be able to play outside the wagon. I feel safe with him playing here. He won't leave the rock area, and we'll be safer here than if we shouldn't make it to Parsons by nightfall."

Jelliroll smiled at Sarah. "Have you ever eaten a jack rabbit?"

"Oh, yuk!" Sarah cried.

"I'm going into the timber and with a little luck we'll eat roasted rabbit, hot-coal baked potatoes and skillet cornbread for supper."

"Couldn't you find a prairie chicken or a turkey? Rabbits are too cute to kill." Sarah was horrified at the possibility "I don't believe I can eat a rabbit."

"Ya can if yer hungry enough," he said. "Besides I'm the cook around here tonight," he said as he grinned at her.

Lord! Sarah thought, they'd created a monster bragging on his take-charge cooking ability.

Roberta looked at him with adoring eyes. "Jelliroll, you're wonderful! I love rabbit, and so will Sarah after she tastes some. Sarah, do you know another man like this one?" Roberta asked as she handed Jelliroll the rifle. "Use this, it won't tear the rabbit up so bad."

"Lord!" Sarah cried and turned away. Later she grinned at Roberta's fondness for the special man whom they were depending on. The surprising factor was his obvious delight in the boy who doted on him. "Jelliroll is one of a kind, all right. You'd better let him go or we'll never eat supper."

Jelliroll gave them a wave as he mounted his big chestnut horse. "I'll be back by the time the fire is hot," he said. "We're only a little more'n an hour from sunset. If ya gals need something, it'll have to wait. Wish me luck, Roberta, Sarah." He waved again, and turned toward the trees that lined the banks of the river-like stream before them.

When Jelliroll was out of sight, Roberta grabbed Sarah so quickly she jumped a foot off the wagon floor. "I'm so happy we're practically on our way to Parsons! What a day this has been!"

Sarah hugged her back and let out a cry of her own, but for a different reason. Johnny had just bitten her leg.

"Don't hurt my mama!" he cried.

Sarah tried to explain that she was hugging Roberta, but Johnny wouldn't be pacified. Finally Roberta took him into her arms to coddle him. Sarah leaped out of the wagon, rubbing her leg. Johnny's sharp little teeth had broken the skin.

"Dear Lord!" Sarah slumped against the side of the wagon, beseeching God to help her keep her mouth shut, or at least, give her the proper words to say.

When Roberta had calmed Johnny, she looked out of the wagon to see if Sarah was all right. "I'm so sorry. I don't know what came over him."

"Roberta, I don't have any children, but if I did, I'd not allow my child to behave as you allow Johnny to do. Did you ever consider whacking his little behind?"

Roberta jumped out of the wagon, Johnny

screaming his head off. "I don't know what to do with him sometimes!"

"Try taking charge — you're the adult, he's the child. Tell him his behavior is unacceptable, and if he continues to bully you, turn him over your knee and whack his bottom until he agrees with you."

"James has told me the same thing, but Johnny's so little. I'd feel like a monster if I hit him."

"You don't have to beat him, for crying out loud, just sting his little bottom once. Tell yourself this, if you let him control you now, when he is bigger, you'll be afraid of him and everyone will despise him for being so ornery. Control is no more than respect when you're training a child. The Bible says in Proverbs, *Train up a child in the way he should go, and when he is old, he will not depart from it.* It's important that you do this, it'll make you a better mother, and someday, you'll have reason to be proud of your son."

Roberta was silent a few minutes, ignoring the tantrum-throwing child in the wagon. Finally, she spoke, "Sarah, thank you, I'm going to try what the Bible says. God knows I've tried everything else."

"You'll never be sorry." Sarah stared at the unique Roberta; she was the easiest person to talk to — to take advice. She never got mad or acted hurt. If Johnny had one tenth of his mother's willingness to learn, he'd be unspoiled in a week. "No question about it, Roberta, you're a special person."

"I've got to do something — I'm expecting another baby in December. How can I handle a baby if Johnny remains so demanding of me?"

"Exactly! I'll help you if you'd like. Oh, Roberta, I'm so happy for you; does James know about the baby?"

"No, I'm afraid to tell him. He has so much to worry about, I don't want to add to it."

Sarah laughed aloud and the sound of it made her realize how long it'd been since she'd laughed so easily. It had become a habit to keep a tight rein on her emotions. She'd nearly forgotten how wonderful laughter could feel. She had denied herself this pleasure because of fear. And, that was what Roberta was doing, withholding pleasure because of fear. "Would you squelch that beautiful expression of happiness by denying James knowledge of his coming child?"

"I don't want to, but he's lost so much. . . ."

"Exactly, so why would you take more from him? He should be sharing this occasion with you, and you need his strength at this time. I'm sorry I came on so strong about Johnny; from now on I'm going to help you more if you don't mind?"

"I won't mind, and I thank you, for everything, especially for telling me about God."

Sarah smiled. She couldn't help wondering why she was so happy. She didn't wonder long;

she knew it was because of the Word that made her able to be thankful — especially that everyone had escaped the flash flood safely, and for the friendship of Roberta and Jelliroll — and for Shadrach. She wondered about him; was he a believer? Good people weren't always God-fearing. But then, being God-fearing didn't mean you were good, either.

She looked up when a shadow passed overhead, and saw the moving clouds blocking sunlight in patches over the prairie. The ragged shapes reminded her of her pinto horse. The dry gulches, edges of flint rock and occasional tree trunks, either rotting or bleached pale-gray by the unrelenting, ever-present Kansas sun didn't daunt her wonderful happiness.

A sudden whiff of a skunk brought her fingers to her nose. "Phew!" she cried.

"It's a polecat." Roberta purred, trying to spot the animal.

"It still stinks. Well, I guess we should start the supper fire. What do you think?"

Roberta agreed and went to tend to Johnny.

The routine preparation of making their camp for the night came off without a hitch, the only worrisome problem being Jelliroll. He hadn't returned. Each kept telling the other not to worry, but Roberta was chewing her nails to the quick. She was afraid to ride a horse and begged Sarah to go find Jelliroll.

Sarah finally agreed. After she saddled Bear, she looked toward the trees where Jelliroll had gone and decided to ride along the stream as she headed for the dense tree cover. Predominant in her mind was the attack on her when she was alone. She didn't want to get caught like that again by another unsavory character. She glanced at Roberta. "I'll not go too far, but if I'm gone longer than you think I should be, don't panic. I'll yell out if I find anything suspicious."

Roberta handed her a knife she'd taken from the wagon. "Here, you take one of James's knifes with you. Jelliroll has the gun. Shadrach would never forgive me if I let something happen to you." Roberta gave her a little knowing smile. "I'll be praying that you find him."

"Thank you. I'll appreciate your prayers." Sarah wondered about her smile — did she think there was something between Shadrach and her?

Sarah waved and headed out. She was surprised when Johnny yelled, "Careful, Sarah."

As she rode along the swollen stream, daylight was fast fading. She urged the horse into a trot because of the approaching dusk. She had no trouble riding her gentle animal.

"What do you think is detaining Jelliroll?" she asked her horse as she rode around a jutting outcrop of rock.

"I certainly don't know of anything but an uncooperative rabbit," she answered herself, knowing that Jelliroll would make every effort to keep his promise for roasted rabbit.

When Sarah reached the widest part of the stream, she looked at the sky. "All right, Bear, we have thirty minutes of light left, at most, forty. We'll ride west for twenty minutes and then come back here while we can still see."

The horse whinnied and Sarah knew they were comforting each other. It was eerie this time of night. "What if I don't find him?" she asked, petting her horse's neck.

Maybe she should go back and get Roberta — then she hoped such a measure wouldn't be necessary because she didn't think Roberta would be much good in a search — not with Johnny. And she'd have to bring him.

Sarah rode in the direction from which she'd seen Jelliroll ride. She searched carefully for any sign indicating a horse had passed along the damp, debris-covered bank of the stream. She was about ready to turn back when Bear's ears perked and he snorted, shying sideways.

"What is it?" she asked, patting the horse's neck while scanning the area. She heard a faint scream — no — it was a whinny from another horse! Instantly Sarah's body tensed. Clicking her tongue and shaking the reins, she edged the pinto toward the sound. The cry piercing the air again sounded more shrill than before. Ahead, she saw Jelliroll's downed chestnut. She kicked Bear into a gallop and closed the distance quickly.

"That ya, Sarah?" came Jelliroll's agonized voice.

"It's me. Where are you?"

"Over here," he cried. "I need help. My leg's broken."

The horse was white with frothy sweat from trying to struggle free of the hole that trapped its hind leg. In the process, the panicked animal had broken its foreleg. As Sarah passed, the horse shrieked and lurched weakly forward.

Bear shied and pranced, her skin flicking nervously. Sarah leaped to the ground beside Jelliroll. "What happened? You're bleeding badly. Are you sure your leg is broken?"

"Yes. Sarah, I can't believe yer here."

His horse struggled and screamed again, and she jumped to her feet to glance at the animal. "How can I help the horse?" she cried, twisting back to face Jelliroll. She couldn't bear to look at the tortured beast.

"If ya can, get the rifle from the saddle holster."

Sarah knew what he was asking of her. "Is that the only way?"

"Yes. Do it now! Look at her, she's been sufferin' over an hour. I've tried to get to her. I scooted backward ta here from where I pitched off the horse. I tumbled down the bank when she went down." Jelliroll winced in pain. "I've bone bustin' through my skin. I can't even scoot now without pain makin' me black out."

The horse screamed and thrashed about. "Don't let him suffer any longer!" Jelliroll pleaded.

"I can't!" Sarah whispered, dry-mouthed and scared. She couldn't kill an animal.

"Yes, ya can. She can't be saved, anyway. Ya must do it! Now!"

CHAPTER SIXTEEN

Sarah shook her head at Jelliroll, clutching her hands to her stomach. The horse screamed again as it lurched in another valiant effort to free itself. She swallowed hard, clamped her jaw and eased toward the horse.

The animal lay still, its huge, frightened eyes watching her as she approached. "Shh! That's a girl. I'm sorry this happened to you. Shh! Let me get this rifle." Quickly, she yanked the gun out of the saddle holster and leaped backward as the animal pitched in a pitiful spasmodic fit. In the terrible seconds that followed, with Jelliroll screaming as frantically for her to kill the horse as the animal begged for freedom, Sarah leveled the rifle and fired.

There was an orange flash, a blast, and the recoiling gun knocked her to the ground. The panicked horse screamed no more. Sarah sat up and gagged, breathing hard and choking while she fought for air. She'd never fired a gun before, never intentionally killed anything in all her life.

With the ensuing silence, her terror began to ebb, letting rational thought return. She struggled to her feet, using the rifle like a stick, suddenly realizing what she'd done. She stood tall and flung the gun from her hands, then dashed to Jelliroll's side. She dropped to her knees beside him, sobbing hysterically.

He placed his arms around her and pulled her head against his chest. He stroked her shoulders, and whispered, "We were both buzzard bait, Sarah. Ya've got backbone."

Sarah jerked up at the strange sound in his voice. He was growing weaker. "I loved that animal," he murmured. "If'n I'd had the rifle, I couldn't of done it. I'll be forever grateful, Sarah."

She laid her head back on his chest for a moment, more to hear how strong his heartbeat was than for comfort — his heart thumped loud and clear. When she calmed down, she asked, "What shall I do, now?"

"Pray fer me."

He was serious, she could see that. "If you're a believer, Jelliroll, you don't need me to do your praying. I meant, what can I do to help you?"

His eyes closed, then opened. He coughed, and spoke clearly despite his obvious pain. "I'm glad yer here, Sarah Daniels. What a stroke of luck ya've turned out to be."

He winced in pain, but bowed his head. *"Here we are, Lord, continue to lead us in our folly."*

"Why Jelliroll, that was beautiful." Sarah straightened up, and swiped at her drippy nose. "Now, It's time to put some feet to that prayer. But what?" she cried.

"Go tell Roberta what's happened and bring the wagon after me, and then we'll decide what ta do. I'll need a doctor, so tomorrow we'd better plan on headin' fer Parsons, but first, we'd

215

best try to stop this blood before I bleed ta death."

"Should we attempt a tourniquet on your leg?"

"Oh, Lord, no! I can hardly breathe fer the pain as it is. Just go get the wagon."

"But, I can't leave you here."

"Yes, you can. I doubt there's nothing yer not capable of doin'. Go now, before it gets any darker. Roberta is gonna to be out of her mind. She probably heard the rifle. I hate fer her to see me like this, but I don't think yer able to stop her from coming, so prepare her as best ya can."

Sarah headed for Bear. She had to step over the rifle and on impulse, she picked it up and took it back to Jelliroll. "I'd just as soon no one knows I killed your horse. Would you mind protecting me from having to tell about this? Could you please let everyone think that you did it?"

He took the rifle and held both her hands. "Yer some special woman. If Shadrach doesn't keep ya, he's a fool."

As she rode as fast as was safe to get help for him, she thought her life would never be as it had been before this trip. Jelliroll's comment about Shadrach had filled her with a disturbing awareness that the man she loved, loved another. But, with that discernment, came a spark of hope.

If it turned out that Leo was dead, why couldn't she fight for Shadrach? As long as he'd not married this other woman yet, it meant she still had a chance. And, after what she'd just done, she knew she could do anything. She wasn't afraid of another woman. The other woman had better be afraid of her.

As Sarah rode out of the trees, she saw Roberta running toward her. "Go back," she yelled, "hitch the wagon. I found Jelliroll and he needs us to bring the wagon. He's hurt badly."

"Go back and stay with him," Roberta cried, "and I'll follow."

"It's too dark. You might get lost. We're not far from the place where he's waiting."

As Sarah rode on to the wagon, she told Roberta what had transpired — part of it, anyway.

Roberta gathered her belongings and shoved them aside as she prepared a bed for Jelliroll. Johnny was throwing a tantrum because he wanted her to hold him. Roberta stopped and took him by the shoulders. "You look at me, Johnny! Look at me, I said."

Johnny stopped screaming and raised his eyes to gaze at her in a state of shock. Carefully, she explained that Jelliroll was hurt and needed the bed. Johnny kicked her in the leg. Roberta had had it. She told him that his behavior was not going to be tolerated, then turned him over her lap and spanked him thoroughly. When she finished, he sobbed and was quiet. "I love you, Johnny, and I'll not allow you to kick me or anyone. You are not to bite anyone ever again —

do you understand?"

Johnny snuffed and nodded his head.

"You speak to me, son."

"I won't kick or bite. I love you. Mama."

"And I love you, Johnny." He flung his little arms around her neck and cried.

Roberta comforted him a few minutes, then set him in the seat beside Sarah. Sarah handed him the reins. "Can you hold these for your mother?"

"Yes, Miss Sarah."

Sarah hugged him, wiped away his big tears and then hugged his mother. "Let's go while we can see." Sarah knew Roberta was shaken up over what she'd done, but felt certain that in the future she would be glad she'd taken control.

Sarah and Roberta spent two hours tending to Jelliroll, and when he was finally resting, Sarah set up her tent so Roberta could put Johnny to bed. Johnny had been a pleasure all evening, expressing his concern for Jelliroll by petting his leg and saying, "It feel better soon."

Two more days passed before they could even think of leaving. Just having one of them climb into the wagon would cause the delirious Jelliroll to scream out in pain. Finally, on the third day, Roberta said there was no more laudanum, and that one of them had to go on into Parsons and bring a doctor.

Jelliroll heard them and said he didn't want

either one of them to leave. "It's too dangerous out there alone." He said he knew he could stand the pain long enough to get to Parsons. He wanted them to leave as soon as possible, but since it was late in the afternoon, he decided it prudent to wait one more night.

At sunrise, the fourth day after the accident, a week since the flood, and eight days since Shadrach and James had left them to go to Cherryvale and visit the Bender Inn, Sarah and Roberta again hitched the wagon. They loaded everything, including the satchel containing James's clothes which was still on the ledge, high and dry. Roberta stuffed all their equipment and supplies around Jelliroll who took up half the wagon.

As Sarah glanced into the wagon, she recalled how hard it had been for them to get him in it. Jelliroll had stood excruciating pain as he helped pull himself to his feet and into the wagon. He'd fainted twice, but had revived quickly. Then, when they'd finally reached their campsite, Roberta had heated water, and together, they'd cut Jelliroll's pant leg off to expose the broken bone. He was fortunate that Roberta had a well stocked medicine chest. Laudanum had put him to sleep after they had cleaned and bandaged his leg.

When the excitement of that early evening had died down, Sarah had made a pan of cornmeal mush, and she, Roberta and Johnny had eaten a bowl for the second time that day, then had gone to bed. Every day since, they'd eaten a little better, but had no meat. They'd eaten mush, water gravy over biscuits, and beans boiled with salt pork for flavoring.

"Roberta," Sarah said as they drove across the flowering prairie, "in case I shouldn't have an opportunity again before we part, I want to tell you something."

Roberta turned to face her. "We aren't going to part, are we? We have to keep in touch, no matter what happens about Robert and your Leo."

Her words warmed Sarah's heart. "No matter what happens," Sarah said, "I want you to know this last week has been the most enlightening of my life." Since she wasn't very good at telling another person about her feelings, Roberta's heartening response gave her the encouragement she needed to say a difficult thing. With a trembling voice, Sarah continued, "In Chicago when I started this trip, I was hopeful about finding Leo, but my hope has turned to realism. I have this feeling that I'll never see Leo again, and the hurt at knowing this is with me every minute. I'll never say goodbye to him until I know he's dead. I loved Leo — he was a devoted husband to me — I can't let go! I'm tied to him in a way that won't let me completely turn loose as long as I don't know what's happened to him."

Sarah was crying and wiped her eyes before

continuing. "I want you to know that in the beginning Shadrach meant nothing more to me
than an employee — he was just the man I'd
hired to help me find my husband. However,
these last two months have changed my life.
There's something very special about Shadrach
Koby, and I find myself highly attracted to him,
but with these feelings for Shad comes more
guilt than I seem able to handle. I want you to
know that if, by some miracle, Leo is alive, I will
live the rest of my life with him. He will never
know about my feelings for Shadrach Koby. Of
course, I've learned that my feelings for him are
hopeless because he is in love with someone else,
and in a way, that makes it easier for me."

"Sarah you don't have to tell me all this. I'm
not judging you."

"Because of your friendship, and that of
Jelliroll, I've learned so many important lessons.
I've learned how to reach down inside myself
and do things I didn't believe myself capable of
even starting. Shadrach and James have taught
me other things also, the main one is that a loved
one, dead or alive, absent or by your side, can
live in your heart and be a vital part of everyday
and everything you do. Roberta, you have
helped me renew my faith that no matter what
happens in the future, I will survive."

"Oh, Sarah, you humble me."

"Let me finish," Sarah said, "I won't say much
more other than to express my thanks to you. I
began this trip as a rather sanctimonious young

woman who thought she was well-educated and capable of anything. I'm ashamed to tell you that I even thought I was superior to you."

"Sarah . . ."

"Please let me finish. I now have another name for myself, a spoiled rotten snob. Since being with you, I've seen the real me, and I don't like me. I'm determined to change. I shall be forever grateful for you and your friendship. The joy, love and camaraderie that you have shown me has given me a new lease on life."

Roberta was crying. "Sarah, every word you said could be from my heart. I've learned from you, also, and know my life will forever be different because of you." They hugged, cried a few minutes, then silently enjoyed the sun beaming on the flowering prairie spread out ahead of them.

The tender, heartfelt remarks from Roberta after Sarah had bared her soul allowed her to enjoy a wonderful feeling of peace. Sometime later, Roberta took over driving the wagon and Sarah rode her pinto ahead as a scout. The terrain was getting rougher and they didn't want to let a wheel fall into a hole that the horses couldn't pull out of.

As she rode, a sudden uncomfortable thought came to her. Today or tomorrow she would surely see Shadrach. Did she have the courage to stay away from him until she knew about Leo? She would try, then whatever she found out, she would deal with the other woman in Shad's life after that.

Sarah looked ahead and saw the roofs of buildings; a rider was galloping toward her. She glanced back at the wagon a long way behind and wondered if she should ride back. Roberta had the rifle. She was turning her horse when she recognized the broad-shouldered rider. It was Shad.

She stopped and waited for him. When he was close enough to be heard, he yelled, "Has something happened? Where is Jelliroll?"

"He's in the wagon. There's been an accident."

"Is he dead?" Shadrach asked as he stopped beside her.

"No, no, his horse threw him and he's broken his leg." Sarah briefly told Shadrach what had taken place on the bank of the swollen stream, and how they were trying to get him into Parsons to the doctor James was working for.

"James is nearly out of his mind," Shadrach said.

"Well, so are we. You've been gone over a week!"

"Sarah, we thought you were safely in Parsons. And we were making good progress in our search so we didn't get in a hurry. James and I have been looking for you since yesterday. We couldn't figure what had delayed you."

"Did you ever think that we might have been in trouble?" she asked.

"Every moment, but we felt certain Jelliroll was in control. Thought maybe he might have gotten lost."

"We were for a while. Where else have you been?"

"We thought we'd found your attacker the day after we left you, before the storm hit. We found a torn piece of bloody shirt near a stream and it had a button on it like the one in my pocket. There was a dead horse nearby. Looked like someone had ridden him to death. We spent three days tracking the man, following boot prints and broken twigs. Once we were close enough to smell him, must not have bathed in a year, but yet, he slipped away from us. We finally gave up. Then we spent another day getting to Osage Mission where we spent the night visiting with a priest. Then we went to the Bender Inn. Another night passed before we reached Cherryvale. We made some inquiries about Robert and Leo, then spent another night. The next day we rode into Parsons, hardly able to tell you what we'd found out. That's when we heard about the valley having been flooded. You can't imagine our concern for you and Roberta, but, because we knew how capable Jelliroll was, we never figured you were in harms' way."

"Well, we were nearly washed away."

"I'm so sorry we weren't with you. How did you escape?"

"Jelliroll saved us. He'll tell you about it."

"I've been searching for you in one direction and James in another. We returned to Parsons last night, discouraged and fearful about what had happened to you. James and I spent the night deciding on a new plan to locate you. As I told you, he left at first light, and I was going the other way, but I came back. Had this feeling right here," he tapped his chest, "that you would be in Parsons today. I'd been anxiously watching for you from town, then when I couldn't stand it any longer, I decided to ride out in the direction you should be coming from. Oh, Sarah, I've been so worried. I'd only gone a mile, when I suddenly recognized you and Bear." He reached out to her.

She ducked under his outstretched arm and turned her horse around, then asked, "What about you? Did you see the hotel clerk who wrote you about Leo's name being on the registry?"

"I have, and I showed him the tintype of Leo. He called another man over and showed him the picture. This man said that Leo was the man who'd signed the hotel book nine or so months ago. I asked him how he could be so certain. He asked me if the fellow walked with a bad limp and did he carry a cane with the head and face of a pretty lady on the handle. That did it! I knew Leo had been there."

"Did he say anything else?" Sarah cried.

"I questioned this second man and found out he worked in the hotel — he said the day Leo was there, he was concerned about starting out so late for Texas. The gentleman said that he told him if he got lost, Benders ran an inn on the

Osage Mission Trail just outside of Cherryvale. That's all he remembered, so I gave the man some of your money which made him extremely happy. That's when James and I rode out of town, intending to find the Bender Inn."

"What was it like?" she asked, eager to hear everything.

"A building twenty by sixteen, with a curtain that divided the store and inn from their private quarters. James and I pretended to be travelers needing some supplies. On one side of the room there was a counter with sparsely stocked shelves behind it. On the other side, a stove and work table. A large walnut table and three chairs sat in front of the dirty canvas divider curtain. Everything was about the way Jelliroll had described it. Old John Bender didn't do more than grunt. I saw a patched shirt hanging on a nail and the patch was where the piece of shirt James and I found would have fit perfectly. The buttons matched the one in my pocket. I asked where their son was and was told young John was nowhere around. Good thing he wasn't. I wanted to see him — see if his face resembled a fight with a bobcat or the fingernails of a woman." Shad looked seriously at her. "How are you doing, anyway?"

"If you're referring to the attack, it's nearly forgotten."

"I haven't forgotten."

"You might as well. I'm only interested in finding Leo. What else did you see at the

Benders?"

"Besides the mother named Kate, James and I saw the very strikingly handsome daughter, also named Kate. I can see why Jelliroll was mesmerized by her. We didn't seem to interest her. I think it was because there were two of us, and we were only trying to buy some flour and baking soda. Then, we pretended we didn't have enough money. She smiled and opened the door for us to leave. What a well put together girl she was."

"Shad, really! I'm not interested in Kate Bender. I want to hear about anything you saw that didn't seem to belong there."

"I saw an old clock, two pair of eye spectacles, a baby's bonnet, and several walking canes. Before you get excited, I didn't see one like the one Leo used."

Sarah slumped a moment in her saddle — she'd had such hope that this was where she'd find out something about her missing husband.

CHAPTER SEVENTEEN

Sarah looked back at the wagon and asked, "What about Robert? Did James find the man whom the Pinkerton Agent had told him about?"

"No, but there is an up side to that."

"What?"

"James had asked Doctor Johnson if he knew a Gary Stone. The doctor said he did, but that Stone had moved to Ohio. When James moaned and sat down, the doctor asked him why his interest in Stone. James told him and showed him a picture of Robert. The doctor said the picture of Robert was the exact image of a badly wounded young man that he had treated a number of months before."

The wagon came rolling to a stop beside them. "Where is James?" Roberta called, a worried look on her face.

Shadrach stretched his neck and looked behind the wagon. "I think he's coming half a mile back there. Hello, Roberta."

"Oh, Shadrach, forgive me. How are you? How is everything?" she said, looking around the wagon for James.

"Just fine, how's Jelliroll?"

"Asleep. Johnny, will you hold the reins for Mama while I go greet your Papa?"

"Yes, I will," the boy said.

Roberta climbed to the ground and gathered

her skirt so she could run, then headed out to meet James.

Shadrach raised his eyebrows as he turned his shocked expression from Johnny to Sarah. "Is this the Johnny I know?" he asked.

"Johnny has grown up a lot since you last saw him. He's a big boy now."

"Big boy," Johnny said standing proudly with the reins held tightly in his hands.

"Is that Shadrach, I hear?" came the voice of Jelliroll from inside the wagon.

"Sure is," Shad cried, riding to the end of the wagon.

Sarah took the reins of his horse as he climbed into the wagon. She heard Jelliroll's emotional greeting and rode back up front to talk to Johnny.

"My mama coming back?"

"Hand me the reins," she said, and when he did, she wrapped them around the brake lever. She reached her hands out to him and he climbed onto her horse. "Look there," she said pointing to his mother and father who were walking hand in hand, leading James's horse. "Your mama will be here in just a little while."

Johnny lost interest in his folks when he realized he was on a horse. "Giddy-up," he cried, his short legs moving up and down.

Sarah couldn't resist hugging him and jiggling the reins so Bear trotted around the wagon with Hominy following.

"See, Miss Sarah, Johnny ride horse."

"You sure are."

229

"Go horsey! Go to Mama — Papa."

Sarah pulled Hominy up beside her and transferred herself to Shad's horse. "Now you hold on to the saddle horn, and we'll walk the horses out to meet your folks."

When Roberta saw them coming, she waved, and she and James laughed at the way Johnny was behaving. "You'd better be careful or you'll create a monster," James said as he greeted Sarah. He reached up to lift the boy into his arms. "Mama tells me what a good boy you've been. Papa's proud of you." James hugged him tightly.

Roberta was beaming. "Did Shadrach tell you what Doctor Johnson said?"

Sarah didn't want to squelch Roberta's happiness. "Tell me everything," she said, getting off Hominy to walk with her friends.

"About eight months ago, some folks brought a badly wounded young man into his office for treatment. The doctor said he was absolutely positive that the young man was Robert."

"Had he been shot?" Sarah asked, having not heard about this.

"No, he'd been hit in the head, twice. The doctor said it appeared to be blows from a hammer or a stone. The fellow was disoriented, didn't know his name or where he was from. Doctor Johnson said he could have amnesia. The man who brought him to the doctor was named Clarence Frank, and he paid to have him bandaged up because the young man was penniless. Frank took the injured fellow with him.

"James asked the doctor if Clarence Frank said where he lived. The doctor said he wasn't certain but he remembered having the impression that the man said he lived on a farm near Independence, Kansas."

"Are you going there?"

"Absolutely, when we can."

Sarah wasn't certain what that meant, but they'd reached the wagon and Shadrach was anxious to go.

"Jelliroll is in a lot of pain."

"I sure am," Jelliroll cried, "and the laudanum is all gone."

Shadrach looked at James. "Is the doctor in his office?"

"He was this morning. I'll drive, we'll be there before Jelliroll can chaw this wad of tobacco I have for him." James pitched him a chunk of brown tobacco, reached down and took Johnny from Roberta, then helped her into the seat beside him.

Sarah and Shadrach rode on ahead. As they waited for the others to reach Parsons, he told her that he'd rented them each a room at the hotel. She was afraid to be where she might be alone with him, but if she refused, he would be hurt. She was going to be strong, she had to be. Until she knew what had happened to the husband, who had been totally devoted to her, she would remember that she was married, and remind Shad that she was if the need to do so ever arose.

Doctor Johnson set Jelliroll's broken bone and gave him a strong pain killer. It took all three men to carry him up one flight of stairs. The doctor had given James and his family an apartment to live in as long as James worked for him. When they had Jelliroll settled in a bed, the doctor left, and Shadrach and James began the arduous task of unloading the wagon. Sarah helped Roberta find a place for every one of her possessions, which were pitifully few.

When late afternoon had come, she'd thought about asking Roberta if she could stay with her and not at the hotel, but after seeing how small the apartment was, she didn't have the nerve. James came in and said the doctor had to leave so he had to go to the apothecary. Shadrach said he would take the wagon and animals to the livery and unload his and Sarah's things.

As Roberta and Sarah continued scrubbing every wall in the neglected apartment, and emptying boxes from the wagon, Sarah noticed how quiet her friend had become. "Roberta, are you all right? Why don't you sit down and rest, I can finish this."

"I'm getting more exhausted than usual."

"Have you told James about the coming baby?"

"No, I'm afraid to." Roberta bent over and started to cry.

"Why?" Sarah went to her side and made her sit down.

"James said that Shadrach would go with me to Independence in the morning, that the doctor really needed him, that he had to work — that we haven't even one dollar left to our name."

"Roberta, dear friend, if the lack of money is what has you so upset, I can loan you whatever you need."

Roberta looked up and shook her head. "James is a proud man, and his ego has been stretched to the limit of his endurance. He'd always swore he'd never borrow a dime, but desperation changes the most stubborn of minds. Sarah, you interest me and if I'm being too nosey, I'll understand. I want to ask you a question."

"What is it?" Sarah asked.

"Your Leo must have been very successful. I've noticed that you speak as if you have money for anything you want, and you must pay Shadrach a tidy sum. . . ."

"Roberta, I'm fortunate to have had parents who left me enough to be comfortable the rest of my life. I'm so grateful, so let me share it with you. James surely won't be insulted if I give you a gift."

"James might not be, but I will be. You are a wonderfully generous person, and I'll never forget your offer, but the subject is closed. We'll be all right for a while. The bed frame he and Shadrach carried up for us isn't paid for. James swallowed his pride and accepted a line of credit at the general store because of Doctor Johnson's reputation. Jelliroll had the only bed in the apartment, and James didn't want me sleeping on the floor — thank goodness, we have our feather ticking. I heard James tell the doctor that he would pay him for treating Jelliroll. When the doctor said the bill was paid, James and I thought it might be you. It was, wasn't it?"

"Seemed the least I could do for him," Sarah said. "Jelliroll accepted my gift with a grateful heart. It was an emergency. Please promise me that if a real emergency arises with you, that pride won't prevent you from coming to me."

Roberta hugged her and agreed, then took a long, shuddering breath.

Sarah stood and started to work again. After she'd washed another wall, she rinsed her rag. When she glanced at Roberta, she saw that she was still distraught. "Are up upset that James is working the rest of the afternoon? I know how anxious you are to go to Independence."

"That's part of it, the worst part is that the doctor said James has to be in the apothecary all day the rest of the week. He asked me to forgive him, but I'm crushed. It's just a temporary job! How can he expect me to wait another week, even another day?"

"I hope you'll understand the plight he's in — he has a family to feed, a bill at the general store, and he probably feels he can't afford to lose this job, no matter how temporary," Sarah said sitting down beside her friend once more. "I was just wondering how you were planning to go to Independence, anyway. You don't ride horses, and if you did, you run the chance of losing the baby."

"Exactly!" Roberta wailed, "what am I going to do? I have to go see if that man in Independence is Robert. James and I are the ones who will know if he is my brother."

"But you can't ride a horse, and you have no wagon."

"James surely isn't selling our wagon, is he?" Roberta cried.

"I don't really know, just heard part of a conversation between him and Shadrach."

"I can ride a horse, I'm just afraid to since I discovered I'm with child. But it can't be much worse than the wagon."

"What about Johnny?" Sarah wondered if Roberta was going to ask her to keep him.

"Jelliroll said he would watch him; he can knock on the floor if he needs James. Thank goodness, the apothecary is right below our apartment."

"Please don't go, riding a horse is too hard on you. Maybe you could rent a buggy?" Sarah suggested, trying to help Roberta out of her dilemma.

"With what? Oh, Sarah, I'm so close to finding Robert, I feel it here," she touched her heart. "I know he's alive. If I tell James about the coming baby, he will make me wait until he can get a day off so he can go."

"Would his going instead of you be terribly upsetting?"

"I don't care who goes, as long as one of us can see if the man is Robert."

"I've an idea, Roberta; why can't you wait on customers, and dust bottles? The doctor's out of town, so why can't James and Shadrach go? Johnny would surely be happier knowing you were not far away, and then, I'll be at the hotel and can help you with Jelliroll and Johnny."

"You won't stay at a hotel! If James will go along with our plan, you can spend the time here with me and Jelliroll," Roberta said, her mood lifting considerably. Sarah was not too happy because, to help her friend, she would have to put her own quest on hold for a week or two. Then she realized that her sacrifice was nothing compared to Roberta's. She was giving up the very good possibility that she may have found her brother to protect her unborn child. *Forgive me, Lord. How desperately wicked and selfish I am sometimes.*

After eating a bite of supper, Sarah and Shadrach said goodnight to Jelliroll and the Jenkins, then Shad walked her to the hotel. He asked her if she would like a cup of coffee before she went to her room. Sarah declined because she didn't trust herself. He was gracious and took her to her room where he said goodnight and left her. She felt dismal and didn't have any clue as to what ailed her — not for a while, anyway.

Unable to sleep, Sarah paced the bare-wood floor of her hotel room. She heard her feet making a padding sound, so she sat down on the bed afraid she might be disturbing someone below her. She had halfway expected Shad to come knocking on her door, but he hadn't. His goodnight to her had been laced with honey. It wasn't like her to be taken in by honeyed words, but she had been — much to her embarrassment. In her mind's eye, she could see his dark, sultry eyes watching her, always saying, I want you — I need you.

She had to be strong. It appeared that he was trying. He hadn't even tried to kiss her goodnight, but what he'd done was just as devastating. Sarah had nearly lost her breath when, at her door. Shad raised her hand to his lips and kissed her palm. The deliberately slow and tantalizing touch of his lips had turned her to jelly. He unlocked her door, handed her the key, and said, "I'm always amazed by your perfect beauty. Goodnight, Sarah." He'd tipped his hat and walked across the hall to his room.

Sarah was weak, just recalling the incident. She lay back on her bed, mulling over her reactions to Shadrach Koby. They were certainly not like any she'd experienced before — not even with Leo. She tried to get comfortable in the bed, but couldn't. All she could see was Shad, broad-shouldered, handsome to a fault, with a smile that melted her resolve like it was ice in July. She jumped out of bed, unable to stand the stifling room another minute. Sarah dressed hurriedly, leaving her long tresses hanging loose around her shoulders, and went to the lobby.

The hotel seemed deserted. Sarah sat down in a green velvet chair and breathed deeply of the outside air drifting through the open door. Suddenly, Shadrach strolled through the door into the lobby. Sarah didn't have time to disappear. She stood and just smiled, trying to hide her embarrassment.

He returned her smile, but said nothing. They both remained silent for what seemed an eternity. "It was so warm in my room, I needed some fresh air," she commented as naturally as she could, although her insides were shaking apart.

Shad said nothing, as Sarah turned slightly to get more of the breeze blowing through the door. She reached up and lifted her hair to cool her neck as well. She saw Shadrach's gaze following her. What was he thinking? Why didn't he say something?

"Look here!" she exclaimed, as she bent over a potted cactus.

"What?" he asked.

"It's blooming. Cacti seldom bloom. Isn't it lovely?" she said straightening up and turning quickly around. She came in contact with his solid chest. As she looked up into his ardent eyes, his arms were holding her. "I'm so sorry," she offered weakly. Time stood still as they gazed at one another. Oh, don't kiss me, her mind begged as he bent his head. Her blood pumped so rapidly she thought her heart would explode. Her gaze was fixed on his tantalizing lips when he slowly moved them to speak.

"You must be a red-headed angel sent to tempt me." He lifted her hair from the front of her shoulders and placed it behind her back. "I want to see all your lovely face when I kiss you." He lowered his mouth to claim hers.

Now, there was not a single doubt in Sarah's mind that her desire for Shad was real. She was lost in the pleasure of his seductive kiss. He pulled her closer, his kiss deepening, his tongue gently tracing the inside of her mouth. She felt herself devoid of every ounce of the resolve she'd made. Even though she thought she was a fool God wouldn't forgive, she could not pull herself away for several seconds. When she stepped back, he didn't try to prevent her going. She was glad, she couldn't handle the sudden raw explosion of passion she was experiencing. It frightened her, more than anything else that had happened between them.

When she finally had will power enough to look at him, he was smiling.

"You taste like honey," he said reaching out to touch her lips.

She backed further away. How could she be so weak? What was it, that in the presence of Shadrach, caused her to forget right from wrong. "Why do you do this? You promised me."

"Are you going to tell me that you didn't want our kiss?" he asked.

"I'm a married woman. . . ."

"Stop that. Just answer my question — didn't you want our kiss?" His dark-eyed gaze held hers, and his deep sultry voice was nearly her undoing. He always caused her such confusion. Sarah couldn't believe what she was feeling. She wanted Shadrach Koby as she'd never desired Leo Daniels — God knew how she felt. She could lie to Shad, lie to herself, but not to God. A sudden image popped unbidden into her mind. It was Leo. Why was he doing this? Was his love so strong for her that he wasn't letting her forget? Was she somewhat clairvoyant like Roberta? The image had stolen the amorous moment.

"Shad, I'm trying so hard to remain a lady. . . ."

"I've no doubt that you are trying, but when two people are meant for one another, it's hard to stay apart. It would be easier on us both if you'd just admit that you want me as much as I want you."

Sarah wasn't certain how to reply. Shadrach's plain talk was making her angry. She stiffened and turned away.

He wasn't deterred by her action. "We desired each other from the first time we met, and now I wonder how long you'll continue resisting?" He reached out and trailed his hand from her shoulder to her fingertips.

She slapped his hand away. He wasn't helping her, he was complicating her decision. *Desired each other from the first time we met* — her flimsy efforts at resistance had been ridiculous. He had been toying with her all along. "Shad, why don't we be honest. I know you can't wait to finish with this job so you can get home to the woman you really love. I'm not going to fire you, but you are free to go any time you want."

"What are you talking about?" he asked angrily, taking hold of her shoulders.

"I overheard you and James talking one evening, and you said, and I'll quote your words verbatim. Lord knows I've repeated them often enough. You said, 'I'm not married, but I'm in love, and this search for Sarah Daniel's husband is hard on me. I'd like to be done with it. I'd like to settle down and raise a family, but until I find Leo Daniels, I'm obligated to stick it out with Sarah.' " He stopped her words with a kiss. Then, as her traitorous body began to respond, he moved away.

She blinked her eyes in shocked embarrassment, and a sudden gust of wind blew her hair into her face. Furious, she started brushing at it with her hands. Shadrach broke out laughing. "What a hell of a couple we're going to make." Then he turned toward the stairs. "Goodnight, Mrs. Daniels."

CHAPTER EIGHTEEN

Still shaken by Shad's last kiss and his arrogant words, Sarah gasped to control mounting anger at him. He hadn't bothered to deny her accusation. She whirled on shaky legs to follow him. "You just hold up a minute, Mister Koby!"

He stopped and faced her with that all-knowing, irritating smile spread across his face. "If I told you that your services were no longer wanted or needed, would you go back to Chicago?"

"Not without you," Shadrach said and turned to climb the stairs.

"You're an insufferable womanizer!"

"And you're the most beautiful woman on earth."

Sarah gasped and lifted her skirt to run up the stairs ahead of Shad. She was in her room and had the door locked when he rattled the door knob.

"Sarah, I know you're upset, but now is not the time to call it quits. Let me make a few more inquiries about Leo, then if I come up empty-handed, I'll resign. You can hire someone else."

"I don't want anyone else," she blurted out through the door, then quickly added, "to work for me."

"Then can't we just forget tonight ever happened?"

She just stood there drawing on all her reserve strength to listen to his beseeching voice. His compelling way had captured her again. "I'll try if you double promise not to touch me again."

"I'll promise — although the Lord knows it won't be easy — now try to get some sleep. James and I are leaving at first light for Independence. We may or may not be back tomorrow evening; if we get here early enough, I'd like to take you and the Jenkins to dinner here at the hotel. What do you say?"

"I'll talk to Roberta."

"Goodnight, again," he said, and she doubled her fists and pushed against the wall to keep from opening the door. She undressed, and threw herself into the bed and cried frustrated tears for the terrible mess she was making of her life. With Leo, her life had been so ordered, but with Shad, she was in constant upheaval.

Sarah hadn't slept a wink when she saw the sun coming up. It appeared so glorious as it shone through the haze of morning. Any other time, Sarah would have spent half an hour watching the changing sky as it turned into day, but not this time — she had too much to do. She dressed and went to breakfast, then to Roberta's apartment. There was still much to accomplish there and Roberta was depending on her.

The day went far better than Sarah had imagined. Roberta was nervous, and anxious to know if the men had found her brother. Sarah spent a lot of the morning encouraging her to be patient.

Roberta was an exceptionally clean person, but Sarah knew some of her energy was expended to make time pass more quickly. Sarah was certain she could have eaten off the floor it was so clean, and when she'd gone to the apothecary to check on Roberta, she saw that her friend was cleaning there also. To keep Roberta from over-doing, Sarah had worked with her until lunch time.

Jelliroll was feeling much better, and hated being in another room, so Sarah helped him off the bed, and he scooted on his buttock into the other room. Johnny was all over him, believing he was on the floor to entertain him. Sarah found herself laughing at Jelliroll who seemed never to tire of the rambunctious boy.

She suggested they eat lunch on a blanket on the floor like they were having a picnic and all agreed. The picnic was delightful. Roberta had come upstairs and joined them. Sarah saw how tired she was and made her go take a nap, saying she would go to the apothecary. While she was there, she decided she might as well finish the task that Roberta had started.

When the sun began to go down, she and Roberta had decided that James and Shadrach weren't going to return until tomorrow. Roberta was disappointed and sighed deeply. They were so tired that both were looking forward to a good night's sleep.

In Independence, James went to the post office to inquire about Clarence Frank. Shad stopped at the sheriff's office to ask if he knew where they could find this man, Clarence Frank.

"Actually," the sheriff said, "his hired man was here yesterday to tell me that Clarence went chasing after some border ruffians who were stealing his cattle. I sent Inman back to guard the rest of the herd because I don't have the men to send after every ruffian that drifts across the border."

"Can you draw us a map to his place? I'm somewhat of a lawman, maybe I can help Mister Frank."

"What kind of lawman?" the sheriff asked as he began drawing.

"A private investigator now, but formerly I was a Pinkerton Agent. Some call me a bounty hunter."

"I see," the sheriff said as he stopped making the map to stroke his chin, "been a lot of them through here the past year. Three Pinkerton men all looking for a crippled man who walks with a cane."

Shadrach's interest leaped at the description of the man being hunted. "Any of them place a name on this fellow?" Shadrach asked, realizing he could well be on Leo Daniels's trail.

"All three were looking for different men, all crippled — how strange is that?" the sheriff answered going back to his map-making.

"Mighty strange. Do you remember their names?" Shadrach asked, his puzzlement mounting.

The sheriff pulled open a drawer and rumbled through some papers. "Here it is, but I only have notes on the second Pinkerton man to stop here. He was looking for a Leonard Daniels from Detroit. I recall the first Pinkerton man was searching for a Lee Davies who was from Arkansas. The last one came through here a couple months ago on the trail of a man who'd absconded from the law after marryin' a poor widow, then stealing her life-savings. Now, here you are looking for Clarence Frank," the sheriff chuckled, "thankfully he isn't crippled."

"Hang on to your hat, Sheriff, I'm in this area searching for Leo Daniels, a crippled man who walks with a cane."

"Sonofabi— you don't say! Damn! This seems a bit more than coincidence."

"I'd say it is, and I'm going to investigate it after I find Frank," Shadrach said, feeling there was more to three missing crippled men than any of them could imagine.

"Want me to deputize you?"

"That won't be necessary." Shad said reaching for the map the sheriff had just folded.

"You watch your back, you hear?" the sheriff said. "There's lots of strange doings going on around here. Just yesterday got a message from the sheriff in Cherryvale. He wants me to send men to help dig up bodies."

246

"What?" Shadrach asked.

"Don't have all the details yet. Seems something is going on at or near the Bender Inn."

"Lord, this is wild country!" Shadrach commented as James arrived. After introducing James to the sheriff, Shadrach told him he had a map to Frank's ranch.

"Great, let's go!" James was out the door, heading for his horse.

"Talk to you later, Sheriff," Shadrach said and closed the door.

James was back in a flash and said he had something to ask the sheriff. "Sheriff," James said as he held out a picture of Robert, "is this man living with Clarence Frank?"

"That's him. Hell of a nice young man; is he in trouble?"

"No, nothing like that," James answered.

"I'm glad to hear it. Clarence thinks the world and all of Inman. Found him crawling in the road up by Cherryvale. He was hurt, and so Clarence had him doctored and brought him here. He is teaching him how to be a cattleman."

"Thanks for the information, Sheriff," James said, signaling Shadrach to come on.

"What do you think we'll find?" James asked Shadrach who was quiet as they followed the map. "The closer I get, the stranger I feel. If this fellow is Robert, it proves there's quite a bond between him and Roberta."

"I'd say it does. Hey, there's the big shag bark

hickory where we're supposed to turn left to the ranch."

As they rode toward the place, they saw a barn twice as large as the neat, white painted house. There was a large fenced corral and several head of cattle. "There doesn't seem to be anyone around," Shadrach said, still baffled, trying to get his mind off what he'd learned from the sheriff.

"Shall we have a look around?" James asked.

"Who's to stop us?" Shadrach quipped.

They tied their horses to the hitch rail and walked first toward the barn. Shad stopped a minute and pulled off his boot to shake out a rock. "There seems to be few comforts for a man that doesn't have a drawback. Look, James." Shadrach held up a pebble, then tossed it aside and pulled on his boot. "Even a man's boots must be worn without obstructions."

"Does that have a meaning that's escaped me?" James asked, grinning at Shad who was trying to get his boot on while hopping on one foot.

As they passed a woodpile, Shadrach pointed to the windmill which delivered water constantly from a pipe into a big wooden trough where a few of the cattle were drinking. A hollowing in the earth beside the water trough where the water overflowed was two foot wide and some animals drank from it.

Shadrach ran his hand over the well-made trough and remarked, "This makes an inviting bathtub." He grinned. "I wonder if the folks here use it." Shadrach cupped his hand and tasted the water running from the pipe. "Sweet water too." Shadrach then went to examining the fence around the corral. "Fine workmanship in this fence."

"Suppose the folks living here have gone to town or after more border ruffians?" James asked. "What should we do, Shadrach? Stay here and wait for whoever lives here to return, or go back?"

"I don't know. I wonder when they were last here? I don't think it was too long ago. James, what's wrong with you?"

"I'm suddenly weak as a cat, haven't eaten all day." James took a deep breath, and rubbed his growling stomach.

"Let's go in the house and look for some food. You're pale and sweaty; and apprehensive about this Inman fellow being Robert, right?"

"I'm suddenly afraid. What if he is Robert and he doesn't know me?"

"We'll just have to help him remember. He's been here seven or eight months, he surely remembers something. Come on, you need something to eat; so do I."

They walked onto the porch and found the door open. "I wish we knew where Frank and Inman were. I'm always leery entering a man's home without an invitation, but they've left their door open for a purpose. Come on, James, there's no need of our standing here waiting, there's got to be some bread and butter." They went into a neat, well equipped kitchen. The room was large and the end opposite the kitchen was a sitting room with a fireplace, a settee and two rockers, several tables with lamps and books on them.

Shadrach called out again as he looked into a bedroom off the kitchen. James sat down at the table and pointed at another room near the fireplace. Shad saw it was smaller than the first bedroom, but it was empty. He didn't know what it was for. The kitchen had a wash stand and a leather strop hanging from a nail nearby; he knew the men shaved in the kitchen. Shad saw a bread box and opened it. "This is great. I'll cut us a slice, and here's a bucket of milk." Shadrach lifted the dipper to his lips. "Fresh too. Whoever brought this can't be far away. Now eat!" Shadrach said as he gave James some milk and bread. Shadrach sliced himself a fair-sized piece, and drank a dipper of milk. As he ate, he walked around the three room house, and noticed there was a loft for sleeping above the bedroom.

Shadrach could see the very edge of the loft and the end of a ladder, obviously used to get up and down. Something else caught his eye. It was on the wall under the loft area. The sun's rays revealed marks on the wall.

James followed Shadrach's gaze, got up and together they examined the wall. "I assume these are days, the longer slash a week — not much of a calendar would you say?"

"It could stand for a lot of things — new calves, trips to the market, deposits in a bank, almost anything. Whoever's kept this record has kept it for — one, two, three, four, five, six, seven weeks, or months. They could mean nothing!" Shad said thoughtfully.

"Those marks must stand for something. Maybe border ruffians they've shot, trips to a bawdy house — hell, let's get out of here." James drew in his breath. "This Inman can't be Robert!"

"Now, James, you're just apprehensive. Relax."

"But, Robert's been gone so long; what if it is him and he does know me and what he's done with my money. That will be as bad as death."

"Not true, James. I'll not let you leave until we know if this fellow is Robert or not. How can you even think of going back to Roberta with no news?"

"All right, Shad, doing that would be unthinkable, and hardly feasible."

They were startled by a sound from the dark shadow of the doorway. Shadrach and James whirled around ready to defend themselves, but stopped. They watched in total shock as Robert Smith leaped into the room with a rifle. Robert stood perfectly still, his eyes glued on James. He shook his head, opening and closing his eyes. He staggered and fell against the door frame.

Finally, he spoke, "I can't recall who you are, but we've met before, haven't we? Why are you in Mister Frank's house?" Robert was still focused on James's face.

"No one was home, and my friend here," Shadrach said taking charge since James was unable to speak, "was growing weak from hunger. Robert, this is your brother-in-law, James Jenkins. Do you remember him?"

Robert blinked several more times, set the rifle down and stumbled to the table. Then he nearly fell backward before gaining some control. "James Jenkins — I think I remember you. Help me, for God's sake!"

Shadrach pulled out a chair for both men. James was still too stunned to say anything, he only shook like he was freezing.

Robert continued, "I remember something — was I buying us a farm? Is this the place we were going to own?" He rose from the chair.

James stood, also, shook his head, fighting to keep his emotions in tack. He tried to swallow, but his astonishment at having found his brother-in-law alive had seemingly overwhelmed him. He reached for Robert and grabbed him in an embrace filled with tears of happiness.

Shadrach saw that Robert was still confused and that he was leaning against the table for support. In a few seconds, James released Robert and sat down.

Robert walked pensively around the room,

keeping his gaze fastened on James's face. Then he turned to Shadrach and asked, "Do I know you?" Tears had filled his eyes and were running down his cheeks. "I've been in such a fog, seeing images flash in and out of my head until I thought I'd go crazy — indeed, I had decided that I had been mentally damaged. Clarence has kept encouraging me to try to remember who I am and where I was from, telling me that someday one of the images I'd see flash in my mind would stay long enough for me to remember something. You called me Robert. Am I Robert — ah — Robert Smith?" he asked sitting down in front of James.

James rapidly nodded his head. "You are Robert Smith."

"I've seen your image many times but didn't know who you were — until this minute." Robert grabbed James around the shoulders in another embrace. Neither seemed able to speak; they only slapped each other's back.

In a few minutes, James used his kerchief and offered it to Robert.

"If you're my brother — ah — I mean, brother-in-law," Robert groped for words, and looked at James and then Shadrach, "then, I must have a sister; do I?" He couldn't stop crying or let go of James.

James and Shadrach glanced at each other, James was still trying to speak.

Shadrach answered for his friend who was obviously too overcome with emotion. "Robert, you have a twin sister. Don't you remember Roberta?"

Robert slowly closed his eyes and shook his head. "No, I don't know what's happened to me. I have flashes of memory, and Clarence tells me that the doctor in Parsons says I may have amnesia. James, you're the first person who has known who I am. Tell me about myself."

"You are my wife's brother, our child's uncle, and my best friend," James said in a clear voice ringing with excitement.

"I remember when we were twelve years old, and you brought me to your home — when you sent me to — to Oklahoma to buy a farm, but not much more."

"That's all correct; your memory will return. Do you remember what happened to you when you reached Parsons? Do you remember getting to Parsons?"

"I don't remember Parsons, but several months ago I started getting quick images in my mind; they were like lightning flashes. Then, once in a while one of these flashes would turn into a dream, but when I'd wake up, the memory would be gone. For the last few months, some flashes have really plagued me, and only this minute are a few making any sense. I feel certain now, that if Clarence Frank hadn't found me and saved my life, I'd be dead."

"Have you any idea how you were injured?" Shad asked.

Robert closed his eyes and shuddered. "Right

now, at this minute, that is the clearest image in my mind. I recall stopping at a roadside inn for the night. I was beguiled by an angel who turned out to be a cunning devil."

CHAPTER NINETEEN

Robert was visibly shaken, looking blankly off into space. His body trembled, his hands were shaking and his lips trembled as he said, "Oh, it's so horrible!" Abject fear echoed in Robert's voice, "I sat at an angel's table and saw her slip behind the curtain which divided the building — the next thing I knew, someone hit me a terrible blow on the head. I fell to the floor, semiconscious, and the demon angel grinned at me and hit me again with her hammer. I passed out, but came to just as her brother opened a trap door in the floor and dragged me over to it. The beautiful — deadly beautiful — girl pulled my head back by my hair and had placed a knife to my throat when her father called out in German, *'Nein, nein, jemand komt!'* Evidently some other travelers were stopping, so the girl shoved me head-first through the trap door." Robert squeezed his eyes closed, and groaned as he held his head.

James started to question him more, but Shadrach saw how distraught Robert was, so he signaled James to wait a few minutes. When James realized that he was pushing Robert too fast to remember, he went to the stove and started a pot of coffee brewing.

When the coffee was done, James served everyone a cup.

"Thanks," Robert said, "I need this."

James waited a few more minutes, then asked, "What happened after you were shoved through the trap door?"

"I hit a rock floor, and after a few minutes — knew, I'd escaped a slit throat and had better get out of the hole I was in or be killed. I couldn't walk so I crawled around the small room which smelled like a butchering block. After my hands left the cool rock onto dirt, I began to sense that I was in a tunnel. When I crawled out, I was behind the building, in a stand of fruit trees. I kept crawling toward more bushes and trees where I could hide in case the demons inside came looking for me. I kept blacking out, coming to and wondering why I was crawling. I'd stand up and fall. Every time I gained consciousness, I'd remember less and less. Finally, I didn't know where I'd been or where I was going.

"When Clarence Frank found me, I didn't even know my name. That was eight months ago." Robert pointed at the marks on the wall under the loft. "I've kept a record of each month, growing more depressed with each one that passed."

"We have news for you," Shadrach said, "we may know where this attempted murder took place, and who the people might be who tried to kill you."

"Take me to them, I'll know them! I've a score to settle!" Robert cried as he drew himself up to his full height.

"I think the law is taking care of them for you. When I left the sheriff in Independence he told me that Cherryvale was asking for help — something big going on involving the Benders. Suspicion is resting heavily against the Bender family," Shadrach said.

James added what he'd heard, "I understood that a search party lead by the brother of Doctor William York was preparing to go to the Bender Inn. The doctor had disappeared after saying he was going to stop at the Benders' on his way to Fort Scott to see his brother who was in the army. The doctor was from Independence, haven't you heard about him?"

"Yes, I knew that, but he hasn't been missing that long. He disappeared last March, but until now it didn't register. Dear God, I wonder how many more men they've killed? Why have they done such a dastardly thing, anyway?" Robert cried.

"Greed. They've robbed and raped because they enjoy the thrill of their outrages," Shadrach said, silently rejoicing that Sarah had escaped the clutches of the suspected rapist, John Bender, Junior.

"So many things are still hazy in my mind. I've had all these images, flashing in and out of my head, and now I know some are coming true." Robert opened and closed his fists a few times. "Do you think the Benders robbed me?" he asked, a sudden gleam coming into his eyes.

"If you don't have fifteen hundred dollars in

your pocket, I'd say you were fleeced good," James said, "but don't let it disturb you. We'll still buy a place of our own. We have years ahead of us."

"Hold on to the table, brother. I remember something that will interest you — let me think a minute so I can get it right." Robert closed his eyes and seemed to be concentrating hard on some matter. He looked up and said, "When I reached Kansas City, I remember thinking that something might happen to me, and I didn't want to lose your money, so I deposited all of it but a few dollars in a bank." Robert walked over to a cabinet and reached on top of it. He pulled down a wallet. "Now I know what this number means." He took a slip of paper from the inside of the wallet. "It's the bank account number. I've puzzled over this for months."

"Damn! Are you sure? You're saying our money is safe! Glory, hallelujah, praise God and Amen!" James was embracing Robert once more.

Suddenly, Robert swallowed with difficulty. "James! You married my twin sister, but I don't remember her. Where is she?"

"In Parsons waiting with Johnny, your three-year-old nephew, for me to check here to see if you were the man Doctor Johnson said he'd treated seven or eight months ago."

"I want to see her; maybe I'll recognize her." Robert wiped away more tears. "This has been like hell not knowing anything — I feel like I'm being reborn."

"Can you leave here?" Shadrach asked. "I mean can you leave these cattle unattended?"

"I really shouldn't, but Clarence should be back by nightfall. We can leave for Parsons at first light if that's all right?"

Shadrach wanted to head back tonight but couldn't resist James's plea to stay. That evening, Shadrach listened as James and Robert talked about things that Robert had forgotten.

"I remember how urgently you beseeched me to be careful as I traveled to Oklahoma — said you'd be praying for me." Robert wiped his eyes and touched James's arm. "God answered your prayer! You can't know how good you look to me!" Robert grinned. "I remember when I left the farm we were share-cropping, I knew that you were truly worried — seemed genuinely concerned — I don't know if it was for my welfare you worried, or for your money."

James chuckled. "You know which."

Robert laughed, then his mood changed. "Just think of angel Kate's hollow victory. Imagine her surprise when I face her alive — Oh, Lord God in Heaven, I want to see Kate Bender brought to justice. I'll even testify against her." Robert's voice trailed off, again.

"Robert," Shadrach said, stepping toward the gaunt young man, "Let's talk about something more pleasant; James and I have a friend who is looking for a farm. Have you any idea where he might find a bargain?"

Robert sucked on his teeth, trying to get a

piece of the beef they'd eaten for supper out from between them. "It's funny you should ask me that. For weeks Clarence has been trying to find a buyer for this place. He's too old to run it alone, and he's tired of chasing border ruffians. When he knows I'm leaving, he'll probably sell it cheap and move to town. This place is too big for him; he owns over a thousand acres."

"That's more than Jelliroll wants or can care for."

"James," Robert said, "if we were going to buy a farm, why don't we buy this and then sell your friend however many acres he wants?"

"Sounds all right to me. Tomorrow, we'll talk it over with Roberta and Jelliroll," James said.

"We'll talk it over with Clarence when he gets here," Robert said, looking out the window at the road.

"If Mister Frank wants to sell, we'd better buy your wagon back and bring Jelliroll out here to take a look," Shadrach said, standing from his chair. "I'm ready to hit the bed if you two will excuse me."

Robert reached up and pulled a ladder from the loft. "You sleep up there. James and I will sleep down here."

"God has surely blessed you fellows," Shadrach said, looking at the happiness on James's and Robert's faces. Shadrach couldn't keep from comparing it to Sarah and her desire to find Leo.

James grinned. "And God didn't make us wait forever, either."

Robert chuckled. "That's what I've missed — your sense of humor. I've been blessed, all right. Blessed with a memory that's flooding back faster than I can keep up with. At the moment, I want to avenge myself by seeing the Benders get their just due — you can't imagine the horror of that night. . . ."

Shadrach watched a shudder pass through Robert. "You don't have to think about them, Robert. Let's just think about the future, which to me seems mighty nice."

Robert was quiet a few moments. "Shadrach, and you too, James," he stopped mid-sentence, then continued, "you two have changed my life. If you hadn't found this place, I'd still be in a haze — maybe forever. If there is ever anyway I can repay you, just name it, I'll be there."

"Forget that! It's you who have changed our lives," Shadrach said, and James quickly agreed.

Still reeling from the unfolding circumstances, Shadrach climbed the ladder and went to bed. He had seen James fighting tears all evening and felt a lump in his throat at his and Robert's happiness. Would Sarah ever experience such joy? Shadrach rejoiced over their finding Robert, but it was mixed with sadness because of Sarah's plight. He could only imagine how she would feel when she saw Robert and Roberta united.

As Shad tried to sleep, the voices from below drifted up to him. Robert was speaking, "I'm sorry, James, I can see this is really hard on you, isn't it? If you don't mind me telling you some more of what I'm remembering, I'd like to. Every man needs a family that he knows loves him. You have no idea what it's like not knowing if you have a family somewhere grieving for you or if you are an orphan with no one.

"I recall that you always treated me as if I were your brother. If you'll let me get this bitterness out, then I'll never talk about it again. At the moment, my happiness almost overshadows my hatred. I don't know how or why you two are here, but this I do know — I'll soon be out of this awful maze in my mind.

"Clarence offered to take me to neighboring towns to see if anyone recognized me, but after several trips, I gave up. Do you know that Frank has fed and clothed me as if I belonged to him. He gave me the name of his son who died three days after his wife delivered him, then she died and Clarence has lived alone ever since.

"Do you realize, I could have lived here and died and have never regained my memory? I never expected you would be looking for me."

James cleared his throat. "You can't begin to know how hard Roberta and I have tried to find you — she never believed you were dead, always said she would know if you were. Listen to this, she said when she thought about you, she felt you were confused and in a haze most of the time."

"I want to meet this wonderful-sounding person. Sounds as if she has an incredible ability to feel what another person feels — I'd almost given up, then — here you were. What a miracle this day had brought!" Robert said.

"What about you, James? What's happened in your life?" Robert asked.

"I've been in nine states following leads to find you. You'll soon remember that I'm married to an extraordinary girl. Who, by the way, when my faith faltered at ever finding you, would say something to kept my belief of finding you at a fever pitch," James said.

"Tell me more about her," Robert said.

"She's never lost that spark of hope she's always had," James said, "and in a few hours, you'll be with her."

"I can't wait, and the feeling in my heart, knowing you two never gave up finding me, is humbling."

Once again, Shadrach knew the two of them were embracing; he heard the backslaps and tear-filled voices, and he knew an aura of disbelief in their love for one another. Shadrach enjoyed the feeling as he dozed off.

He woke up when Clarence Frank came home, but didn't get up. Shadrach lay there, listening as Robert told Frank what had happened.

"It's hard to believe a woman so lovely could have such a diabolical streak, such a scheming mind. If James hadn't found me, I'd probably have been here forever if you didn't kick me out."

Shadrach heard Frank denying that he'd do such a thing, then Shad's mind turned to what the sheriff in Independence had told him. Actually that conversation had not left his mind since he'd heard it. He was now beginning to believe that Leo Daniels was alive. Shad didn't know how he was going to approach Sarah with what he was starting to believe.

The more he studied on the subject, the more conclusions he was drawing. Leonard Daniels could be a fancy way of changing the name Leo Daniels. Lee Davies still carried the initials, L. D. If Shadrach was right, Leo was probably alive, married to someone he hadn't yet bamboozled out of any money. Leo could be a bigamist! Poor Sarah — she'd been so sure of Leo's devotion to her. Soon, Shadrach knew he would be on another quest, because he had to prove to Sarah what he was coming to believe.

As he turned over, jabbing his pillow to get more comfortable, Shadrach heard Robert speaking. He sounded so upset, Shad looked over the edge of the loft. "Right now, hatred for the Benders is gnawing at me." Robert let his head fall into his hands. He stood several minutes, then lifted his head, his eyes narrowing with a far-away look in them. He spoke with hesitancy, "I don't understand what's happening to me. I feel so strange sometimes, and I'm all mixed up. I've these peculiar flashes of living somewhere else — I see a young boy — a woman — I think. Could I be married?"

"I can almost guarantee you that you're still single," James said.

"Oh, Lord, I think I'm losing my mind!" Robert looked at James and Clarence Frank. "I may be talking to a figment of my imagination this moment."

"You're not losing your mind, Robert. James and I are very real. You're just confused," Clarence said, "but don't despair, think how much you've already remembered just this evening."

Shadrach heard the anxiety in Robert's voice. "I've still got amnesia. When will it all go away?"

"Give it time, son," Clarence said. "Eight months is a mighty long time to be without your memory."

"What are you saying?" Robert looked at him, puzzled, then terrified. "How old am I?" he asked James.

"You're twenty-six years old."

Robert moved closer, his eyes wide with bewilderment. "I can't believe this is happening to me."

"Believe it, Robert, the quicker you come to grips with the present, the easier it'll be to believe the past. It's a dreadful thing that's happened to you," Clarence said, "but don't lose sight of the fact that you could have been murdered. Stop dwelling on the Benders. They will be apprehended."

Shadrach recognized the gentle comfort in Clarence's voice, and hoped Robert was aware of the man's deep concern.

Clarence moved across the room to the water bucket and got a drink.

"You okay, Clarence?" Robert asked when he saw his friend's pale countenance.

"Here," Robert said quite easily, "sit in my chair."

"Thank you, son. I'm all right," he said, and sat down.

"It's just that I've grown so fond of you, I'd not considered that you'd ever leave me," Clarence said.

Robert said, "And I have grown dependent on you; you're like the father I always wanted. I want you to know that no matter what happens next, I'll always be here for you." Robert proceeded to tell Clarence about James's friend who was looking for a few acres, about James wanting to buy a farm to raise his family on, and as they discussed all the possibilities, Shadrach sat on his bed, wondering about getting dressed and leaving for Parsons.

Robert spoke so softly that Shadrach thought he was talking to himself. "I don't understand how one young girl could have the power to steal my memory from me."

Shadrach realized how heavily Robert's loss of memory was weighing on him and tried to think of something to get his mind off of it. Before he could speak, Robert said, "Kate took sadistic pleasure in what she was doing. I'm a blasted idiot! I let her beauty beguile me."

Shadrach realized that Robert had integrity — that he could admit his mistakes.

Robert reached out and grabbed James's arm,

"Promise me something!"

"Name it, Robert."

"Keep me away from Kate Bender. I'll kill her as ruthlessly as she tried to kill me."

"Then, you'll end up in jail," Clarence stated firmly.

"You have my word," James pledged. "I'll keep you with me until the Benders are apprehended."

"Boys, are you ready to catch a few winks?" Clarence asked, standing on his feet.

"Sure am." Robert smiled.

"You two take the bed," Clarence said, "I'll curl up in the empty room."

Shadrach decided it was too late to leave so he lay back down, but sleep wouldn't come. He couldn't get Leo Daniels off his mind, and what he was beginning to think about him. Poor Sarah, he thought again. Then he couldn't stop the thrill rolling over him when he remembered the kiss he'd given Sarah. He loved her so much it hurt. Would she ever look at him with pale green eyes filled with love — love for him?

Suddenly, he knew sleep was not in him. He sat up, pulled on his boots, spread up the bed he'd messed up and descended the ladder. He went to the stove and poured himself a cup of lukewarm coffee.

"You Shadrach Koby?"

Shad looked around and saw an elderly man he knew was Clarence Frank. "Sure am, Mister Frank. I can't sleep, so think I'll head back for

Parsons. Will you do me a favor?"

"Name it," Clarence said.

"Tell James and Robert, I'm not going near Roberta so the good news is all theirs to share. I'll be at the hotel when they want me."

"Not really too safe at night. Sure you won't reconsider?" Clarence asked.

"I'm certain. Nice to have met you, Mister Frank."

"Same here."

CHAPTER TWENTY

Roberta yawned wearily as she climbed the stairs to her apartment. "I don't know when I've ever been this tired. I think not knowing about Robert is half of it."

"I've heard that worry is as hard on the body as physical labor," Sarah said, hanging scrub rags on a nail to dry.

"Then I've had a double dose of fatigue this day," Roberta cried. "I'm ready to fix supper, if I don't drop."

"I have to go to the hotel and get a change of clothes," Sarah said, "— why don't I order dinner for us and bring it back when I come?" Sarah asked.

"Sounds great, and I'd be glad to loan you anything you need, but I'm afraid my clothes would swallow you."

"I don't mind going to the hotel. I might even bathe before I return, if I don't fall asleep first."

"Sarah, you could grab a few winks before you come back; it's not all that late. That way I'd have time to bathe Johnny and myself. You'll enjoy the evening more if you aren't so exhausted."

"I just might rest twenty minutes or so, then I'll stop at the restaurant and get our dinners so we don't have to cook."

Roberta replied, "It's agreed then. Jelliroll will

enjoy eating with us. I'll put Johnny to bed and take care of my needs while you're gone."

"I may oversleep," Sarah said, "so don't worry about me if I'm late."

"Tell you what, if you're not here by eight o'clock, I'll figure you've overslept and come get you. That way I can help you carry back our supper. Don't worry, we had a late meal at noon. We'll be fine until eight o'clock."

Sarah left the apartment and walked the short distance to the hotel where Shadrach had rented their rooms. He'd unloaded the pack animals and set every item at the foot of her bed. Last night all she'd done was dig out her nightgown, now she had another job to do.

She looked around the sparsely furnished room and went to work. After shaking wrinkles from her clothes, she hung them in the chiffonier, and placed her toiletries on the wash stand. She laid her nightgown and a change of clothes on the end of the bed, then took the provided towel, soap, washcloth, and her robe down the hall to the public bath. This was an experience she didn't enjoy, but few hotels had private baths. She locked the door and bathed in the cold water as quickly as she could. The water appeared to be clean, but the thought that someone else might have bathed before her kept her from sitting in the tub. She only kneeled in the water. She'd have loved to sit down and relax, but knew the bed and a nap were waiting for her; she'd relax then.

Sarah finished bathing, scurried back to her room, changed her clothes, and made a decision. She'd go downstairs and order three dinners boxed to go and delivered to her door by seven thirty. That way she wouldn't over-sleep.

In the dining room she waited for a waitress, surprised by the lack of patrons. Everyone seemed to be gone. Earlier the town had been full of activity, but now, all was quiet.

A very attractive lady about thirty years old sat waiting at a table, fumbling with a folding fan. "There's only one waitress," she said a bit disgustedly, "hope you're not in a hurry. You're welcome to sit here with me if you'd like. I'm waiting for three dinners to go. My husband isn't feeling too well," she said, fanning herself furiously, "so I'm taking him and our driver dinner. We can eat as we travel and save time if the kitchen would hurry up with my order. Leodis doesn't want to stop here for the night. Why, I don't know. He wants to get home to Tulsa, to our own bed. He says we'll stop in Independence for the night." The woman took a breath of air and continued talking.

"He's such a dear, so devoted to me. So different than my first husband, God rest his soul. All Burt thought about was making money. What did it get him? An early grave is all, but thank the good Lord, Leodis came along. We fell in love the moment we met. He's so devoted to me, won't hardly let me out of his sight.

"Well, look at me, sitting here talking your ear

off. I'm Isabella Danner." She stuck out her hand.

Sarah was breathless just listening to the lady. "I'm Sarah Daniels."

"Do you live in Parsons?" Isabella Danner asked.

"No, I'm from Chicago, but I've fallen in love with Kansas. I may just stay."

"This part of the midwest has a way of growing on you. My Leodis used to live in Chicago. In fact I met him a few miles from here in Cherryvale. He was a drummer; this was his route. He sold women's clothes, but he never worked a day after he fell in love with me. Never even needed to work, but then, he didn't have to, he was independently wealthy. We were married three weeks to the day after we met. It's been a wonderful nine-month honeymoon."

The waitress bought a box to the lady. She paid for it and looked around at Sarah. "It's been a pleasure visiting with you. Good evening." The lady headed for the door.

Several minutes later, Sarah noticed Isabella's fan still on the table. She snatched it up and followed the lady out of the hotel. Just as Sarah came up behind the covered buggy, the head of a cane came out of the window and knocked on the side of the buggy. Instantly, the buggy surged forward, but not fast enough for Sarah to miss the head of the cane she'd seen. It was the one Leo had carved while in the hospital — the one with her face on it!

For a few minutes, she couldn't move. Adrenaline had flooded her body, making it hard to stay on her feet.

"This is insane!" she finally cried, gathering her skirt so she could run after the buggy. Her effort was in vain. She watched the buggy disappear, but she didn't stop. She headed for the livery.

"Saddle that pinto; I'll be back here in ten minutes," she ordered. Sarah turned from the startled livery man and raced to the hotel. Oh, God, she silently cried as she bounded up the stairs to her room, what am I to do?

She had never wanted Shadrach Koby more than this minute. He'd know what to do, but he wasn't here. It was up to her to find out who had Leo's cane and how it had been obtained. Had he been killed for the money he carried? Quickly, Sarah wrote Shad a note telling him what she'd seen and where she was going. Then she ran to the room across from hers and shoved the note under Shad's door. Back in her room, she changed into trousers and boots. If she was going to ride hard and at night, she might as well wear her boy clothes. She was certain that would be what Shad would have had her do.

True to her word, she was back at the livery in ten minutes. Sarah patted Bear's neck. "You've got to get me to Independence," she said as she stuck her foot into the stirrup and slung her leg over the saddle.

"That's not a safe road to travel after dark,"

the livery man said, having overheard her speak to her horse.

"Have you a pistol I could borrow?" Sarah asked.

"Well, sure, but a slip of a girl and one pistol ain't no match for border ruffians, the Dalton boys, or even the James brothers. Where's the man you were with?"

"Sorry, but I don't have any more time to lose. Do I get a pistol or not?"

"How do I know I'll get it back?"

Sarah reached into her pants' pocket, where she'd shoved some money, and pulled out a ten-dollar certificate. "You can hold this until I return."

He took the bill and handed her a pistol. "It's loaded. Six shots. That's all. Watch your back, girl. Feels like rain; you got any gear?"

She shook her head, not wanting to go back to the hotel. "I'll take my chances," she said, lifting her eyes to Heaven to say a quick prayer; then she jabbed Bear in the flanks and galloped down the road in the direction the buggy had gone. She didn't hesitate to take the secondary road as she followed the buggy, but did wonder why the driver had taken the cut-off road. To her it seemed the main route, called the Osage Mission Trail, would've been smoother and safer, but she wasn't making the decisions.

Shadrach couldn't resist making a slight detour to see what was going on in Cherryvale.

He passed more wagons and buggies than you'd usually see in any town on a Saturday. Shadrach flagged down a passing rider, and, after offering him a drink asked why there was so much traffic. The man swallowed half Shadrach's flask of whiskey, then sat and talked a few minutes. Shad was glad to see the man was giving his horse a chance to rest.

"Surprised you haven't heard — Colonel York from Fort Scott went looking for his doctor brother from Independence who was missing like a dozen others from around here. He traced his path from Independence, to Osage Mission, to the Bender Inn. The Benders were questioned about Doctor York, but denied having seen him. It seems Colonel York was suspicious of the Benders from the first, but when his search turned up nothing, he and his men went home.

"The Colonel recruited a larger group of men from Independence and they went searching again.

"Guess what they found when they reached the Benders this time? All four Benders were gone. They'd left most of their belongings behind.

"I was at the Bender Inn about two weeks ago," Shadrach said, "and all of them but the son were there. He was probably hiding outside somewhere."

"That's exactly how long they figure the Benders have been gone. They left their animals to starve to death, but you can bet they took the money and jewelry they'd stolen from passing travelers. Some figure they robbed folks of ten thousand dollars. I think it was a lot more. They're digging up the orchard, finding bodies everywhere. I've had a cousin missing for six months. I want to see if he was one of their victims." The man mounted his horse and waved.

Shadrach whistled for Hominy. What he'd heard was in line with what the sheriff in Independence had told him. Shadrach decided to detour to the Bender Inn and look around for himself. What if one of the bodies being unearthed was Leo's? Shadrach almost wished one would be. His cold-blooded murder might be easier for Sarah to take in the long run, better than what Shadrach was beginning to suspect about the *devoted husband* of Sarah Daniels.

Shadrach passed more travelers, obviously intrigued with the mystery unfolding at the Benders. It always struck him as bizarre the way folks developed a morbid curiosity about death. The way people were flocking to the Benders proved his theory correct. For a quick moment he wondered if that was his reason for going, but he knew better — he was searching for a missing man, maybe a victim of multiple murders.

As Shadrach rode into sight of the yard, he saw folks coming from every direction. Some were running, others walking, many riding in buckboards, wagons, buggies and on horseback. As he looked around, he estimated there was near a thousand people. Word of a crime of this magnitude had spread rapidly.

Shadrach tried to find the sheriff, but the crowd was too large. Shad tied his horse and walked around. The stench from the dead farm animals about gagged him. He headed for the house and couldn't believe his eyes. Folks were carrying off the possessions the Benders had left. They were even taking pieces of wood as souvenirs.

This shouldn't be happening. Shad searched more diligently for a lawman, but again found no one. He wished he'd have let the sheriff deputize him. As it was no one paid any attention to him. One man took a punch at him for telling him that he shouldn't be busting up the boards to the house — that everything ought to be left alone until the sheriff had examined the crime scene. Shadrach had ducked the fist leveled at him, and when he looked around, the man was gone.

Shad went into the cabin and saw a deputy trying to stop people from taking anything else out of the house.

The trap door was open and the terrible odor coming from that hole couldn't be mistaken. Shadrach had smelled decaying, human blood too often in the war. Men went down with torches. When one came up vomiting, he was asked what was down there.

"I thought I was standing in soft dirt, but the torch light revealed it to be a thick layer of dried blood. Under it was a solid rock floor.

"There's a tunnel. Some are following it. I

can't go on, this is horrible." He vomited again.

Shadrach left by the back door, and saw men examining places in the ground they said were graves. Several were already opened.

Men with shovels began digging. Shadrach heard that the first body exhumed was Colonel York's brother. The man telling him this said, "I saw the colonel break down and sob, then he cursed. It was his brother, Doctor York."

The man shoved a shovel into Shad's hand and said, "You might as well help us finish this."

Shad helped dig, and by the end of the day eleven bodies had been unearthed. The grave that would live forever in Shadrach's memory was that of a little girl baby who appeared to have been buried alive with her dead father. All the uncovered bodies were identified, all of them having been reported missing. Most of them were said to have been carrying large amounts of money. Some men were buying cattle, some farms, and several were wanting to buy lumber for new homes in Cherryvale.

It was suppertime, and the men who were working were weary. They talked about coming back tomorrow to dig some more. Shadrach was too saddened and worn out from his work to stay any longer, nor was he coming back. The corpses were getting harder and harder to uncover and identify. He wouldn't know Leo or any article of his clothing. Shad wasn't about to let Sarah come out here and see the way the Benders butchered their victims. Even if she couldn't identify Leo, she would always believe that he had died at the hands of this Godless, evil family.

When the baby girl had been found, people had wept. Such an atrocity had angered the hardest of men. Shad was looking at a mob who now wanted vengeance. This was a good time to leave.

He rode about eight miles as the crow flies before he reached Parsons. When he'd crossed a river, he removed his boots, emptied his pockets, then jumped in, clothes and all.

He rubbed himself and his clothes until he couldn't smell the terrible odor of death any longer. He got out of the water and removed his clothes, wringing out all the water he could, then dressed again, he combed his hair, and, when his feet were dry enough, he pulled on his boots, mounted Hominy, and rode for Parsons.

His clothes were drying but still damp when he passed the apothecary heading for the hotel. James saw him and ran out of the building. "Shadrach," he called, an anxious look on his face, "is Sarah with you?"

"Sarah," Shad repeated, "isn't she with you?"

"Roberta said she left for the hotel before six o'clock this evening to bathe and change clothes. She was exhausted, so Roberta told her to take a short nap before coming back to sleep with her. Sarah also said she'd bring dinner for Roberta and Jelliroll. When Robert and I got here, Roberta sent me to the hotel to help Sarah since she hadn't shown up and I wanted to get food for Robert and me."

"Was she asleep or what?" Shad asked anxiously.

"I made the clerk open her room when I couldn't get any answer. She wasn't there. I went to the livery and her pinto was gone. I was hoping you would have intercepted her. No one knows why she has done such a fool-hardy thing."

"Oh, dear God," Shadrach cried as he stared at James. "I'm going after her. I need a fresh horse. Can I ride your roan?"

"I'll go get it saddled for you," James said.

"Take Hominy to the livery." He gave James some money. "Tell the smith to give him extra food and rub him down. I'm going to the hotel; I'll only be a few minutes."

Shadrach took the stairs two at a time, stopping at Sarah's door. It was locked. He put his shoulder to it and with one thrust, it opened. He saw her nightgown and the unslept bed. Her clothes were strewn over the room. He looked in the chiffonier and saw her riding trousers, boots and hat were gone. She'd left in a hurry, disguised as a boy — but why? Shad knew she'd disappeared, and hastily at that. All her toiletries were on the wash stand. A lady doesn't go anywhere without her personal items, so Shad deducted she'd left in a frantic state of mind.

He went to his room, and, on the floor was a note in Sarah's handwriting. He unfolded it and read:

Shad,

I met this woman, Isabella Danner, in the dining room. She forgot her fan. When I ran after her, I saw the head of a cane tap the side of the buggy signaling the driver to go. The cane was exactly like the one Leo made in the hospital. I'd know it anywhere. Whoever has that cane has to know what happened to Leo. You weren't here to advise me, so I decided to follow the buggy to Independence. I'm scared, it's dark outside, but I have to know who has Leo's cane.

Shad, if something should happen to me, I have to tell you, you've been the best thing that ever happened to me. I'm just sorry I didn't meet you before the woman you love ever knew you existed. Hope to see you in Independence. If I get back before you do, I'll be at Roberta's and James's apartment. Sarah.

Shadrach changed clothes. The night was too cool to wear wet clothes, and when he left the hotel, James's horse was waiting at the hitchrail.

"If that woman comes back before I do, don't let her out of your sight," he called to James.

"You're sounding more like a husband all the time," James said as Shad mounted his horse.

"Not yet, but I'm gonna be, God willing," he yelled as he galloped down the road, heading west toward Independence. He looked at the sky and knew he would run into rain before much longer. He hoped Sarah had taken her rain gear.

CHAPTER TWENTY ONE

"Bear," Sarah said to her animal as she looked at the road ahead, "take care, I wouldn't want you to stumble and throw me off." She saw a flash of lightning and glanced at the black clouds swirling overhead. "Bear, I'm wondering it this was such a good idea — but I have to follow — I have to know what happened to Leo. I wish I had a lantern, but I'd probably just burn myself or you." She patted her horse's neck, trying to see in the near darkness to stay on the road.

She counted on the lightning to help her keep on the path. She was certain she would be seeing the lantern on the buggy anytime. If she ran into any danger on the road ahead, she might not catch the buggy. "I'll just stop if I see a light that seems like it's not on a wagon. I'll get off the road into the safety of the trees."

She snapped her riding crop to the side of the horse's back. "Come on, faster!" she cried. The horse balked and Sarah snapped her crop again.

Sarah flinched at the sound the crop made. Of all the noises she'd ever heard, the swishing rasp of the crop, or the whip, chilled her spine more than the hiss of a cottonmouth.

Each time she heard the sound, she remembered the awful beatings the horses had endured at her father's stables. He'd whip a horse anytime his fancy dictated.

Sarah often thought of the pain and brutality suffered by the racing horses her father owned, and never understood how he made so much money, using his animals as he did. To her recollection, not one of the horses deserved the treatment they received. Her father was unique and brilliant, a smart horseman, and he owned several very successful champion racing horses.

Leo was so different, he treated animals like people. In his heart he had two dreams. One, to be treated as the man he knew himself to be, and the other, to embrace success in business as he would a woman, with all his heart and soul.

The word "embrace" caused Shadrach to come to mind. He had powerful strength, and was a conscientious investigator, often doing much more than he was paid to do. He was compassionate, and generous to a fault. Down deep inside, Sarah figured she resented Shadrach and wanted him to be more like Leo, or Leo to be more like Shad. Then she'd have something to compare so she could judge one against the other.

Shadrach had told her that distance should not be able to keep a man from getting in touch with his wife, and this gnawed at Sarah more than any other remark. She knew in her heart of hearts that Shadrach was such a man. He always kept her informed even when he was away. She'd been given messages by strangers if he was going to be later than he'd told her he'd be, or if he wanted her to meet him somewhere different than he'd planned.

Shadrach seemed to have a reason for his life. Sarah wished she had reason for hers; all she had was a confusing, hopeful memory of Leo Daniels, mixed with feeling for Shad that shouldn't be. Poor, long-suffering Leo, she thought, and her heart twisted in bewilderment. She found herself wishing for Shadrach, when a few weeks ago, she'd been wishing for Leo.

Sarah felt she knew one thing for certain: Shadrach probably wanted to be with her — to break her intended fidelity to Leo, or maybe he just wanted to be through with her so he could go back to the woman he loved. What a state of turmoil her life was in!

As Sarah rode around a sharp bend in the road, a brisk wind pelted raindrops into her face. She saw the light of a buggy ahead. She slowed her animal, trying to decide what to do when she caught up. She wasn't even certain this was the buggy — but it almost had to be. Oh, how she wished Shad was with her. She tried to think what he'd do — hold back, stay unnoticed, and follow the buggy.

The buggy had been moving swiftly down the rutted road, now it slowed down. The approaching storm was pelting them with rain, forcing them to slow down. As Sarah followed, it rained spasmodically for several minutes. She'd ridden off the road, hugging the tree line. This offered some protection, no mud, less rain and shadows to keep her from being spotted.

The starless sky, void of the moon, and occasionally filled with an ominous flash of lightning, warmed her that more rain wasn't far away. She regretted not having any rain gear.

Sarah couldn't keep her mind off Leodis and Isabella Danner riding in the buggy ahead. Who were they? And what did they know about her husband? They had his cane, they must know something. In anguish, she begged God to let her find out what had happened to Leo. *"Lord, don't I deserve to know about him? But then, maybe I'm better off not knowing."*

Sarah saw the driver of the buggy stand up, then pull his hat low and his collar high. He drove the buggy hard, obviously trying to beat the storm. Sarah knew the jolts of the buggy wheels dropping in and out of the ruts must be hard on the Danners'.

Sarah rode, ever mindful of the lightning and rolling thunder, as she tried to guide her horse safely, but the wash-outs and intermittent rain was making her task nearly impossible. She was growing more miserable every minute. Sarah wished she was back in the hotel — warm and sleeping.

For over an hour, she carefully followed. Her gaze strained to see the splash of light up ahead telling her the buggy was still moving.

A lightning flash allowed her to see the buggy wheels sink low in the mud, and at one place where two roads nearly paralleled each other, the driver seemed forced to take the adjoining road or get completely bogged down. He urged the horses onto the narrow, more solidly packed road that Sarah assumed to be the Osage Mission Trail.

She was glad the driver had taken the better route. It was smoother anyway, she thought to herself. She tried to calm the fear she felt riding in the dead of night in a storm and virtually alone. She'd heard from the liveryman that local people tried to steer clear of this road at night. They were surely getting close to Cherryvale where killing and robbing too often occurred.

"In the daytime, this road's well traveled," the livery man had said as he'd tightened the cinch of Bear's saddle.

"Come nightfall," he'd continued as Sarah had mounted up, "it's as if the Indians who first made the trail come out to haunt it."

Sarah shuddered. The night sounds, plus the flashing lightning, made the road spooky with ghostly shadows.

The livery man had also said, "The worst of southeast Kansas marauders and border ruffians comb this trail at night looking for weary travelers, so guard your back."

"If we're in such danger traveling this road, why would Leodis Danner take a chance with his wife alone?" she said talking to herself, trying to calm her fears.

When nothing seemed to ease her pounding heart, she prudently changed her thoughts, thinking about the road on which she was traveling.

She'd heard Shadrach and Jelliroll talking and Jelliroll had told Shad that he avoided the road when possible. He'd tried to make light of it by saying, "I don't want some aging prostitute or murderer catching me unprotected. They might like the way I look and keep me. They use the road after sunset, because darkness hides their true identity."

Sarah knew darkness hid much, much more. She jerked her head up when she heard horses riding fast out of the trees just ahead of her. She quickly guided Bear behind some scrub oak and sumac bushes. She could barely see the buggy, until a streak of lightning revealed how dangerously close to it she was hidden. She was closer than she wanted to be, so she prayed Bear didn't give her presence away.

Before the driver could react, six horsemen were upon them. One snatched the reins from the driver and stopped the carriage. Another yanked the occupants from the wagon. The woman was Isabella Danner. Sarah could see her clearly in a flash of light. She couldn't see who the man was on the other side of the wagon.

The driver grappled to regain the reins and was hit in the head with a gun butt. He huddled in the seat seemingly unable to move. The woman from the wagon screamed, and another man shoved her to the ground.

Sarah wanted to scream, but knew she would be in danger like them if she revealed herself. One of the men brought his hand down hard across Isabella's face to stop her from screaming, then he yanked at her bodice.

"Finish him!" a voice commanded of the man still holding the gun on the driver.

Isabella yelled, then scrambled to her feet, throwing herself at the man, but another fellow yanked her off her feet again, onto the ground, and threw himself astraddle her.

Sarah's mind was racing over every option open to her — but anything she tried would result in her being caught. Was she being prudent or cowardly? She closed her eyes, not wanting to see what was taking place, but Isabella's blood-curdling scream snatched Sarah's eyes wide open.

She saw the outlaw with the wounded driver fire directly at his head. A flash of lightning revealed the driver's eyes open wide as his tall hat fell to the ground ahead of his body.

The man staring down at Isabella said, "If you value your life, don't fight, you understand me?" All the time he talked, the other men were going through her purse and satchels.

The man with Isabella seemed to be the leader. The lantern from the buggy revealed his large frame and pock-marked face. He presented an appalling sight to Sarah who struggled to remain where she was hiding.

Sarah shuddered as she imagined what was happening to Isabella's husband. Since she hadn't heard him yell or seen him fighting, she figured they'd killed him. Sarah's concentration was drawn to Isabella, who was fighting like a cornered wild cat. The eyes of the man over her exposed one emotion, his hankering for a woman, any woman. Sarah knew that Isabella, and she, if she were discovered, were in for a bad time at the hands of these marauders.

"For the love of God, you can't be serious!" Isabella cried. She had hidden her valuables in her bosom, and quickly opened her blouse. "Here, you can take my money, my jewels, but don't kill me."

"Madam, you are most generous and caring, and I'll take this," he snatched the valuables from her, "and I'll have these, too." He grabbed both her breasts. "See, madam, I've been locked up and deprived the pleasures of the ladies for several years. I don't plan on letting any escape me, not even one."

Sarah was gripping her pistol, ready to fire at the man, but his words stopped her. There were six of them, and she had only one gun. The outlaw reached up and took Isabella's hat from her head. He pulled her combs loose, so her hair fell around her trembling shoulders. "There," he said in a randy voice, "I like my women this way."

"Have mercy," she pleaded, "don't do this terrible thing."

"I'm next," yelled the man waiting beside Isabella and the outlaw.

The man shoved another one away, and shouted, "I'm next!"

The leader, the one with Isabella, smirked. "You bastards be patient. A highbred, haughty lady like this is cold as ice, but it makes me hotter than fire. I'll be a while."

"You're a fool if you think I'm gonna stand here and watch you wear yourself out. Hurry up and get off her."

"Don't call me a fool! Keep giving me trouble and I'll have your head blown off," the man said, looking at the cold-eyed gunman, waiting his turn at the woman.

The man with Isabella laughed, enjoying the struggle within her. He ripped her bodice completely open to rake her breasts with his lusting eyes and calloused hands. Sarah was biting her cheeks to keep from screaming.

Thunder rumbled after lightning streaked across the dark sky like fiery spears thrown down from heaven. Sarah pleaded with God while there was reason to hope, then watched in horror unable to help.

Sarah begged and wept for Isabella. Despite the horror of what was happening on this side of the buggy, a sudden moment of desperate concern clouded her thinking — why wasn't anything being said about Isabella's husband?

In all her life, she'd never known this feeling of impending doom like she felt this moment. Then, gunshots filled the air. The outlaw taking his turn with Isabella looked up and said, "Did he tell you where his money is?"

"Sure did. He was pitchin' a fit 'cause we're

havin' his wife. Said he didn't bargain for this — he just wanted her dead and himself wounded. A man evil enough to hire us to kill his wife deserves to die."

"I agree. Come on, drop your trousers, it's your turn." The man got to his feet, pulled up his pants, then shot Isabella.

"Damn you! Why'd you kill her? It was my turn."

"Hurry up, you'll never know she's dead. She wasn't moving anyway."

Sarah knew Isabella's husband was an evil killer, and the man who had killed him was a madman, as were the other five; they obviously would rather kill than eat. Her mind reeled from their words and actions. She'd never experienced such evil. She turned away from the horrible sight to glance behind her. Had she heard another horse coming? More border ruffians? She backed her animal deeper into the brush and waited.

The vibrations in the earth beneath her told of an approaching horse. The rider was carrying a lantern. Sarah's heart twisted in her chest when she thought of Isabella, but not as much as when a flash of lightning revealed the rider was Shadrach.

The lantern suddenly disappeared, and a volley of gunfire flashed from several positions. Sarah knew Shad had brought a posse of men with him. She looked at the buggy in time to see the six men rushing for their horses.

"Let's get the hell outa here!" the leader yelled. They mounted up and rode pell-mell down the road.

Sarah stayed hidden until she knew she was safe. The last thirty minutes seemed like a day in hell. She saw Shadrach riding stealthily forward. She pulled Bear behind her and called his name.

He was at her side in seconds. Sarah flung herself into his arms and sobbed. "Sarah, dear God! You don't know what I've been through trying to find you. What's happened over there?"

It took her several minutes to be able to talk. Then she told him the gruesome circumstances, and how she'd stayed hidden because she knew she'd have been killed like Isabella.

"Shad, you know why I was following the buggy?"

"I got your note, and left immediately, but got turned around when I lost your trail. You left the main road, then got back on it, but I finally found you."

"I heard the leader of those horrible men say that Leodis Danner hired them to fake a robbery and kill his wife. I can't imagine such evil. He hadn't bargained for them to rape her. Oh, Shad, I couldn't do anything but watch the ordeal." Sarah looked around. "Where are the other men with you?"

"I'm alone."

"But the shots and yells . . ."

"An old army trick to fool the enemy. I saw I was outnumbered and figured a robbery was taking place, so I just tried to scare them off."

"What are we going to do now?" Sarah asked.

"You wait here while I go gather the dead and place them in the buggy. We're only a few miles from Cherryvale. I'll drive the buggy to the sheriff's office. He'll know what to do."

"I can't ride in that wagon!" she cried.

"You can ride ahead of me so I can keep you in my sights."

"I can do that," she said, letting go of Shad's hand.

He walked to the wagon and to Isabella. "Lord, have mercy!" he exclaimed as he reached into the buggy for the lap blanket. Shad wrapped the lady in the cover and carried her to the buggy seat. Then he lifted the driver in beside her, and went to the other side of the wagon. He stumbled over a stick, then set the lantern down and picked up a walking cane. It was the one he'd heard described a couple of times. There was a man lying on his stomach beside the buggy wheel. He rolled the man over on his back and moaned an oath. He was looking at Leo Daniels.

Shad began placing the pieces of the puzzle in place. Leonard DaNiels, Lee Davies, Leodis Danner, and Leo Daniels were all one and the same.

CHAPTER TWENTY TWO

Shad quickly lifted Leo Daniels into the buggy and covered him with the second lap blanket. Poor Sarah! How am I going to tell her about Leo? Shad shut the door as Sarah rode up. She stayed back a short distance.

"Are we ready?" she asked.

"Yes, here, you take my lantern and watch the road ahead. When your arms grow weary, you can let the lantern rest on your saddle horn. Be careful and don't let it slip. Bear won't like it and neither will you." Shadrach went after Hominy and tied him to the rear of the buggy. He climbed to the seat, adjusted the buggy lantern and said he was ready.

Sarah hesitated, "So much remains unanswered; I can't believe this has happened. With Leodis Danner dead, how will I ever know what happened to Leo?"

"Sarah, sweetheart, we're only a few miles from Independence. Let's take these bodies there. The sheriff will know what to do. I'd like for you — and me to talk to him. Maybe he can shed some light on this situation."

She took a long shuddering sigh, and rode on ahead. Despondency had never laid so heavily over her. She'd been so close to finding something out about Leo. The brutal attack on Isabella Danner stayed sickenly in her memory.

She'd never forgive herself for staying hidden — what a coward she was! *Lord will you ever forgive me?*

Up ahead was a deep rut, and the smoother trail around it turned sharply left. Sarah rode back toward the buggy and yelled, "Stay to your far left."

"I'll do it, thanks," Shadrach called. He waved as Sarah rode on. How was she going to respond when she saw who the dead man was? Damn! he hated this part of his job. She'd been so certain of Leo Daniels's love. How would this affect her self-esteem? Maybe, if she heard what the sheriff had told him about the three Pinkerton agents searching for the same crippled man with the same distinctive walking cane, she would begin to realize what had happened.

Shadrach knew he'd figured it out. When Leo absconded with Sarah's ten-thousand dollars, he'd taken a job as a drummer. That would explain his being seen so many times in this area. He sold clothes to the general stores in Parsons, Oswego, Cherryvale and Independence. That's how he'd meet his rich widows, or young women with a substantial inheritance — like Sarah. Isabella Danner must not have been as gullible as the others. His only hope of getting her money must have been the robbery in which she was to be killed. What a shock he must have had when the gun was turned on him. Leo was a moldy crumb of humanity!

Sarah signaled when she saw the town ahead.

She waited at the edge of the road.

"Follow me," Shadrach called, taking the lead. This has been a bad scene for everyone, especially Sarah. He could see the toll of what she'd been through on her face. A face that should only be reflecting happiness. She'd had a tough life. He had found out about her father. He knew that she and her mother had been abused by a cruel man. Sarah had survived him, the death of her mother, and finally the heart attack of her father in the middle of whipping her for trying to protect a horse he was set on beating to death. The horse had lost a race he had bet heavily on. Would she survive Leo Daniels's premeditated deception? Shadrach could only pray her strength was strong enough.

He pulled the buggy to a stop before the sheriff's office. Leaping to the ground, he walked around and unified Hominy, tying him to the hitchrail beside bear. "Let's see if the sheriff is here," he said smiling at Sarah whose countenance reflected her emotional state.

Inside the office, a deputy told them the sheriff was not in, but that he was due any minute. "You can wait in here or outside. There's a bench by the door. Nice place to sit and watch the sun come up."

"Thanks," Shadrach said as Sarah stepped outside. "Deputy, last night, the lady and I came upon a robbery and murder on the Osage Mission trail. We've brought the bodies here. Do you want to take care of them?"

"Are they from around here?"

"I believe they're from Tulsa, Leodis and Isabella Danner and their buggy driver. That's all I know."

"You'd best wait for the sheriff. He might want to talk to you," the deputy said.

"I've told you all I know. If the sheriff doesn't get here shortly, we're not waiting, but if he needs to learn more, we'll be staying at the Parsons Hotel."

"What's your name?"

"Shadrach Koby."

The deputy was writing as Shad left. He stepped outside and saw Sarah, weaving unsteadily on the board walk. As he took her arm, she staggered against him. He put his arm around her and walked her to the bench. "It will all work out, sweetheart. Here, let's sit down."

"Why are you calling me sweetheart? That's the second time this morning," she asked tonelessly as she sat down.

"You are my sweetheart," he answered.

"Do you call all women sweetheart?" she asked, talking about anything to keep her mind off what had happened.

"You're the only one," he said.

"No sweetheart in Chicago?"

"You've hinted at that before. I have no one in Chicago, never have, never will. You are the only sweetheart I've ever had, or ever wanted."

Sarah turned and stared at him. "One evening on the trail, I overheard you and James talking. I suppose I am the woman you were wanting to marry and start a family with."

Shadrach grinned. "You were the woman."

"But I'm married," she said lamely.

"Or you're a widow," he answered.

"Am I?" she asked studying his face.

Shadrach decided not to hedge anymore. "You are a widow," he said gently.

Sarah turned away and said nothing for a few minutes.

"Shad," she finally said, "if you know something you haven't told me, now's the time."

"Are you certain you're up to it?" he asked.

"It can't be any worse than Isabella Danner's death, and knowing that her husband had hired those men to kill her breaks my heart. I hate to say this, but he deserved the double-cross against him. Actually death was too good for him."

"Sarah, don't say that — at least wait to make such a judgment until I've told you what I know."

Sarah grabbed his hand and asked, "Oh, Shad, is it that bad?"

"It's that bad," he answered.

She took a deep breath. "All right, tell me."

He gently related to her every word that the sheriff had told him. "I've been wondering about the similarity in names, Leonard DaNiels, which is really Daniels spelled differently, Leon Davies, and Leodis Danner. . . ."

Sarah held her hands in tight little fists. She

299

was swallowing rapidly, the color draining from her face.

Shadrach started to speak, but she shook her head at him, then rose unsteadily to her feet. She walked to the buggy, opened the door, picked up the walking cane off the floor of the buggy and examined it a moment.

Shad was right behind her, afraid of what she might do. She laid the cane back where she'd found it, then slowly pulled the lap blanket away from the body. When she saw Leo Daniels, she dropped the blanket cover, and grabbed her mouth to stifle the scream that wouldn't stop for a few seconds.

Shad reached out and tenderly turned her away. She stopped him and looked up into his face. "Remember when I told you I'd never give up looking for Leo until I found him or stood over his grave and told him goodbye?" she asked, barely able to control her voice.

"I remember," he said.

She turned back to the buggy. She lifted the blanket and placed it back over his head. "Goodbye, Leo. This is the ultimate deception — too bad it backfired on you. May God have mercy on your soul."

Sarah walked to her horse. "Can we leave now?" she asked in a voice barely above a whisper.

"Yes, we certainly can. I've much to tell you. We found Robert alive and well."

"I'm so glad — Shad, let's ride for a while so I

can gather my thoughts, then I want to hear every detail about Robert and Roberta."

"I understand," he said, clicking his tongue for the horses to go.

Sarah reached across the space between them and took Shad's hand. They rode that way into the sunshine of a new day as they traveled back toward Parsons.

THE END

POSTSCRIPT

The bloody Benders as they have become known, did exist and did commit horrible murders against travelers stopping at their inn for a night's lodging, supplies for the trail, or a rest stop and a meal, especially if they appeared prosperous.

Eleven bodies were dug up and identified. But the number of victims not found could number closer to one hundred. When the Benders realized they were under suspicion, they hurriedly left Kansas. Posses searched for them, but came back saying they had found no one. To this day, the record stands, the Benders were never captured.

Cherryvale has lived over a hundred years with notoriety of being the site of the first serial killers in the United States — the first mass murders in Kansas history.

James and Roberta Jenkins bought the ranch of Clarence Frank. Robert fully recovered his memory and became the herdsman on the cattle ranch. Clarence Frank and Jelliroll became fast friends and built themselves a cabin on the north edge of the ranch. When they felt like it, they rode in round-ups, assisted in the branding, and helped plant the fields of feed needed for the cattle.

Shadrach bought three hundred acres from Clarence Frank and became a wheat farmer.

Shad and Sarah were married six months after the death of her husband. Sarah had thought Leo treated her devotedly, but Shad was the wonder in life. She had never been so happy, and her life with Leo soon faded away in the light of her happiness with Shadrach Koby.

THE ULTIMATE END